GREAT MEN OF SCIENCE

BRIAN BOONE

PINE STATE PRESS

Library of Congress Control Number: 2019948494

ISBN: 978-0-5785-6022-9 (softbound)

ISBN: 978-0-5785-6024-3 (ebook)

Cover design by Bossman Graphics
www.bossmangraphics.com

Published by Pine State Press

PRAISE FOR GREAT MEN OF SCIENCE

"Brian Boone's work reads like Thomas Pynchon, if Pynchon were 10% funnier and 15% more photogenic. *Great Men of Science* is a hilarious romp from a truly demented mind — and I mean "demented" in only the kindest sense of the word."
— **Tim Long, writer and producer, *The Simpsons***

———

"I didn't know much about science before reading this book, but I learned a lot! That Einstein invented the cheese-in-the-crust pizza. That Da Vinci was the inventor of the Hacky sack. And that Einstein was the great mind behind the Spice Channel. Okay, I made that up. But here's an alternative fact that's more than true: This is a funny-ass fucking book and it made me laugh many, many times."

— **Mike Sacks, author of *Stinker Lets Loose* and *Passable in Pink***

———

"*Great Men of Science* is about a rivalry among scientists, but when it comes to joyfully zany prose, Brian Boone has no rival. This is a dangerously funny read — remember to wear your safety goggles."
— **Geoffrey Golden, author of *Wet Hot American Summer: Fantasy Camp***

For M. and B.

No scientists were harmed in the making of this book.

Nor were any consulted.

1

———

To think that scientists used to just throw away their leftover tungsten bits. Now, of course, they collect that scrap-and-waste tungsten and store it in beaker-shaped duffel bags. Then, on December 25th — yes, Enrico Fermi's birthday — they gather in major science towns, climb to the roofs of research facilities, and at the stroke of midnight, toss the contents of those beaker-shaped duffel bags up into the sky. Truly there is no more beautiful or uniting a moment for the scientific community than this definitive tradition of Science Day.

It's quite a sight: A billion tungsten flakes drift slowly to the ground, glimmering like tiny diamonds as they do. Scientists gaze upon this, "The Great Tungsten Cascade," as they reflect on the year, their work, and the ceaseless amazingness of science. They also sing songs about science and sip drinks which glow, because bits of tungsten fell into them.

Those fortunate enough to make good on the previous year's Science Day toast of "next year in San Verguenza!" congregate for the world's biggest Science Day celebration in San Verguenza, California, home to Gray Labs, the most aggressive force in science since Thomas Edison smashed a bunch of light bulbs in Nikola Tesla's face at the latter's wedding to his beloved pigeon. Fun fact about Gray Labs: Every cutting-edge scientific breakthrough of the past 40 years happened at Gray Labs. (All except for crack, because it bid too high on the government contract.)

Under the direction of its enigmatic founder Eli Gray, Gray Labs put on one hell of a Gray Labs Presents Science Day. Holographic and robotic vendors sold scientists' favorite refreshments: popping candy rocks, freeze-dried astronaut-style ice cream, and 1990s throwback transparent cola. Street performers entertained revelers with large-scale versions of junior high science class tricks, like freezing a thousand tomatoes in liquid nitrogen and shattering them, writing messages on the side of a building in disappearing lemon juice ink, and the "Human Newton's Cradle." The more exhibitionistic celebrationgoers would dress as iconic scientific figures of the past, their costumes growing more provocative with each passing year. A "Sexy Edmund Halley," which consisted of little more than fishnet stockings and a comet bra, became a titillating if trite standard.

Despite being a scientist by blood and choice and growing up in San Verguenza, Albert Malfort had never properly attended the local Science Day festivities. There was always a reason; he'd been too young, or he wasn't allowed to, or because he worked at Gray Labs, and his job included cleaning up the campus the morning after Science Day. This year, however, was different. He was finally able to observe The Great Tungsten Cascade, albeit from above and from the interior of a prison cell — one of those hovering, two-dimensional ones that had become very popular with local authorities for its space-saving properties.

As he floated about in complete flatness, Albert contemplated how, if he could do it all over again, he'd play a few situations just a hint differently. He also agonized over how he could possibly escape his jail cell, or get the message out that the cell had a design flaw. If struck by a laser at precisely 35 degrees, the dimensional compression would fail, and restore the third dimension for Albert, freeing him from this literal prison and also make him fall out of the sky at a tremendous velocity.

Albert's thoughts were interrupted when quite suddenly he was a third-dimensional being again, and one who was falling out of the sky at a tremendous velocity, and into the path of a young woman holding a laser cannon.

ABOUT TEN YEARS EARLIER

2

The Western Scientific Institute ranks among the most prestigious and expensive establishments devoted to the most marketable of scientific disciplines. As the Da Vinci quote etched into a gigantic, fiber-optic needlepoint sampler in the dining hall read, "Produrre scienza, acquisire denaro," or "Make science, get money."

It was at the Institute on the night before graduation where Albert Malfort tried to make science and, subsequently, if things went according to plan, get money. But before Albert could get on with his glorious future, he first had to weather the odious present, particularly the final rounds of the end-of-year pomp and circumstance.

Instead of a reading of names and the playing of "Pomp and Circumstance," WSI held a Presentation Presentation. Graduates prepared a project to demonstrate the total of their four years (give or take) of study in a public setting and to show off to administrators, professors, other students, and, most importantly, representatives of major research-and-development corporations. Sure, it was a science fair, but it came with much higher stakes. And, usually, a shit ton of lasers.

With the Presentation Presentation just hours away, Albert furiously worked on his project in his lab space, one of the rent-by-the-semester rooms ("Marked for Demolition," as they were officially called by the Facilities Department) used by students who couldn't afford well-appointed off-campus lab spaces. Consequently, the lab was also Albert's living space; he didn't think it was all that bad. The previous tenant's synthetic sheep had spontaneously combusted, leaving behind a queen size mattress's worth of odor-and-moisture-resistant wool. And with the abundance of open microwave technology bouncing around campus, Albert could place a frozen dinner in the room's southwestern corner, and it would cook in seconds.

Albert predicted that he would one day look back on the ignominy of his college years with wistful nostalgia and gratitude for helping him stay hungry, metaphorically and literally. This notion sprang forth — fully developed in its entirety — on this, Albert's last night of college, the night Albert figured out time travel.

Well, not "figured out." He was about to conduct a time travel experiment that he *knew* would work. He was equally confident that the success of this experiment would directly lead to his being offered a research fellowship at Gray Labs, allowing him to get so rich and famous that he would never again have to live secretly in an abandoned building.

Although there are many schools of thought on how time travel *may* work, Albert was of the mind that time and space were wrapped up with one another because they're the same thing — that time was an element of the physical plane, akin to the weather or the mineral makeup of the soil. "Time is wallpaper" was how Albert would describe it if anyone ever were to ask. (No one had.) "Time is wallpaper" was also what he had written at the top of his Presentation Presentation poster board in glitter.

As of 3:30 a.m., Albert had been awake for 20 hours, and he looked it, although he always looked like that, what with his greasy, bromine-colored hair beset by both dandruff and bald patches, and eyes that were so red from strain that it overwhelmed their natural color, which was probably blue. On top of a tall lab bench, his centrifuge spun somewhere in the vicinity of 3,600 revolutions per second, which is very fast, and also how many seconds there are in an hour. This was not a coincidence. The centrifuge whirred and screeched and threw off tiny, triangular blue and purple sparks. Albert had wired in two digital clocks, and he used some conductive wire to connect them to a small mound of russet potatoes.

The clocks, the potatoes, the centrifuge — all sat at an arm's length from Albert, flanking the evening's real stars: two single-use tungsten abysses, each about the size of the single eating plate that Albert owned. They were infinitely black, darker than the dark in the absolute darkness of an underground cave that the senses aren't comfortable with, so the brain starts imagining or inventing little flecks of light to prevent itself from going mad. The little flecks of light in the abysses, however, were real, and they appeared, Albert noticed, exactly once every 1,700 centrifugal rotations. Albert was proud of his ability to count very quickly, and rightfully so.

Albert placed each clock in front of an abyss and noted the time displayed on both. He took a deep breath, then a giddy sigh, and reached under his workbench for a very scientific-looking cardboard box. He tossed back a flap and, from inside, removed an adorable miniature pig. While monkeys and rats had long been favored by commercial science as test subjects, in academia, tiny pigs the size of chipmunks were the sacrificial lamb of choice because their flesh was most like that of humans.

"Carl," Albert said to the tiny pig, "I'm going to be wealthy beyond my wildest expectations. But you know what? Even if I weren't, it's still all about the science, you know?"

Carl had little opinion on the matter, choosing instead to sniff around the table for crumbs. He wouldn't find any; Albert couldn't afford to waste food. At least both got to eat plenty of truffles, which Carl would find underneath the fir trees on campus during his morning root.

"When they see what I've accomplished, Carl. When they see..."

Carl snorted in a cute, piggly kind of way.

"Who? The people from Gray, and Orange East, and all the others! When they see what I've done, I'll be beholden to no man! I'll chart my own path. I won't even have to change my last name. The scientist named Malfort that people think of will be *me*! And it will be in a good light!"

Carl snorted again, this time with a palpable note of judgment.

"What, you think I should call him 'Dad'? No way."

Carl, wisely, said nothing.

"I won't just be famous in the scientific world," Albert said, continuing to fantasize aloud for the benefit of a pig, "I'll be famous in the *regular* world, too. My name will be the name normal people associate with science, the way that Frank Lloyd Wright is the only architect that anyone has ever heard of!" Albert fully believed that once his achievements in time travel became known, he'd outrank and render forgotten the greats of science, the big-time luminaries like Thomas Edison, Linus Pauling, and even his namesake, the most popular and recognizable scientist in history, the great cytologist Albert Claude.

Albert picked up Carl, and the animal squealed with delight, or possibly in panic or desperation — who can really tell with miniature pigs — as Albert strapped him into a tiny-pig-sized helmet covered in blinking diodes and topped with a vibrating antenna.

"That's a good little piggy," Albert said as he carefully threw Carl into an abyss, the one on the left. Carl's squeal echoed ominously, from both nowhere in particular and also everywhere. Albert lunged for the shelf below the table and grabbed the large circuit box with inch-thick red wires that connected everything — the potatoes, the clocks, the centrifuge, even the abysses, at their crispy and gelatinous edges. Albert flipped a switch, not without some difficulty, as it was controlling a lot of electricity, which is surprisingly heavy.

A pulse, or rather a wave, blew through all those items. The world went blindingly white for a few seconds, then black, then white again, then back to the usual grey that characterized Albert's existence. Quickly, Albert replaced the circuit box and took the goggles hanging around his neck and put them on his face, where they should've been already. He peered into the left-side hole, and, getting no response at all, stuck his ear up to the expanse, but immediately reared back by its strong, sucking force. He was just about to examine it in a highly clinical manner — by sticking his finger in there, or at the very least, a pencil — when from the right-most abyss, out came Carl, shooting upward at high speed.

Carl, covered in a thin layer of bluish-purple goo, landed at Albert's feet, walked around in a little circle, and rolled around on his back. Then his own corkscrew tail distracted him and he gave chase. Albert looked at the clock on the left, corresponding to where he'd thrown in the pig: 3:47 a.m. The one by the abyss from which Carl had emerged read 3:42 a.m.

In a controlled laboratory environment, Albert had time traveled a pig five whole minutes into the past.

Albert hooted, hollered, then hooted again, and hollered once more, throwing his hands up in the air near his head to form a crude "H," the traditional scientific gesture of celebration, spontaneously devised by Edward Teller immediately after he invented the H-bomb.

"Hello! You are friend!"

Albert naturally looked at Carl, assuming for a fraction of a second that an excursion through time gave his pig the power of human speech. But Carl could not have talked, as he was eagerly slurping up as much water as he could from the petri dish that had "CARL" written on it. The matter required more scientific inquiry. Albert looked around the room and hypothesized that the human voice came from the other human who was in the room.

3

———

Standing before Albert was a man blessed with the unearned confidence of an 18-year-old, plus the smug self-satisfaction of a 50-year-old with a prematurely vested 401K. Additionally, he was unfairly, bile-risingly handsome. Although Albert admittedly didn't take too much pride in his appearance, and he usually looked like he was in the middle of a long, slow battle with a degenerative disease, he wouldn't call himself ugly. But when placed next to this guy, he was repulsive by comparison.

But then, as if suddenly aware of his shameful attractiveness, the stranger flashed a specific goofy smile, the one that's the universal sign for, "I have no idea what's going on." And he just stood there, with a big dumb grin on his face and his eyes as wide as a petri dish that a thirsty pig drinks out of when it returns from a brief jaunt through time.

"HELLO!" the stranger said so loudly and with such zeal that Albert stumbled backward a little.

"Hi," Albert coughed out.

"HELLO!"

"Can I help you with something?" Albert asked, cringing, quite aware of how awkward he sounded. But then he hadn't talked to a non-pig in weeks.

"YOU. ARE. BEST. SCIENTIST…HERE?" He pronounced the words carefully, as if he had learned them phonetically. Still, he'd said "here" obtusely, as if pausing briefly on a silent "J" that was in there somewhere. Based on that observation, Albert surmised that this man was a Scandinavian.

The stranger's posture relaxed. He jauntily strolled around the room, casually tossing into the air, and catching in his long-fingered, delicate hand, a toy geyser, its grey smoke shooting into the air and dissipating upward. *Okay*, Albert thought, *this guy is definitely Scandinavian*, as everybody knows that Scandinavians love geysers.

"Hello, you hear me say this? You are best science heeeeeeeere," he repeated, waving his arms around in wide circles. Albert took this to mean not just the room, but also the building, or maybe even the entirety of the Western Scientific Institute. He blushed.

The stranger stood squarely in front of Albert, no more than a foot away. Their eyes met, but only a little, because the man was a good six inches taller than Albert, who at 5'6" was on the short side for someone who claimed to be full-grown. As he stared, Albert noticed that the stranger smelled objectively fantastic, like phosphorus sulfate, but also of vaporized gin and with just a touch of the cloying sweetness of astronaut ice cream.

He's a scientist! Albert realized.

The man broke the stare, smiled kindly, and then grabbed a chair from the table. He went to sit down, but then flipped it around and sat in it backward, like a young substitute English teacher. Albert gasped in admiration.

"Is name Alan, yes?"

He knows my name! thought Albert, before he remembered that his name wasn't Alan.

"Albert. Albert Malfort."

"Mal...fort? Is like same as Ronald Malfort?"

Albert felt his face turn hot and his rectum clench.

"No!" he lied. "Different Malfort."

"Oh, this is *very* good. Anyway, hello!"

The stranger leaped up, curiously without making any sound as his hypnotically shiny shoes hit the ground, and he vigorously shook Albert's left hand with both of his own hands with such force that Albert's wrist briefly dislocated before relocating itself.

"Hello, hello, helloooooooo! We are friends now, you help me. Okay!"

The stranger took a deep breath as a smile crossed his lips, as if he were about to tell Albert the most exquisite secret in the universe and then slip away into the mist.

"I am Magnus. Magnus Bigfaker."

It was a very Icelandic-sounding name. Albert congratulated himself for his correct hypothesis that the stranger was, indeed, Scandinavian.

"I am from, I am not sure of word, but..."

Magnus wrapped his arms around himself, shivered, said, "Brrrrr!" and then stomped on the ground with both feet.

"Hug...floor?" Albert guessed.

"NO. IS NOT HUGFLOOR!" Magnus yelled, shutting his eyes so he didn't have to look at Albert, which Albert knew was the tell-tale sign of an angry Icelander.

"I'm sorry, it was just a joke! A joke!" Albert desperately tried to explain. "Iceland. Iceland, right?"

"Yes, yes! Iceland. *Not Hugfloor.* Battle of Hegflur terrible battle in 1263. Denmark win. Many die."

"Oh, I'm so sorry, I was just trying to -- "

"Is joke!" Magnus said, releasing his elegant fists, and opening his sensational eyes.

"Is joke, friend! We are friends. Friends, they joke! Okay, Alan? Ha-ja-ha! As to become we are as friends, you can help me with the big graduate presenting...thing."

Magnus sat back down, solemnly, and once again, backward. Then he darted up and kicked the chair across the room.

"I work on project for *three year!*" he howled. "Three year! Then tonight, it gone!"

"Oh, no!" Albert said as he walked over to Magnus, not having the faintest clue as to how to console him. "What was it?"

"Made by man antimatter of waste product of corn farm factory."

Pinpointing antimatter alone was notable, but to make it out of industrial waste certainly gave it commercial applications, Albert thought, as he felt a twinge of relief that this project was gone, and that he would not have to compete with it for attention at the Presentation Presentation.

"But roommate. He eat. I leave note that say 'DO NOT EAT, JERRY.' But Jerry, he eat! It yellow triangle. Look like snacking corn chip. Jerry love snacking corn chip," explained Magnus. "Alan no has, say... some kind of project from first year that get good grade? Project you give to Magnus, so Magnus have something for presentation Presentation Presentation?"

Albert felt bad for Magnus, he really did, seeing as how the poor guy was getting an unfair punishment from forces that were beyond his control. And so, Albert replied to Magnus's request in a manner that would similarly curse his life for a decade.

"Yes."

4

The Western Scientific Institute Ballroom was like any ballroom, but with more eyewash stations. Its perimeter was lined with cheap, foldable tables covered in maroon table-cloths standing on an ugly maroon carpet embroidered with Vitruvian Men. As every ballroom smells like vegetarian lasagna due to frequent catered events, this one did too, but that was because of the graduate presenting instant vegetarian lasagna pills.

Albert's table sat at the back of the room, just to the side of a pair of metal doors that led to a hallway, which led to the bath-rooms and a little area where the custodial staff kept the buckets they used to clean those bathrooms. He wasn't getting many visi-tors. From his un-vantage point, Albert could make out only a few of the other projects, and he didn't think that they were very compelling. "The Word Calculator" seemed like museum gift shop junk, as did "Individual Household Moon." Albert counted 15 separate students claiming to have built a superior tool with which to catch rodents. Other projects were less than curiosity-piquing, such as "Semi-Semi-Conductors," "The Artificial Appendix," and

"HD Microfiche." One project was obviously just a bucket of stem cells. Attracting a particularly large crowd was "The Living Meat Coat." The name was misleading, as it was more of a vest.

Of all the graduates present, Magnus Bigfaker was notably not among them. Albert presumed the empty stall next to his was for Magnus, so he hopped over for a second and carefully placed underneath a table the project he'd promised to deliver, carefully stuffed into a plastic shopping bag (an invention unveiled at the 1971 Presentation Presentation).

Albert turned around to check on his project, but really to see if anybody important was checking out his project, then turned back around, only to be startled by the sudden, almost magical appearance of Magnus.

"Hello! Best friend!" said Magnus, a little too loudly. From behind him, a crew of six young women, all the same height (tall), build (lithe), and hair color (blonde) emerged and descended upon Magnus's unadorned stall. They all wore aquamarine lab coats constructed out of some kind of shiny tungsten-vinyl alloy and embossed on the back with a stylized "Magnus" in black stitching.

The crew sprinkled little metallic beads onto the stall's table-cloth, which was immediately devoured and replaced with an aquamarine one boasting a thread count so high it could be visible from space. On the partitions surrounding the table, the women hung translucent sheets, each which projected a holographic, three-dimensional "X?". Albert thought each "X?" really seemed to jump out at him, which they did, because they were holograms.

"Is big day for science, yes!" Magnus said, distracting Albert by vigorously shaking his hand. After, they stood in silence for 10 long seconds.

Finally, Magnus spoke, sounding just a hint irritated. "So you have project for Magnus?"

Albert nodded to the table. Magnus zipped over, and before even opening the bag, his eyes lit up, a smile crept across his face, and his eyes gushed huge tears of joy, which made Albert feel awkward. But then, he was a scientist, and most displays of emotion made him uncomfortable.

"You are true friend, Alan. If I win contest, I give you all of the credits!"

They laughed, Magnus obnoxiously, and Albert as if he were imitating someone who was laughing obnoxiously.

"I am not for win with last-minute project."

Albert understood what Magnus meant, but he was still a little miffed. What he'd given him was old, and had just been sitting around, but it was still a very nice project.

"Just, just be careful with it," Albert said to Magnus, who hadn't heard or listened, as he was already in his stall, addressing in hushed tones his crew, fresh-faced and beaming like a bunch of first-day interns.

Albert noticed that Magnus had not prepared a poster board, which would surely be frowned upon. But none of that mattered; today was going to be *his* day. Albert smiled, closed his eyes, and pictured himself at the Nobel Prize banquet in Stockholm, taking a third trip to the all-you-can-eat meatball buffet.

5

Magnus spent the evening before the Presentation Presentation the same way he'd spent all of his evenings in school: recreationally trepanning. That entailed drilling a hole into his head and all the way through the skull to tickle the pleasure centers of the brain, directly and literally with the duck feather Magnus would affix to a surgical-grade drill bit.

Sitting on the floor of his bespoke dorm room, he held the drill up to his head and giggled as the feather caressed him just behind his earlobe, which four years of field study on that very floor had proven was the ideal place to enter the skull to guarantee maximum fun. Just as he was about to fully push in, he looked away, distracted for a fraction of a second by the flash of a shiny object in the corner of his eye; the object was a mirror.

The drill bit bore into his head, resisting the hard, bonelike substance that comprised his skull, before finding the spongy, welcoming flesh of his brain. He collapsed, falling onto a pile of graduation presents, instantly breaking some dumb gold disc labeled "VOYAGER" that his father had tearfully presented to him earlier that day.

He believed himself to be freshly high when he was, in fact, still high from a trepanning session earlier that day. His latest attempt had not actually unlocked any more euphoric nodules; in his distraction, he'd missed them slightly, albeit completely.

While an unsuccessful trepanation may cause viscous, dark red goo to seep out of the head from the site of puncture, the notable aftereffect of this trepanning session was that *yellow* goo gushed out of the hole Magnus had just drilled. He was rightfully terrified, but kept this untoward show of weakness to himself, as he, a wealthy person and a Scandinavian, had been trained. Plus, there were girls there. Mostly though, he was just too high to get all weird about it.

While some currently unreachable part of his brain alarmed another part of his brain about the jeopardy facing a third part of his brain, the rest of Magnus's brain directed Magnus to bolt up onto his feet and shout, "I shall experiment on this. In the name of SCIENCE!" All this meant was that he intended to taste the yellow stuff presently gushing out of his head and onto the marble floor. It's a common saying in the scientific world that "Science is 90 percent tasting weird things and observing what happens."

As he went to do just that, Magnus felt feelings he'd never felt before. He felt like how he imagined other people must feel. Uneasy. Unsure. *Ugly.* This was a very troubling 15 seconds, but things lightened up as soon as Magnus ate the glop that had spilled from out of his skull.

After he had his fill, he sucked up the ooze with a large household syringe, injected it back into his brain, and then sealed the borehole with one of the many marble skull plugs he necessarily kept stockpiled. Instantly, he returned to his baseline state of invincibility.

As he had felt sad, very briefly, and then back to his normal state of extreme self-confidence, Magnus realized that he had made quite the discovery. He had uncovered a natural, physical source of what had heretofore been but a concept, and an unquantifiable one at that: charisma. He figured that such a breakthrough would make for an ideal Presentation Presentation, his capstone project which he had not yet started. Magnus understood that he'd have to run some experiments to prove that what came out of his head really was charisma, and that it was a useful tool in the field of human manipulation.

Certainly, he thought, there had to be some sap still working on his final project in the middle of the night before it was due. Magnus wondered: Could he get that person to help him, to their own detriment, on this, the most important night of their life, using only his prodigious charisma? Magnus was not immediately convinced, but he thought that it was possible if some other powerful element was involved.

The expensive escorts trepanning in the room were quite high by that time, and they started to make goofy grins and speak in silly voices.

Magnus had his thesis.

6

Magnus stood near the back of his stall, matching his pressed, floor-length lab coat with a white privacy mask. The ultra-thin globe (Presentation Presentation '04) fit around the head, and its wearer could neither see nor hear living creatures, only objects, giving the appearance that the vicinity had been struck with a neutron bomb (Presentation Presentation '74). Magnus couldn't even notice all the people milling about his area: R&D reps, most of the other graduates, and reporters from both *Science Beat* and *Science Beat Teenz*.

An older, distinguished-looking gentleman glided up to Albert's stall, dressed in the same lab finery as Magnus, although his coat featured gold braiding, indicating a high-ranking science official. Albert knew exactly who he was: Andreas Riptide, chancellor of the Western Scientific Institute, chairman of the International Scientific Board of Regents, and Honorary Moon Colonel.

As Albert was a student and Andreas Riptide an administrator, they had of course never met face-to-face, although Andreas Riptide had been the subject of a "Who I admire" report Albert wrote his sophomore year of high school. Even if his home had contained any research materials besides the "R" volume of a grocery store encyclopedia with a 1985 copyright, Albert still would've chosen to write about Andreas Riptide.

Albert could still remember a few fun facts about him:

• He had changed the original spelling of his name, "Ryptyjdj" to "Riptide," which was phonetically identical and also very cool.

• He was born in Iceland.

• He'd married Karolinka Wakimovich, an East German super-model and nuclear engineer.

• He's credited with developing significant scientific break-throughs such as particle collusion, telescopic diffusion, and the microwavable crisping sleeve.

Two older, paunchier men also dressed in ornate lab coats flanked Riptide. From their name tags, Albert could tell that one represented Gray Labs, and the other was from Orange East, the upscale scientific boutique offshoot of Thomas Edison's Edison Labs. Also in the group was the WSI mascot, Mr. Molecule. The character's costume, said to be built from actual dark matter, was decorated with thousands of sequins that were also tiny, opera-tional Tesla coils. Rumors had persisted around the school for years that there wasn't actually a person inside the costume, and that Mr. Molecule really was a giant molecule. Regardless, Mr. Molecule's sole function was to appear at WSI functions and charge $40 for photos.

"Good afternoon, Mr. Molecule. Good afternoon, Dr. Riptide. Gentlemen of the science industry," Albert choked out.

"Good afternoon to you as well, student! What are you going to show us today?" Dr. Riptide excitedly asked while absolutely beaming.

Albert launched into the spoken part of his presentation,

which he'd optimistically written two weeks before he'd made the time travel breakthrough with Carl a few hours earlier.

"Let me ask you a question. What *time* is it?"

"Uh, well, I don't really carry a watch, but I imagine it's about — "

"Well, let's not lose any *time* here, sir!"

Albert had meticulously calculated his words for maximum hilarity. But he did not get to share any more of his prepared marks because the house lights had gone out, and a hush had silenced the ballroom. A beam of what seemed to be pure, intense white light, like that of a toy star outfitted with fresh D-batteries, illuminated Magnus's stall.

In one fluid motion, Magnus tore the bag off the object Albert had given him, as well as his privacy mask, which imploded into nothingness. Strobe lights flashed on Magnus as he struck poses and recreated memorable tableaus from great moments in scientific history. His constant prop was the object given to him to be his presentation: Albert's beloved, sixth-grade-science-fair-winning photon ray.

"What is that? Is that a space pistol?" someone whispered.

"No, it's a gun. An earth gun. Yeah!" someone else whispered.

"It's a photon ray!" Albert said to no one in particular, and, likewise, being heard by no one in particular over the booming, synthesized human voice delivering lines of code over the room's public address system.

Magnus continued to vogue and vamp with the gun, his scientific re-creations segueing into cowboy tropes — pointing the gun into the crowd over his shoulder, under his arm, between his legs, out in front of his body, spinning the trigger guard around his finger, and then spinning the tip of the gun on his finger as if it was a large, orange sports-ball.

Albert began to suspect that maybe Magnus was not exactly the person he'd claimed to be the previous night.

As the strobe lights triggered seizures for several spectators, another voice on the P.A. shout-whispered, "Charisma!" Then the flashing of lights, recitation of code, and projection of holograms came to an abrupt stop. Magnus was suddenly illuminated, but from within, as if he'd eaten a large bowl of phosphorus just before his presentation, which he had done.

"What actually makes the world go 'round?" Magnus asked the crowd, which collectively wasn't sure whether or not it was a rhetorical question.

Albert's suspicions and alarm increased. He thought it strange that Magnus, who just a few hours earlier was an exuberant but hapless student with a poor command of the English language, was now speaking with the perfect diction and non-regional accent taught to aspiring newscasters. Also, he seemed to have his presentation very much ready to go, not to mention an extremely well-funded one. Magnus hadn't once mentioned a uniformed staff.

"What makes our planet turn? Is it the sun's gravitational pull? Rotational mites? Invisible space magnets?" Members of the audience verbally cast their votes for each option. "All of the above, obviously, but also...*none of the above*. Science does all of these things. Science generates money, and money comes freely and easily to those of us who are excellent at science. But what allows some of us to be handsomely rewarded for even the slightest effort when so many other worthy scientists remain unseen, toiling in dank underground labs, never to have their work realized or appreciated?"

Albert felt a twinge of understanding. He wasn't sure why.

"Charisma!"

Magnus went on to detail the previous night's events to the crowd, relating how he came to discover the charisma center in his brain. A less charismatic man would have lied and made up a story to present themselves in a better light; Magnus told the audience that he discovered charisma when he'd been drilling into his own brain while getting high with prostitutes. If anything, it proved his point — he just had *that much charisma.*

The story made Albert feel incredibly yucky on the inside.

"My brief flirtation with depression was alleviated by the reinjection of this substance back into my person, and I had an inkling, a hypothesis —a science guess, if you will — that this was, in fact, charisma.

"But how could I know for sure that this was charisma, and not just some other, useless brain fluid? And how could I find out in such a limited amount of time? The clock was ticking. I tell you, friends, I wished I'd had a time machine."

"I have a time machine!" Albert shouted. No one cared.

"Friends, let me introduce you to a very important member of my research team."

Magnus turned, and his internal phosphorus spotlight shined on Albert, who was very confused but sensed that things were about to get worse. Still, he did what human beings by their nature do when summoned by a spotlight: He went up on that stage, which wasn't really a stage, rather more of an elevated bubble.

"His name is not important. I think it's Alex."

"Albert."

"I said it's not important. Guess what, Alvin? You were my control group."

"Huh?"

"How do you not know what a control group is?"

The audience laughed.

"Then," Magnus said, shifting into his imbecilic accent, "if smart scientist are you, why for then you not know I manipulate you into giving effort for toward my project on very most important night of Alan's life?"

"Why did I help you?" Albert searched. "Kindness?"

The audience roared with laughter.

"I would call that," said Magnus, in what Albert was now convinced was Magnus's real speaking voice, "manipulated out of your own interests, at a time when your interests mattered the most, and toward *my* interests. On a chemical level."

Magnus held up the photon ray.

"My control group gave me this photon ray. *Today.* While he should have been working on his own project, he took time out to find one for me. Why? Because 'I am making for talk like this to him and tell him Jerry eat Magnus project, *boo-hoo-hoo* Magnus.'"

The crowd roared again. Albert peed his pants just a little, but his rented lab coat was extra-long, and thus quite forgiving against any stage accidents.

"I call that proof that charisma is real, that it's in my brain, and that it can make anybody do what I want."

What Albert wanted was to disappear. He wished Magnus would just shoot him with that photon ray. He contemplated grabbing it out of his hand and ending himself. Or Magnus.

"In fact, I have so much charisma that you'll all still applaud me and give me lots of money even after I destroy this guy's project."

True to his word, Magnus fired the photon ray directly at Albert's final school project. His Presentation Presentation presentation. His time travel setup. His ticket to a better life. His ticket to *any* life.

Blue light shot up from the table and turned instantly into yellow smoke. The time travel display was, simply, no longer there, nor was the table, nor the dividers, nor Albert's poster board. Poor Carl skittered away at top piggy speed, squealing in pain over a burnt tail-tip.

"Carl, come back!"

The crowd laughed again. Someone repeated "Carl, come back!" in a whiny, high-pitched, mocking tone.

"Charisma!"

The crowd applauded wildly.

The house lights came on, and Andreas Riptide, along with Mr. Molecule, skipped jauntily up to Magnus's hover-stage. The old man slapped Magnus on the back in a paternal way. In an even more paternal way, he hugged him for a solid minute. And then, in an extremely paternal way, he shouted, "My son! I'm so proud of my son!" That's when Albert finally figured out that these two were father and son.

Andreas Riptide reached into the breast pocket of his formal whites and took out a butter-colored object about the size of a sugar cube. Then, he carefully unfolded the object 17 times, at which point it took its true shape, that of an oversized novelty check.

"The WSI Board of Regents, in a generous cooperative agreement with Gray Labs, awards its first-ever $5 million research grant to Magnus Bigfaker Riptide." Andreas handed the giant, already made-out-to-Magnus check to Magnus, who amusingly pretended to endorse the back of it with Albert's photon ray. Once more, the audience roared.

"And in an unprecedented move, the Board has voted to award another prize, a 'nice try award,' if you will."

Albert, who could barely stand up, or hear, or prevent himself from dry heaving, perked up his ears. More accurately, they popped in the middle of a dry heave.

"It goes to a student whose project may not have obvious commercial potential, but that which still has important scientific ramifications."

Albert held his breath and listened carefully.

"And it goes to Magnus Riptide! His project was that good!"

From his back pocket, Mr. Molecule produced another giant novelty check, already unfolded, and already made out to "Magnus Bigfaker Riptide" in the amount of $2 million.

Albert swallowed a mouthful of his own stomach acid and said aloud to himself, "At least I'm still graduating."

7

"Albert Malfort will not be graduating."

There were many events over graduation weekend beyond the Presentation Presentation. They included "Gray Labs Presents: A Laser-Light Show Tribute to Gray Labs," a father-son rocket golfing competition, and "Schrödinger's Brunch," in which everyone on campus was invited and also not invited.

As most of those were family-and-friend-type events, Albert hadn't planned on attending any of them. Which is why he was completely unaware of the existence of the Post-Presentation Presentation Non-Graduation, a reading of names and subsequent public shaming of those who failed at the Presentation Presentation or had in some other way embarrassed themselves during their time at the Western Scientific Institute.

"Once again," said Mr. Molecule in a deep, guttural tone that was technically an audible, ultraviolet stream of light, "Albert Malfort will not be graduating." He paused. "This concludes the Non-Graduation."

"Did they say Malfort? Oh, my..." and, "I hope that sad sack isn't his son," and various iterations thereof rippled through the crowd.

Albert looked around until he spotted Magnus, surrounded by young science groupies and old scientists. He smiled at Albert and laughed, and gave him a shrug, as if he'd just made him the victim of an impish, good-natured prank rather than a catastrophic, life-changing act of callous cruelty. Albert stood his ground, maintaining eye contact as he vomited all over himself. A swarm of cleaning nanobots from a few stalls over made short work of the mess.

Albert, still hunched over, noticed the swirling black tornado of feet inches from his own. He looked up, and there was Mr. Molecule, who handed him a translucent card.

"You did not present a presentation at the Presentation Presentation," the card stated.

"You saw Magnus. He destroyed my proj —"

Mr. Molecule gestured to Albert to keep reading.

"Showing a presentation at the Presentation Presentation may be your final duty as a student at the Western Scientific Institute," this card read, "but it remains compulsory."

"I made a *time machine*. It got wrecked."

Mr. Molecule nodded at the card, a little more annoyed this time.

"Then you should have gone back in time and prevented that from happening..." the card stated. Albert flipped the card over. "...And if you can't, well, then your time travel presentation wasn't very good..." Albert flipped the card over again. "...Or far enough along, anyway, and you probably would not have passed anyway."

As hard as it was to own up to it, he knew that Mr. Molecule was right. If he *really* knew time travel, he'd travel through time and fix what had just happened, no big deal. But he couldn't, because his entire project — the whole of his research — had not only been destroyed, but it had been a happy accident in the first place. Albert had no idea how he had done what he did. It had just...worked.

As he found himself lying on his side, curled up atop the scratchy carpet of the ballroom floor, stared down at an angle by a Vitruvian Man who had long ago lost the fibers in his right eye, Albert admitted to himself that he was a fraud. A humiliated, shivering, vomit-covered fraud.

He felt the hefty punch of self-loathing in his stomach as he thought about all tossed-off projects and experiments he'd made throughout his young life, some for fun, some for school, some for necessity, like the nutritional cakes he'd made out of garbage and septic tank waste to feed himself as a latchkey tween. Or there were those other projects, ones he'd given to classmates he barely knew that were then used to cruelly sabotage his own tenuous ticket to a lovely future. Like that fantastic photon ray he'd given to Magnus a few minutes earlier.

Any number of Albert's childhood creations could have been viable, competitive final projects, Albert realized. It was cold comfort when it dawned on him that no, they wouldn't have, because he still would have been in a graduating class with Magnus Riptide, who still would have destroyed his project, no matter what it would have been. Because that was *his* project.

Albert had no options, and what was worse is that he hadn't had any time to plan for his lack of options. Which meant Albert had only one option.

He was going to have to go home and live with his father.

8

———

With his complimentary bus ticket that American colleges provide departing non-graduates (it discourages loitering), Albert took the 90-mile, seven-hour ride to San Verguenza, a Northern California valley town surrounded by both majesticish brown hills, and crumbling missions left behind by 19th-century Spanish settlers. Gray Labs had purchased a vast amount of acreage here years earlier for a large sum. It issued annual bonuses to the municipal government so long as it honored three simple requests: 1) Let Gray Labs police itself, 2) Don't ask questions, and 3) Seriously, don't ask questions.

Upon the most elevated part of this garbage land, once home to a beloved community center and a landfill, sat the sprawling research and production complex of Gray Labs. It was a shining city on a hill, looking down on the rest of the world, literally, what with the solar panels and metallic beams of its octagonal buildings reaching infinitely skyward.

A quick glance of the Gray campus from 500 yards away was the highlight of the bus trip for Albert, outranking even the incessant screaming from the 17 babies on board that distracted him from thinking about why he was on a bus heading to the part of his hometown that wasn't Gray Labs. Albert gazed from afar at the luminous facility. He wondered what kinds of experiments were underway in there, and how he could almost have played a part in those experiments, and what the scientists there were having for lunch, and what he could have had for lunch if he'd gotten to work there.

Despite being a San Verguenza native with a father who was at one point one of Gray Labs' most valuable employees, Albert had never set foot on the grounds. The company had worked out a deal with the California attorney general's office that it wasn't liable if anyone over the age of 13 incurred injury during a visit to Gray Labs. Anyone *under* that age who got, say, sprayed with radioactive super-pollen, the state would still have to consider Gray responsible. Thus Gray Labs enacted a strict "nobody under the age of 13 allowed" policy.

Albert's father, Ronald Clark Malfort, had been terminated on the eve of Albert's 13th birthday, which certainly made for an unwelcome, last-minute change in the primary activity planned for the budding young scientist's birthday: a VIP tour of Gray Labs. The cake his mother had ordered, a scale replica of the Gray Labs complex, was especially and suddenly heartbreaking. Seeing his mother try to throw the cake away without him noticing was the last thing he ever saw her do; she left later that day. He still wasn't sure where she went; he heard his father mumble something once about following Stephen Hawking around on the lecture circuit.

Ronald Clark Malfort, or "Ron," as his own son called him out of spite, was one of the most accomplished and important scientists in the world. Once. Ron Malfort had led some of the first cloning experiments of pigs, both guinea and miniature. His work with the latter revolutionized science, as tiny pigs would one day replace the commonplace scientific practices of testing on dogs, rats, and in some seedier locales, short people. Ron Malfort subsequently became a pioneer in the nascent discipline of gene therapy. His work involved extracting all the DNA from a body, removing the offending genes and replacing them with better ones, and then re-inserting the "clean" DNA back into the body; he called it "The Find and Replace."

The hype and the importance of it all went to Ron Malfort's head, where it festered and contorted. Because the world viewed him as the foremost expert on genetics, he, too, saw himself as the world's foremost expert on genetics. He mistook this privilege for permission to make some disturbing choices only tangentially related to his area of study.

As part of the special, souvenir, $20 issue of *Science Beat* to commemorate an annual Gray Labs Presents Science Day, a reporter was tasked with calling famous scientists and/or their representatives to obtain quotes for a cheesy spread called, "What Does Gray Labs Presents Science Day Mean to Me?" The reporter found Ron Malfort in person merely by going to the place where Ron Malfort could usually be found on a weekday evening: drinking vaporized Manhattans at a local bar called The Manhattan Project, where the specialty was vaporized Manhattans.

The reporter asked Ron Malfort her one question: "What does Gray Labs Presents Science Day mean to you?" Ron Malfort dutifully answered to the best of his abilities. But his quote was not going to fit into the two-line bubble reserved for his remarks. He spoke casually, fluidly, and lengthily on a number of topics. *Science Beat*, a wholly-owned subsidiary of Gray Labs, published Ron Malfort's comments in full, in a special standalone edition (with a cover price of $40).

Some highlights:

What does Science Day mean to me? What it means to me is that it's a bunch of chicken shit.

It's just a way for old Eli Gray to put on a big party and have everybody tell him what a great guy he is. Well, I don't think he's a great guy!

You want to know the truth about Eli Gray? The truth about Eli Gray is that Eli Gray is more than 150 years old, and he is being kept alive by artificial means. Eli Gray isn't the son, or the grandson, or whatever he says. You know, the guy who invented the telephone five seconds too late and Bell got the patent, and he became a footnote? That Eli Gray is the same Eli Gray. Why do you think they don't allow phones at Gray Labs?

He's Elisha Gray. Still alive, all this time. He's got Linus Pauling down there in a room at Gray Labs, making time and keeping it in bottles for him. Then he takes those bottles and takes what's in 'em, and somehow that makes him live.

I heard the secret messages they left for me. John Knitty did. He did, that's who. He left them for me in that song, "I Wish I Could Store Time Up in Bottles Forever." I've heard that song a thousand times. You listen really closely to that song, it tells you everything. It's all there, right in the song. You've just got to listen to it backward, and really loud. That's why John Knitty is dead. Killed in a plane crash. Eli Gray didn't want the world to know his secret. He killed Knitty. Eli Gray killed him. I want another Manhattan.

These comments made Ron Malfort come across as a mentally ill person, to say the least, although he did accidentally expose the strange-but-true fact that phones had never been allowed at Gray Labs. Curiously, they were installed just days after Ron's controversial statements were published, although company policy dictated that they be called "Grayboxes." As for "I Wish I Could Store Time Up in Bottles Forever," it was hard to gauge John Knitty's intent to place secret messages in recordings because he had, in fact, died in a plane crash.

Ron Malfort was immediately fired from his position at Gray Labs. It's something Eli Gray had been itching to do, as the upstart was getting dangerously famous for his breakthroughs, leading to a company policy of officially crediting all discoveries, innovations, and patents developed at Gray Labs to Eli Gray, and Eli Gray only. After the termination came an Eli Gray-led systematic destruction of Ron Malfort. This included death threats, modestly sized letter bombs, and a significant number of unordered pizzas all sent to his home from Spazzatura, the pizza parlor widely acknowledged to be the fifth-worst in San Verguenza. Worse still, Gray made sure that Ron Malfort appeared on the cover of *Unpopular Science* for a record seven consecutive issues.

The ordeal had left one of Albert's definitive if mundane memories of his father instantly and tragically ironic. "I just want to be like Linus Pauling, you know?" Ron Malfort would say to Albert at least once a week while driving him to school. Albert hated these drives. His father always listened to the same cassette, a homemade mixtape of maudlin '70s soft rock like "I Wish I Could Store Time Up in Bottles Forever," and his father invariably droned on about Linus Pauling, the Nobel Prize-winning chemist who risked his reputation to zealously advocate that all biological problems could be eradicated with high doses of Vitamin C. Never quite conclusively proven, these assertions left Pauling a pariah of science up until the day he passed away in relative obscurity.

But what truly made Ron Malfort seem a bit off was his tenacious insistence that everything he'd told *Science Beat* had been factual, and in doing so he took his rivalry with Eli Gray to new, ill-conceived heights. Mere weeks after the publication of his interview and resulting termination, Ron Malfort released a statement, announcing plans to "defeat the evil Eli Gray and his time bottles" by amassing an army of "super-genius scientist-soldiers."

A week after that, and unable to recruit anyone to his cause and also running out of the pricey mood stabilizers that his Gray Labs health insurance had once paid for, he released a second, more specific statement:

"The only way to build up an army is to do it from scratch. Today I announce the creation of the Ronald Clark Malfort Depository for Germinal Excellence. With donations from the world's top scientists who know the truth about Eli Gray, and the assistance of young, fertile women with expansive birthing hips, we shall build this army, one by one, until the day of reckoning. Children are our future!" In other words, it was a sperm bank, but one that accepted only the seed of the world's most remarkable and paranoid scientific minds.

Now, the Ronald Clark Malfort Depository for Germinal Excellence *was* a real place. It was not centered in the breathtaking tower of iron and glass pictured on its brochures, but rather in the garage of Ron Malfort's ranch-style home on the outskirts of San Verguenza. It consisted entirely of some freezers, a pre-owned centrifuge, an old voting booth to provide privacy, and racy magazines to carnally inspire the scientific gentleman, such as *Lab Brats* and *Science Beat Forum*. Such gentlemen were not forthcoming. The Depository ultimately attracted genetic material from just two parties: 1) A sample from a world-famous scientist, donated by his family and who wished to remain anonymous, and 2) Ron Malfort.

9

———

As buses always drop off passengers in the worst part of town, the bus unloaded Albert in front of his childhood home, and also and the headquarters of the Ronald Clark Malfort Depository for Germinal Excellence. The place wasn't in the best shape; the paint peeled, the roof sagged, one of the two large windows in the front room had a rock-shaped hole in it. Dead brown grass around the house concealed spent freezers, vintage centrifuges, and other, less easily identifiable technological waste. To Albert, it looked the same as it had the last time he'd seen it, years earlier.

Despite no lead-up in the way of footsteps or the sounds made by a vehicle, Albert was surprised to find himself suddenly no longer alone on the street. Whoever it was would have had to have used advanced scientific trickery, thought Albert, an accurate assessment, because the man standing beside him was Gray Labs founder, president, and spokesman Eli Gray.

He stood there gleaming in his signature uniform of shoulder-to-toe grey bodysuit, grey utility belt, and grey tennis shoes. Albert had read in Eli Gray's authorized biography *Shades of Gray* that

Gray had seven of these outfits, all in his legally trademarked color of "Eli Gray Grey," and it was all that he wore. He also rocked a helmet, of which he only had the one, and which he wore all the time both publicly and privately. Eli Gray could carry on one conversation inside the helmet and another outside the helmet; rumors said it's because his remarkable brain contained two speech centers.

"Hey!" he said, a little too loudly.

"Hey," whispered Albert, slightly confused.

Eli Gray dropped into Albert's hand a perfect cube of tungsten. Eli Gray reared his arm back and hurled an identical cube at the Malfort home. It satisfyingly smashed right through the middle of the front room window, leaving a gaping hole in the glass next to the one that was already there. Albert heard a faint string of shouted profanities from inside the house before the angry, hulking mass that was Ron Malfort lumbered outside.

The intact glass around the new hole began to vibrate faster and faster until it shattered, then turned to black powder, and disappeared.

"Gray Labs rules!" Eli Gray shouted, throwing his arms up in a celebratory "H" formation. He bolted away as Albert stood still, paralyzed with what was becoming a familiar combination of confusion and terror.

Ron Malfort shot something at Eli Gray, but missed, or at least he missed Eli Gray. The weapon's discharge had left a manhole-size black hole in the ground. Those were all over the place in San Verguenza.

"And you..." he said, turning to Albert, about to wrap his thick, hairy, tremoring hands around Albert's throat.

The sneer on Ron's face immediately melted into an expression of warmth and pride, and the near-strangulation became a one-sided hug. "Albert!" he exclaimed, his voice scratchy and cracked from years of puffing on homemade e-cigarettes.

The Malforts hadn't seen each other in three years. Toward the end of Albert's freshman year at WSI, his father had jumped out at him from behind a bush while he walked across campus one morning, asking him to hang up on school grounds some posters seeking "Quick Money for 'A' Students, Men Only." Ron looked a lot different now. Only three years had passed, but they were those eventful three years in which a man in his sixties does all of his aging at once. He certainly wasn't a living example of the genetic superiority he preached. His head was bald, his belly round, and he had a grey mustache that upon closer inspection was actually just a whole lot of untrimmed nose hairs. Close to but unattached to the mustache was his beard: long and wild, like that of a third-rate wizard. He would've stood well over six feet tall if he weren't permanently hunched over. He wore a greasy, smear-covered lab coat. It wasn't buttoned, and he didn't have anything on underneath.

Ron Malfort was, Albert thought, super-gross.

In the split-second it took Albert to take all of this in, he also realized that he was in no mood to see his estranged father. He bolted on foot, and as he ran, wildly threw the tungsten cube in the general direction of his father's home. It hit one of the six small windows on the garage door protecting the Ronald Clark Malfort Depository for Germinal Excellence. Albert was pleased that he'd made contact; he'd never thrown in an athletic situation before.

Then he felt something graze his left ear, and looked back to see his own father, devastated and humiliated but still quite angry, holding a weapon. As he ran, Albert felt around his ear and found that part of it was missing. He no longer felt too bad about running away from his father, as his father had tried to kill him, or at the very least, displace his molecules.

"Come on!" he heard Eli Gray yell as he rounded a corner. There, Eli Gray was waiting for him, atop a SegGray, one of those two-wheeled gyroscope-powered electric stand-up scooters. He held a second SegGray upright and waved at Albert to hop on. Albert did. Eli Gray zoomed away, and so did Albert.

Albert followed Eli Gray through the dusty outer neighborhoods of San Verguenza. He followed him past his old grade school. He followed him through the downtown area with the many businesses that catered to scientists: The Unified Theory, the science pawnshop; Elements, the high-end bar; and several Gray-branded decontamination centers, which had replaced all the mom-and-pop ones.

They whizzed past various powdered orange-flavored space-drink carts, laser tag centers that used real lasers, and a Shuttle Commander Jimmy Howard's Moonbounce Emporium. They rode past the Theremin outlet store, the small theater that only performed plays in C++, the all-male strip club Hardon Colliders, the chemical supply company Barnes' Nobles, the Christian Science Reading Room, and the municipal office where citizens paid parking tickets and filed for building permits and stuff like that. San Verguenza was a science town, but it still needed a place for routine town business.

Albert followed Eli Gray through the disreputable areas. Albert saw the street performers dressed up as robots that really were robots; he thought he saw Joules Newton, an old friend of his father who dealt in black market scientific equipment. Albert followed Eli Gray on his scooter out of the downtown area and through to the beginnings of the Gray Labs-owned and operated section of town. He followed him through the employee housing projects, and under the overhead pneumatic transportation tube they had to install because the interns got so lost in thought that cars and SegGrays hit them while crossing that very street. Still, Eli Gray almost hit some random intern, and then Albert almost hit the same one.

Finally, Albert rode behind Eli Gray around a hilly bend, through a grassy field, the hills in the near distance looking down on them as they wound up, up, up to the main entrance of Gray Labs. Albert felt his heart flutter as the metallic gates opened, and Eli Gray pulled his SegGray into the "SegGrays ONLY" parking lot. He waved for Albert to park next to him, and so Albert did.

Then Eli Gray jumped on top of Albert, and Albert couldn't breathe. The last thought Albert had before he passed out was how much an ether-soaked rag tasted like honey-roasted peanuts.

10

When Albert regained lucidity, he found himself sitting on an inflatable ball-chair in a white room with no apparent means of entry or exit. And by the looks of the work in front of him, he was almost done with an inch-thick stack of paperwork, and he had apparently already signed and/or initialed every page.

After momentarily noticing that Gray Labs uses and probably also makes fluorescent light bulbs that don't leave a room in a sickly yellow pall, Albert realized that he had no idea how he got there. He felt at first a little cheated that he didn't know how he got to the inner sanctum of Gray Labs, much less talked himself into a job, and agreed to sign 500 or so forms confirming as much. But he was no less thrilled that he'd pulled it off.

Also, he was wearing new lab whites and a tie. The tie, which he didn't know how to tie, was tied, and it had little pictures of quarks on it. Right then and there, Albert decided that this would be his "casual Friday" tie if the legend about Gray Labs having casual Fridays were true.

Albert hoped that during his lapse in consciousness that he

had filled out all of the forms correctly. He turned the page at the top of the pile, signed it, and added it to the stack, this one acknowledging understanding that payments for radiation poisoning treatments would be paid by Gray Labs at an annual cap of $50.

"Hi, Albert. Have you been bold today?"

This startled Albert, and he and jumped in his seat, but then he chuckled. Eli Gray had referenced "Be Bold," Gray Labs' classic advertising slogan. Gray Labs ads invariably depicted Eli Gray hanging upside-down in exotic locations, such as over a cannibal tribe's stewpot, or mountain biking down the face of the least-popular president on Mount Rushmore, all with the simple caption, "Be Bold." Despite Gray Labs pioneering photo enhancement and manipulation software with its EyeLie suite of programs, none of these photos were ever doctored — Eli Gray really did visit all those places and perform the stunts. He even took the photos himself.

Eli Gray was also a control freak, obviously, which was precisely why he insisted on interviewing and approving even the lowliest of low-level hires. A CEO interviewing employees and procuring recruits semi-against their will are just two of the things the Gray Labs prospectus listed as examples of Eli Gray's propensity to "be bold."

"So, how did I get here?"

"You came here willingly. Your signature on one of those pages confirms that."

Eli Gray slammed his hand on the table and deftly pulled out a single sheet of paper from the bottom of the stack, turned it over, and slapped it on the table. He pointed to the signature.

"Okay. But how did I get *here*?" Albert asked, waving his hands around to indicate the room.

"You came here willingly."

Even though Albert couldn't see his face, and nor could Eli Gray see Albert's, because inside that helmet he was composing an email, Albert could tell that Eli Gray was silently glowering at him to drop the issue.

Eli Gray noticed Albert notice the big bowl of candy on the table. Eli Gray grabbed a piece out of the bowl, a hint that Albert took to mean that he too could and absolutely must have one as well.

"Candy transistor radios. They really work!" Eli Gray said as he flipped a tiny switch on the candy. Albert could faintly make out some music until Eli Gray held the candy transistor in front of the helmet where his mouth would be, after which the candy dissipated like a sand pillar.

"Osmotic eating. It's very new."

"Okay."

"Well then," he took a breath. "Welcome to the Gray Labs... family," he said, unsure of the last word.

"Thank you," Albert replied with a slight quiver in his voice. "I wasn't quite sure this would be a possibility."

"On account of you not graduating?"

He was hoping that Eli Gray had not found out about that.

"Well..."

"You're not your father, Albert."

Albert grinned.

"That was a test back there, Albert."

"It was?"

"If you turned on your father and followed me back here, you got a job. If you'd sided with him, well, then you would never have worked in legitimate science. You made the right choice."

"He sure was angry," Albert said with a chuckle.

"Do you know what line of work *my* father was in?" Eli Gray asked.

"No, sir."

"And I don't remember. But I know what *I* do, and that is to be bold. Be bold, Albert. Let the crazy old man watch you thrive! It'll drive him crazy. More so, I mean." As he said those last words, pixelated images of nuts, bananas, and cuckoo birds briefly flashed up on the surface of Eli Gray's helmet.

"How else do you think you got into Western when your last name was 'Malfort'?"

Albert *had* always wondered how he'd been accepted when his last name was the same as that of the most scorned man both in science, and now he finally knew: a good old-fashioned spite recommendation, courtesy of his father's enemy.

"We saw your work at the Presentation. It was good."

"Thank you, sir!"

"Good. Not great."

"That's fair," Albert admitted.

"No. Good. Not fair."

"Sorry."

"It's too bad what happened," Eli Gray continued as he paced around the room. "I mean, it was *hilarious,* but also bad. All things considered, you didn't graduate from college."

"But you said --"

"Here. Have this. Every new employee gets one."

While he appeared to have no pockets, and the single table in the room had no drawers, Eli Gray produced for Albert a small, fist-sized cube. Like the room, it was white and had no visible means of entry. Eli Gray leaned down and softly pressed the top. The cube unfolded into six flat sides and presented its contents: a grey strap, a tiny LCD screen, and a golden-brown lump.

"Thank you!" Albert said, feigning enthusiasm but telegraphing confusion.

"Do you know what it is?"

"I do."

He did not.

"Albert, it's a Gray Labs TotTimer. One of our teams figured out a way to miniaturize potato clock technology and make it portable. Now you can wear a potato clock on your wrist."

Once he knew what it was, Albert thought that it was the most wonderful thing that he had ever seen. As he was left-handed, he excitedly went to put it on his right wrist, noticing a half-inch-wide hole in his right arm. It was the second new hole he'd received that day.

"Pre-employment biological screenings," Eli Gray explained.

It felt a little weird to have a hole in his arm, but not as weird as wearing his watch on the wrong wrist would be. He put the watch on. It looked great on him.

"Can you remind me what, exactly, I'll be doing here, sir?"

"Research and development."

11

———

In his excitement and self-destructive tendency toward believing what he would like the truth to be, as opposed to the actual truth, Albert had misheard Eli Gray. He hadn't said "research and development" — he'd said "research," then paused for a comma-length amount of time, and had then said "development." The "and" was an optimistic invention of Albert's woefully hopeful brain. "Research and development" was a very specific and terrific thing — exploring time travel, or running the time travel department, to list two hypothetical examples. However, "research" and "development," taken separately, meant nothing in particular in most situations. At Gray Labs, it meant grunt work.

Albert spent his years at Gray Labs testing hundreds of products either in development, or which the company would stop developing. That all depended on how badly they affected Albert.

• In a space-capsule-like chamber, Albert reviewed synthetic oxygens in solid, liquid, and gas forms. The winner, or the one sold to the space program: chewable, watermelon-flavored oxygen, because that was the one that caused Albert to pass out for the least amount of time.

• While being an astronaut ice cream tester is a dream job for any child, it wasn't so romantic for Albert. He didn't care for the flavors designed with the scientist foodie niche in mind, such as Pelican, Thanksgiving Dinner, and Spruce.

• A Gray Labs manager had told him that his DNA was exceptional and that they were studying it, but the guy finally broke down and told Albert that they used the nine ounces of fat they sucked out of him each week as a starter for Bertloaf, the world's second-best-selling synthetic human-meatlike frozen meatloaf dinner product.

• It was only one day a year, but Albert was the main guy, the *only* guy, in fact, to enjoy the privilege of cleaning the corporate campus of vomit chunks and tungsten flakes the morning after Gray Labs Presents Science Day.

• His summer weekend task was entertaining at area children's birthday parties dressed up as Eli Gray. All he had to do was show up, yell out "be bold" a few times, and cut a sheet cake with a laser. Albert never understood why he couldn't wear a helmet and a jumpsuit to the gigs instead of the stiflingly hot Eli Gray character suit made out of reticulated foam.

It was all worth it for Albert, even though he was paid less than minimum wage, legal in California if the employee had attended college for four or more years without graduating. What little money he did earn was paid out each week in a three-minute session in the Gray Labs ¢a$h Money Hurricane Booth.

While that would net him only around 40 bucks in singles, the benefits were generous, particularly the free employee housing in The Residence at Gray Labs Heights. Automation and comfort were paramount, and that attitude manifested in amenities such as central heat, air, and decontamination; deodorant-applying robots; a toaster that sensed when the user might want toast and would prepare it to be ready slightly before the brain recognized the desire for toast; and a bidet. His apartment came with a sleep-number bed, a sit-number couch, and an excreta-number toilet.

After six years of loyalty and a willingness to be placated, Albert was rewarded with a promotion into a permanent position in Research and Development. For real this time. Sort of. Albert was stationed in a basement, where he was tasked with creating space-savers, kitchen gadgets, and other novelties to be loudly sold on television. While it was a subterranean, windowless cave of concrete, Gray Labs referred to this division as "The Garage. If anybody working down there ever developed anything that funda-mentally changed the human experience, the company's marketing department could promote it with the romantic notion that "it was developed in a garage" without invoking the ire of the Federal Trade Commission, which had a whole task force devoted to sniffing out phony garage-origin claims.

Albert's five top-selling creations were, in reverse order:

5) The CheesePlease, which explained to lactose-intolerant people what any dairy product poured into it tasted like.

4) The Family AirLoo, a space-saving hover toilet.

3) Springform pants.

2) Joke contact lenses that purported to predict the wearer's exact day of death and superimpose it into their line of vision, but which analyzed body chemistry to actually and accurately predict the date of the user's 50th birthday.

1) Car-B-Que™: The Barbecue For Your Car™

Having most of his hours filled with work and the rest filled with relaxation made Albert forget all about what he had really wanted to do with this life. In other words, he had become an adult. He was happy, or, at the very least, he had a good thing going and had kept it going for almost an entire decade, and he didn't want to screw it up.

But then he started to get bored.

12

———

Albert lollygagged in the Gray Labs break room, drinking a midmorning beverage of his own creation: coffee-flavored freeze-dried beverage crystals; a few heaping tablespoons of a Gray Labs Foods product called Smart Cream, which consisted of Ginkgo biloba genetically modified to actually work, then chemically bonded with high fructose corn syrup; and a pinch of powdered orange-flavored space-drink.

The break room sat on the second-to-top floor of the main Gray Labs building, and cheesy old '70s scienceploitation films played on a loop on a TV in the corner, stuff like *Bunsen Beakers, Chemistry Set-Up,* and *Red Smoke, Black Hearts.* The employee manual said that this, and this alone, was how Gray Labs kept things "fun."

As he went to sit down in his favorite spot, a red velveteen number made with memory foam that anticipatorily contoured itself to a person's dimensions from 20 yards out, he eavesdropped.

"You could starve 'em. If they're smaller, you can fit more in, right?"

"If I could legally do that, I wouldn't need you."

"What about smaller cells?"

"We've got a place down by Chula Vista, not even open yet. We built it to hold a maximum of 4,000, and we've already got 12,000 ready to go. So I don't think we can go much smaller."

"So, then, what do you want us to do, exactly?"

"Can't you just, like, science it up?"

"Yes!" shouted Albert as the two men glared at him from halfway across the room. He lumbered over, slowed down by an extra 50 pounds he'd packed on since coming to Gray Labs; he had never gotten over the novelty of having access to three or more meals a week.

"What you're looking for is something in the area of spatial displacement, am I right?" Albert asked.

"Well, yes," said the man wearing a suit. "Who the hell is this?" he asked the man in the Gray Labs lab coat.

"Good question," he said as he stared down Albert. "Who the hell are you?"

"Albert Malfort. I work down in the Garage. Impulse Tech."

"Oh, right, the as-seen-on-TV crap."

"Yes, sir."

"What do you know about prisons?"

When Albert was 15, his school guidance counselor had sent him on a "Scare the Crime Right Out of 'Em!" field trip to a nearby federal penitentiary, thinking Albert was an at-risk-youth just because his father had been in prison once or twice. At the time of Albert's visit to this prison, Ron Malfort was incarcerated there, doing a stint for trying to smuggle into the U.S. what he had been told was the preserved sperm of Genghis Khan. It was the last time he'd ever see the inside of a prison, Albert told himself, right after he witnessed his father get shanked by his cellmate over a disagreement about cold fusion.

"What do *I* know about prisons? I know they're incredibly inefficient wastes of space and money."

The smirking guy in the suit paused and then chuckled.

"Hi, Albert. Eric Bates. Chief technology officer at LockedIn."

They shook hands, then took a small bottle of hand sanitizer spray out of their pockets and sprayed the other man, as was Gray Labs company policy on the rare occasion that anyone ever actually touched.

"Um, yes," the Gray Labs associate said, clearing his throat. "Albert here is one of our, um, top developers, across the board," he improvised, trying to make Eric think that this was all planned. "I was hoping you were around today, Alan."

"So, infomercial stuff, huh? Anything else?"

"Have you ever heard of a little thing called Bertloaf?"

Eric's eyes lit up.

"I'm Bert."

Together they recited the Bertloaf advertising tagline, imitating the TV announcer, which was Eli Gray. "Bertloaf. It's the family dinner, for families, that tastes like...family." They high-fived, which hurt Albert's hand a little, and then they repeated the hand sanitizer ritual. The Gray Labs rep looked on in contempt.

"Well, if you know about cheap approximations of food, then you understand what prisons are all about."

"What's the problem?"

"Same problem we always have. We have to fit more people in. You guys are my Hail Mary pass."

Albert didn't fully understand the statement, beyond the sense that it was both sports- and religion-related, subjects for which he had no frame of reference, and so he just stared awkwardly at the man.

"Can you help me fit more people in?" he clarified to Albert, vaguely annoyed.

"Oh, yeah, that's easy."

"It is?"

"Sure. You got a piece of paper?"

From the table next to the chairs, Eric picked up an order form that had fallen out of a catalog. Magnus Riptide graced the cover; Albert saw it and bristled. He hunched down over the table, between the two men, and started to feverishly draw out his idea as it came to him.

"Last week I was toying around with temporal displacement," Albert said as he drew a line image of a wall eating itself. The idea hit him when he'd been trying to design a grease trap that would fit into a USB-powered deep fryer. "I couldn't get something to fit, so I made more room," he went on, drawing a box with only two sides, recalling how he made the inside undercarriage of the fryer larger than the outside using a tungsten alloy.

"I don't understand," said Eric, wincing at Albert's doodles.

"I do," lied the Gray Labs rep, squinting at Albert's drawing as if that would help.

"Oh, well, it's pretty simple, actually," Albert said, entirely too fast. "Once in a while, three dimensions are just too many." He demonstrated by drawing a cube, and then he erased several of its sides. The cube still, as a surprise to Eric, resembled a cube. "Like in prison, space is a luxury."

"There are no luxuries in prison, Albert."

"Exactly."

"Exactly!" repeated the Gray Labs rep, trying to say it at the same time as Albert but missing by a glaring half-second.

"So, I cut out the third dimension."

"How do you just cut out the third dimension? Isn't a third

dimension, just, sort of, you know, *there*?" Eric asked, waving his arms around.

"Tungsten, Eric."

"Yeah, tungsten, Eric," the rep said, playfully punching him in the shoulder. He was utterly ignored, and so he angrily swiped the *Science Beat* off the table and pretended to read it, jealously peering over the top at Albert.

"What's tungsten?"

Albert was appalled that a man in a science-adjacent profession had never heard of tungsten, but also very excited because he rarely got the chance to just geek out over his favorite element.

"Tungsten is, from a scientific point of view, the *best*!" Albert enthused. "I mean its chemical symbol is a W, which looks like two birds soaring while holding hands. That can't be an accident."

Albert flipped the order card over and started listing all the fun facts he could remember about tungsten, many of which he first learned from the *Superstars of Elements* trading cards he'd collected as a boy.

"It's 18 times as dense as water. In Swedish, *tungsten* means 'heavy stone.' It's used in jewelry, industrial lubricants, light bulb filaments, yacht ballasts, darts. Basically, anything good you can think of is made from tungsten."

"Cool, but how does it factor in here? You're losing me."

"You're *losing* him, Albert!" intoned the Gray Labs rep, pretending to read an article about mosquito cloning.

"What's unique about it is that it absorbs nitrogen and carbon dioxide vapor, and converts them into oxygen."

"What, like some kind of metal tree?"

"Yes, exactly!"

"Yes, exactly, exactly!" said the Gray Labs rep, once again trying to seem on the same page as Albert.

"Hey, Paul, you can get out of here if you need to. I think we've got this under control."

Paul's eyes almost popped out of his skull as he glowered at Albert and stomped away, never breaking eye contact with Albert, quietly muttering promises of revenge.

"Anyway, as I was saying, it generates oxygen. That makes it an ideal building material in atmospherically hostile environments. People can breathe where they ordinarily couldn't, which is another property of tungsten. It shrinks, or, more accurately, it *absorbs* physical space."

"The third dimension."

"Yep."

"How is that even possible?"

"It's just what it does."

"That's so weird."

"It's no weirder than the fact that there are five chemical elements that serve no other purpose than to explode."

"But how do you put people into two dimensions? You'd squish 'em, wouldn't you? That would kill 'em. And we can't kill 'em. Well, not all of them. Not, you know, right away."

"Yeah, you'd think they'd die," said Albert, taking the free seat next to Eric. "But tungsten is a temporally flexible element."

"Wait, that means it's only flexible...sometimes?"

"No, not temporarily, *temporally*. Because it shrinks space, it takes anything enclosed inside its walls outside of the time-space equation."

"So that means..." Eric hoped Albert would cut him off because he didn't know where he was going with that thought.

Albert took the hint. "It means that there's no time or physicality inside. Which also means a suspension of biological needs."

"You're saying I don't have to feed anybody."

"Nope. No food. No water. So no human waste issues. Only the occasional dump of used-up tungsten flakes, which you're going to get with any high-tech gadget these days."

Albert talked a good game, but, as it had been with the time machine project in college, everything he had just said and reported to Eric had been a massive, happy accident.

"Huh," Albert said to himself, making an interesting discovery in that moment.

"What's that?"

"It floats?" Albert blurted out. "I mean, *it floats*."

"What floats?"

Albert showed him his chicken scratch of math, science, and dimensional anomalies. Eric nodded in concentration, pretending to understand it all.

"It floats!"

"What does that mean exactly, for the, uh, prisoners?"

"It means gravity is a side effect of the third dimension."

"Yeah?"

"Yeah. You can just set these things loose in the sky!"

"Albert, can you get this thing to market in, say, a month?"

Creating an entirely new technology from scratch was a tall order, and making a working version that was ready for public consumption took the notion from improbable to downright impossible.

"Of course!" Albert said.

"Brilliant," Eric said. "I'll talk to who I need to talk to, and you can get started."

13

After he graduated from the Western Scientific Institute even more advantaged and cash-flush than he'd been previously, Magnus Riptide did what anyone with immeasurable talent, opportunity, and a financial safety net would do — he walked away from it all. He was the kind of person who needed to find what *he* wanted.

Magnus never did stray too far from the world in which he was raised. In short order, Magnus became science's most popular model, appearing in catalogs and ads for Gray Labs and Orange East posed suggestively atop superconductors, industrial centrifuges, and quasar simulators. In these spreads, Magnus wore tiny, bulge-flattering lab shorts and an unbuttoned lab coat. This became a common costume for physically fit young men who attended Gray Labs Presents Science Day. *Popular Scientists* called him "The hunkiest slice of centrifuge-adjacent beefcake this side of Scandinavia."

Contrary to the lies told by other models, Magnus really did eat what he liked, and for him, that meant traditional Icelandic dishes: pickled sheep heads, pickled shark bowels, and pickled rotten bread. As these were revolting and subsequently unavailable outside of Iceland, Magnus had figured out a way for Magnus, his supplier in Reykjavik (most Icelandic men are named Magnus), to upload food items to the Internet, where they were then transmitted via Wi-Fi and downloaded right into the mini-fridge aboard *Bohrs, Oars & Libertine Ladies,* Magnus's home-yacht. It was a fun little hobby for Magnus — a little "light" science, like astrology, or building a potato clock.

Magnus was later shocked to learn that he'd invented the digital transmission of food. He did think it was pretty cool that he brought esoteric homemade treats to as many as 40 expatriate Icelanders around the world; as it turned out, the technology worked solely in the transmission of Icelandic folk dishes. It had something to do with the chemical makeup of pickling spices.

But he still won the Nobel Prize for Physics (*and* for Chemistry) for his troubles, as well as the Nobel Peace Prize, benefiting greatly from the Scandinavian-biased voting board. He was only the second male model to win both prizes in a single calendar year.

The day he turned 30, Magnus decided that it was time to quit modeling and embrace his destiny to be a scientist, a decision he was thrust into when his 30th birthday card arrived from his modeling agency: a small square of entirely black paper. He understood immediately — his modeling career was over. But now he could be "hungry," thought Magnus, forced to act and succeed when failure was not an option, although he'd saved up a fortune from modeling in addition to his inexhaustible trust fund.

First, Magnus drafted a press release to announce to the scientific community that he would be "returning to their fold to bask in their love." Then, he opened a desk drawer lined with narwhal leather, shooed away a boat koala (an invasive species that took hold during Americans' obsession with Australian things in the 1980s), and pulled out the latest, although slightly chewed up, Gray Labs "Wish a Wish for Christmas Wish" catalog. Its cover depicted Magnus in novelty antlers, a red nose, and an open lab coat while licking a candy-cane-striped test tube. He appreciated the electronic catalog's "press down to buy" option, very convenient because he was buying everything because he'd need to stock a new lab. For him, money was no object, which is the best way to shop.

Next, he'd need to get caught up on the latest scientific breakthroughs. Apart from the food-over-Wi-Fi, Magnus hadn't paid much attention to the news, so he went scrounging around his yacht for science magazines. As he had never bought any, the closest thing he could find was a box marked "college things." It contained a thin stack of papers stapled together, just some photocopied research about calcified cremains of amoebic protein strains in fossilized dinosaur exhalations with some equations in the margins and "MAGNUS" scrawled on top of the first page. "A+ amazing!!!" a professor had written on it. "SEE ME AFTER CLASS AT HOME (I BOUGHT A NICE BOTTLE OF AQUAVIT!)"

The professor hadn't read it, nor had Magnus paid much mind to the assignment. If either had put in just the least bit of effort, they would have discovered something amazing therein. Right there, in one of Magnus's handwritten calculations, between a seven and an eight, was a brand-new number. Magnus pulled out a calculator and ran the data. He got an error message, so he did the math the old-fashioned way, with a pen, on the back of his assignment, carefully carrying the 7, and then carrying the 8, accounting for the remainder and the cosine. Still, this other number kept coming up.

This new figure simply *was*, and it followed all the innate the rules of math. Magnus was in rare company in his find; a new number hadn't been discovered in more than 300 years, not since the banner year of 1688 for Sir Benjamin Billions.

At the end of his drafted but not sent press release, Magnus added, "P.S. I found a new number, and it's called *M*." He didn't win a Nobel Prize for this, because there is no Nobel for mathematics, although he did secure the Fields Medal, and the Nobel Prize for Literature. He'd inadvertently written the press release announcing his discovery of *M* as a haiku, as well as an acrostic, and with some symbolic imagery that reminded more than one critic of the long-lasting ramifications of the Opium Wars. Within six months, his press release became the bestselling poem of all time.

But Magnus wasn't going to just let humanity "have" the new number. The World Numbers Board offered him a flat, one-time fee, with a modest bonus every *M* years. Magnus sensed he was getting cheated, so he proposed a commission system. Every time *M* was used anywhere on the planet, Magnus would receive the deceptively minuscule-sounding 1/10,000th of a cent. The members of the World Numbers Board thought *they* were getting the better deal; such is the power of Magnus's charisma. He stood to earn tens of millions in passive income each year, roughly *M* times what he'd been initially offered.

Magnus's re-emergence and celebration happened to dovetail with TV pilot season. Producers of a crime drama, about a scientist who solves crimes using only the power of science, approached Magnus to play the lead. Within three months of the debut of *The Scientist,* starring Magnus Riptide as Police Detective Lieutenant Dr. Claude Von Scientizt, M.D., the bestselling T-shirt in the non-scientific community, and the bestselling novelty lab coat pin in the scientific community, bore Magnus's character's catchphrase,

"Let's make a science guess!" Critics were impressed with Magnus's performance, with many comparing him favorably to Carl Sagan, on account of how, as one writer said, "his uncanny ability to look sexy in a turtleneck."

As he came to terms with his wealth, fame, and influence, Magnus knew he'd have to change his behavior; being an asshole was a young man's game. For good things to keep happening to him, he knew that he'd have to pretend to be gracious. During a break in shooting on *The Scientist* one day, Magnus opened his laptop (the only thing from his Gray Labs shopping spree he'd ever actually used) and typed in a query:

how to be a rich person

The results primarily returned information about a book called *How to Be a Rich Person*, written by a popular prop comedian who became an art collector and highbrow satirist. *How to Be a Rich Person* was, in fact, a tongue-in-cheek work. But, as the stereotype about Scandinavians having no sense of humor proved accurate, Magnus couldn't tell that the book was a joke.

As he read excerpts of the book, he skimmed over the things he already did "correctly" as a rich person, unaware that the book was making fun of him, and excitedly absorbed all of its many "tips," such as:

A rich person has everything in the world, which puts him in the unique place of being able to make a "vision board" and have everything on it come true. It is the duty of a rich person to make this "vision board" — a physical document admitting to all that you want and somehow do not yet have.

On his tablet, Magnus drew everything he wanted, nay, that he *deserved.* He didn't have magazines around to clip from, and also, he was a magnificent illustrator. He could have done that professionally if he'd really wanted to.

As he thought about what else he could want, he didn't notice as his hand, talented even without his direct attention, started drawing. Magnus's hand knew what Magnus wanted before his brain could even weigh in: It had drawn a picture of Thomas Edison.

Like every outwardly confident male, Magnus's swagger masked a deep longing for male approval. His father, Andreas Riptide, was far too kind for Magnus to admire, and Magnus had long ago transferred his hero worship to a more viable role model, one that was cunning, ruthless, and who didn't care about setting an example. For Magnus, that was Thomas Edison, a scientist, innovator, and savage businessman. Magnus wanted to meet Thomas Edison and make him be his mentor. Unfortunately, for both pupil and teacher, Thomas Edison had been dead for decades.

For this to work, and Magnus was too rich and consistently successful to think for even a second that it wouldn't, Magnus would have to make the biggest sciences guesses of his life. He was going to have to clone Thomas Edison, and it wasn't going to be easy. As the old saying goes, "Every worthwhile scientific development began with the desecration of a corpse."

He tried his best, haggling over the phone with representatives of Orange East for more than an hour, but they were unwilling to part with the remains of their founder, lying in state in their flagship store, for any price. Magnus got so mad that he did what all men do when they're frustrated, confused, or angry. He threw something — in his case, his phone — and it flew out of an open porthole window, barely missing a boat koala on the outer deck, eating a putrid onion it had dug out of the trash.

"Orrrrrrrrrrr!" The plaintive but pathetic, whale-like moan came from outside, as if from the sea itself. Magnus looked out the window, driven more by intellectual curiosity than culpability, and when he saw what he saw, he gulped.

"Bohrie, what was that?" Magnus asked the boat's operational and navigational system.

The feminine A.I. voice delivered the scary news as gently as a robotic voice could. "Sir, it's walruses."

Walruses had once been the biggest menace of the sea, attacking fishing vessels and plundering their cargo, until the late 1940s, when the scientific community trained these pirate walruses in the ways of banking. Both sitting around all day and hoarding money came naturally to walruses, and all they wanted in return were buckets of fish, delivered regularly.

Prominent scientific families soon established their own private walrus banking pods, where their money was kept safe, by walruses, in undersea vaults, free from taxation and other silly laws. (This system is the origin of the phrase "offshore banking.") Still, these walruses had piracy in their blood and could revert back to their old, violent ways at the slightest provocation, such as being struck in the head with a phone.

Magnus noticed a particularly angry member of this walrus pod holding his discarded satellite phone in its flabby flipper, rubbing a welt on his tusk with its other flabby flipper.

"What the hell was that?" the walrus shouted in Walrus, spoken with a thick Walrus accent, which together sounds very much like American English with a Queens accent.

Magnus ran out onto the deck.

"My apologies, Mr. Walrus," Magnus offered. His Walrus was flawless, but his voice quivered with nervousness.

The walrus sneered and turned to the other walrus, which sat with his arm-flippers crossed, eyes digging sight-daggers into Magnus. "Mr. Walrus? Did he just call me *Mr. Walrus*? Just because I'm a walrus, my name must be Mr. Walrus?"

"I meant no harm. I just didn't know what to call you," Magnus calmly stated. "What is your name?"

"It just so happens to be Mr. Walrus."

"So what if it is?" the other walrus chimed in.

"Look at that hair and that jawline. I bet everybody thinks you're Icelandic. Well, nice to meet you, *Magnus*."

"I, I am Icelandic."

"Really?"

"Yeah."

"What's your name?"

"Well..."

"Ah, jeez," Mr. Walrus demurred. "It's Magnus, isn't it?"

"Yeah. Nice to meet you."

"Magnus what?"

"Magnus Riptide."

"How come your name don't follow traditional Icelandic naming conventions?"

"Yeah," the toady walrus added, "how come your name ain't whatever-your-dad's-name-is, then 'son'?"

The walruses double flabby-flipper high-fived twice, first up high, and then down low. Magnus had a prepared response for when smartasses asked him that question.

"In 1263, my ancestors found a way to manipulate the ocean

with electrical currents, bringing untold fish and boats to Iceland. King Magnus VI renamed the family 'Ryptyjdj,' which is pronounced like, and means, 'riptide.'" He took a breath. "That connection to the sea is also why we're talking to each other in your native tongue, and not mine."

"Oh yeah? Well, you know what I'd like to know? I'd like to know why someone with such supposed kinship for walruses would throw a phone at one."

"Well, I was angry with the person on the other end."

"Was I the one that you were talking to you on this phone, and made you angry with my words?"

"No, sir."

"Then why did you throw this phone at me?"

"It was just bad luck that you were there."

"Bad luck for me? Bad luck for you. What say my associate here logs on to your banking accounts while I make sure nothing happens to this lovely yacht of yours?"

Magnus panicked.

"Hey, maybe I can make this up to you," Magnus stammered while searching his brain for ways to make good on that spontaneous promise. "I have the means to get you whatever you want."

"I doubt it," the assistant walrus muttered.

"Hold on," the head walrus interjected. "You said you're Icelandic, right?"

It took Magnus about five minutes to set up food-over-Wi-Fi on the walruses' computers; being as how they were walruses, they didn't mind at all that the unlimited quantity of food that Magnus could provide was fermented fish. What he didn't know was that the walruses were especially grumpy because they hadn't eaten any fish in weeks and were considering the prospect of living off each other's blubber. The family whose vault they guarded had missed a couple of payments; as it's just a few buckets of fish delivered once a week, there was really no excuse. The walruses were so appreciative that they allowed Magnus into the vault of its deadbeat owners. "Take whatever you like," the head walrus had told Magnus through mouthfuls of a profane variation of lutefisk.

Magnus didn't need the money they were offering, but it would've been rude to decline, and walruses respond to rudeness by breaking legs. He entered through a phony-rock façade into the cavernous, sub-oceanic vaults it concealed. Before him stood two, thick, brown metallic doors, rusty and green under the constant presence of salty ocean air and algae both naturally-occurring and theft-deterring.

Magnus was under the impression that there would be one door to one vault, and he was to help himself to a cursory amount of money — not too little as to be impolite, not too much as to seem greedy. But here were two doors. The words scratched into the doors didn't help much either. One said "MALFORT" and the other "MALFORT PRIVATE RESERVE." Having a difficult time choosing, he decided to just take whatever he could grab from both vaults.

In the vault marked just "MALFORT," there was only a small table with a few stacks of bills atop it. Magnus examined them and found that while there weren't many bills, the bills were large — $1,000 notes — and held together with a paper band marked "Gray Labs — 40 bills." Each stack was $40,000, and there were three stacks, and so Magnus took advantage of his guests' hospitality and slipped the three stacks into his pockets.

Magnus went out, closed the door, and immediately entered the "MALFORT PRIVATE RESERVE VAULT." There was no money in the room, only a small freezer made entirely of glass. In the freezer was a single object. Upon further inspection, it was a rack of vials. Upon even further inspection, there were precisely a dozen vials, each filled to the top with milky white goo, then sealed with a cork. Upon even still further inspection, Magnus saw words on the sticker on the side of one of the vials: "T. Edison."

14

———

Albert sat in the second-to-last row of the auditorium perched atop the main building of Gray Labs, waiting for the Product Announcement Event to start. Even though it was his product that was being unveiled that day, the strict seating protocol remained in effect: top clients in the first five rows, and media in the back row. The rest of the 400 seats or so were up for grabs to any of the company's 3,000-odd rank-and-file; the Event started at noon, so Albert had arrived at 5:30 a.m., just in time to get the last seat available.

The tater-tot on his wrist said it was 11:58 a.m. He'd killed the last six hours alternately napping with his hands territorially clenched to his armrests and eavesdropping on other attendees' conservations as to their theories about what products Eli Gray would personally announce from the iconic "Black Stage" that morning. The consensus heled that it would be nanobots, or nanobots that ate failed nanobots, or maybe some kind of non-biodegradable, non-disposable jetpack.

Now Albert was just doodling in a notebook, writing bubbly versions of the words "Sky Jail," "Sky Jail 2000," and "lesser dimensional physical incarceration unit" in the margins. The rest of the page was taken up by Albert's theoretical idea of what it would be like if he were on the cover of *Popular Scientists* magazine and also had big muscles.

Suddenly, the lights went out, and then they came back on, row by row, from the back of the house to the front, continuously illuminating Eli Gray as he made his entrance, flying in on a jetpack chugging exhaust. Albert and most everybody else coughed when Eli Gray flew past their rows, but that subsided and turned to bemusement when they all looked down at their bodies and found that the exhaust had stained a Gray Labs logo, permanently it would turn out, on the backs of their hands. The assemblage clapped in appreciation.

"Ladies and gentlemen, the Gray Labs Flyer!" boomed the voice of Eli Gray from the auditorium's sound system.

More applause. A reporter behind Albert fainted, partly from hysteria, partly from breathing in too much jetpack exhaust.

"Like it? Well, look under your seats. Be bold!"

Everyone did so and found not a Gray Labs Flyer, but a black-and-white photocopied Gray Labs sales brochure — a Gray Labs "flier." It wasn't all that funny, but the reporters laughed uproariously when they finally got the joke. The scientists, meanwhile, many not blessed with a sophisticated sense of humor, murmured amongst themselves variations of "Flyer. Flier. Right. I understand this."

"Just a little joke to start things off," Eli Gray said as he landed in the mathematically exact center of the stage, in front of a wall of video screens. He removed the jetpack, and an underling ran onto the stage to get it. She was dressed entirely in black, including a mask, and she was visible only because she was moving.

"Hold on, Jennifer. Watch this everybody."

Terrified, Jennifer stood utterly still except for the trembling. Eli Gray took the jetpack back with one hand, and with the other, crushed it down to the size of a microchip. Then he handed it back to Jennifer.

"Go on, Jennifer."

"But I'm —"

"*Be bold*, Jennifer."

Jennifer took a deep breath, removed her mask, and swallowed the tiny speck of compressed jetpack. She gulped and panted.

"Show them, Jennifer."

Jennifer opened her mouth to reveal a set of teeth so straight and so perfectly white ("Not just white, but Pantone 11-0601 TCX white!" assured Eli Gray) that Albert could tell from all the way back in the second-to-the-last row.

Jennifer hurried off the stage, waving to the cheering crowd, crying in relief and sobbing in appreciation.

"Alright, let's settle down everybody. Thank you all for coming today. It's been a big quarter for us here at Gray Labs. The numbers are bigger. The innovations are more innovative. In short, things are bold."

"Be bold!" shouted one guy in the front, misreading the moment. He was summarily escorted out of the arena by one of Eli Gray's personal goon robots, waist-high and made to look exactly like Eli Gray if he were a Japanese cartoon character. The seat was filled with a seat-filling robot that also resembled Eli Gray.

"Let me ask you a question. What's the fastest growing industry in the world today?"

On the screen behind him, words flashed on and off, barely perceptible to be subliminal, but then repeated thousands of times a second to negate the subliminal effect, words like "technology" and "innovation" and "computers."

"Technology? Innovation? Computers?"

A wave of self-satisfied applause spread across the elliptical arena.

"Friends, the fastest growing industry is whatever Gray Labs says it is."

In three different sections of the auditorium, five separate people passed out, slid down to the floor, were removed by robots, and then replaced with more robots.

"Specifically, though, the fastest growing industry in the world is incarceration. Prisons."

Images of depressing, cement, cell block-style prisons filled the screens.

"By the time I finish this sentence, another three people will have been placed behind bars. And this was not a particularly long sentence."

The crowd laughed at the pun, but only a little.

"This may not sound like the kind of industry Gray Labs would have any interest in. But we innovate. We motivate. We *revolutionize.*"

Eli Gray snapped his fingers. The scary prison images gave way to more images of prisons — converted prisons. The same human storage lockers previously pictured were now filled with children at desks, and families clad in head-to-toe American flag apparel buying enormous kegs of mayonnaise.

"We go where there is *innovation*, and where *we* go, there is innovation."

The images on the screen disappeared, replaced by the word "BOLD."

"It's no secret that I don't believe in the death penalty. I think it's wrong. I'm very progressive."

"Because he prefers to let them suffer!" Albert overheard a

reporter behind him whisper to another with a self-satisfied chuckle.

"So, what's the alternative?" Eli Gray continued. "Prisons. While we can all agree that everyone even remotely criminal should be locked up, no community in the world actually wants a prison within its city limits. So what do we do? We innovate. We... be bold."

The screens began to rise, very slowly, gradually revealing a blindingly white room. Albert knew what was coming, and he had never felt such pride, not since his father had gotten thrown out of his son's fourth-grade science fair for telling one of Albert's classmates that his pinhole camera was "baby garbage made by a garbage baby."

"What if we could take all these prisons and make them into something more useful? And what if instead of traditional prisons, we could make one that didn't take up any room at all? What if there was a way we could eliminate the costliest parts of prison: food, housing, and the third dimension?

"What if...we did? What if...*I* did?"

The crowd shouted back in unison, "Be bold!"

The screens shot up the rest of the way. All of the black on the stage disappeared, as did the black carpet, the black paint, and the black fabric that covered the non-stage parts of the auditorium. The hall became completely white.

"Presenting the latest innovation from the ancestral homeland of innovation, Gray Labs, founded by yours truly, Eli Gray."

The audience, in various stages of gasp, stared at the stage in confused silence. Upon it stood, evidently, something. From Albert's point of view, it looked, quite gloriously, like nothing. In other words, his invention worked. Albert hadn't beamed like that since that time he'd taste-tested Gray Labs' glowstick-flavored ice cream.

"There's nothing there!" a man from the middle of the auditorium shouted, tearing large clumps of hair out of his head.

"Fraud!" screamed another reporter. The sources of both outbursts were dutifully and brutally escorted out and replaced with seat-filling robots.

"Where there once was something, let there now be nothing. Where there appears to be nothing, there is but a something, but that something bears all the hallmarks of nothingness."

The crowd remained silent, except for a couple of people who sobbed.

"A few weeks ago, I was toying around with temporal displacement, as one does."

With a stylus, he drew in the air a vector-style image of a wall eating itself. It hung in the air in front of him as he drew it. "I couldn't get something to fit, so I made more room," he added. Then he drew a box with only two sides. It was all very familiar to Albert because it was the same off-the-cuff presentation that he'd given a few weeks prior.

"You see, once in a while, three dimensions are just too much. They're unnecessary."

He drew a cube, as Albert had done, and then erased some of its sides. The cube remained a cube.

"So you cut out one of them."

"How?" an audience member desperately called out. "Tell us!"

"Tungsten," Albert murmured to himself, deflated.

"Tungsten!" shouted Eli Gray to a thunderous round of applause.

"I don't have to tell you guys about tungsten. How it's 18 times as dense as water. How it means 'heavy stone' in Swedish. That it has the highest melting point of any element. Gosh, I just love tungsten!

"What you may not know about tungsten is that it also, for lack of a better word, generates oxygen. It converts other gasses into breathable air. That makes it an ideal building material in atmospherically hostile environments. It also absorbs physical space. The third dimension.

"But how do you put people into two dimensions? You'd squish 'em, wouldn't you? That would kill 'em. And we can't kill 'em. Well, not all of them. Not, you know, right away."

Inane audience laughter ensued.

"So then, how? Tungsten again. It shrinks space. It takes anything enclosed inside its walls fully outside of the time-space equation. It means that there's no time or physicality inside. Meaning no biological needs for anybody. No food, no water. Not even waste, other than a monthly dump of used up tungsten flakes. Which, of course, just adds to the Gray Labs Presents Science Day festivities."

This time the crowd laughed uproariously, and a few people whistled in approval.

"This, friends, is a lesser dimensional physical incarceration unit. Or, as it will be known from here on, the Gray Labs Grey Area. The world's first two-dimensional prison cell."

The crowd exploded in rapturous applause and jumped to its feet in a standing ovation.

"Oh, and one more thing."

He paused for dramatic effect. The room fell silent, save for one very frustrated and long-suffering scientist who said quietly to himself, under his breath, "This is *bullshit.*"

"It floats."

The crowd gasped and high-fived, but as they were socially and physically inept types, none of the high-fives landed.

There was laughter. There was weeping. There was rolling around on the ground. There was speaking in tongues.

"Oh, hey, well, I'm not going to take credit for that remark."

Albert listened expectantly.

"I think that's a quote from Albert…"

Albert listened expectantly, but more so.

"…Claude. The great cytologist."

More applause. One fevered participant tried to rush the stage and get in the cell, but goon robots assured that that didn't happen.

"I don't mean to toot my own horn or anything," Eli Gray said before literally making the sound of a horn emanate from his helmet by pushing one of the many metallic buttons on his cuff, "but this hasn't even reached the open market yet, and it's already a rousing success. We've shopped the prototype around to prison-building companies and secured contracts in the neighborhood of $6 billion. It's a lock for the Nobel Prize for Physics."

Eli Gray produced a plaque-mounted golden baton, not like a drum major's baton, but more like a prison guard's baton.

"This here is the Golden Baton. Given out each year to the inventor of the Prison Technology Innovator of the Year award."

By that point, Albert had buried his head in his hands and his own lap. He blacked out, but only for a moment, returning to consciousness when Eli Gray called Paul, the Gray Labs rep he'd disregarded when pitching the two-dimensional jail in the break room, up to the stage to give him a bonus in the form of a $500,000 novelty check, something that, according to Eli Gray, "had never before been done in company history." The bonus, he meant.

"Of everything I've ever thought of, of every innovation I've humbly given the world, I think the Gray Area might be the most important," Eli Gray said. "I'm so proud to share it with you all today.

"Be bold!"

From out of his pocket, he pulled out a tiny black pill, uncrumpled it into a jetpack, put it on, and flew out through a hole in the ceiling right above the stage that opened for him as he flew upward. The audience stormed out of the arena, trampling each other in their excitement.

Albert hung his head low while clutching his stomach, moaning as he rocked back and forth. This position allowed Albert to see something under his chair that he hadn't noticed earlier. It was an envelope, with the Gray Labs logo, and the name "Albert" written on it, so Albert figured it was probably for him.

He tore the envelope open. Inside was a brief form letter from Eli Gray, thanking Albert for "his many contributions," recognizing him as "a credit to the entire organization," and finishing up with a reminder to "be bold!" Also inside was another, smaller envelope marked in script type, "Your Boldness Bonus." Albert popped it open and into his hand poured out four perfectly round gold pieces, each about the thickness of a name-brand chocolate sandwich cookie.

For all of his efforts, gold coins weren't nothing. They were close to nothing, but not nothing. They would just about cover a night of heavy drinking.

15

Magnus had Thomas Edison's DNA in his hands, or to be more specific, he had a vial that contained a suspended solution in which the main ingredient was a substance that held Thomas Edison's DNA in his hands. He wasn't yet quite sure what the middle step was between "Thomas Edison's DNA" and "Thomas Edison clone." His first, best, and only idea of how to proceed was a vague memory of a shopping spree purchase of a KopyRight!, a high-end 3-D printer that took everyday blank carbon, available at any science supply store, and converted it into any object.

This technology was not without some controversy. Its manufacturer, Gray Labs, which had bought the rights from a WSI graduate, had been investigated for false advertising. While a widely televised KopyRight! commercial depicted a plucky, little-girl scientist using the device to clone her dead twin brother, the machine was designed only to replicate inorganic objects, although in stunning, molecular-level detail and with unique imperfections intact. The KopyRight! simply didn't work on organic materials, or with living things. If it were attempted, the results were reportedly catastrophic.

The Federal Trade Commission forced Gray Labs to state "FOR THE REPRODUCTION OF INORGANIC OBJECTS ONLY" on the KopyRight!'s box, website, billboards, and in commercials, which became straightforward affairs demonstrating documents, jewelry, and famous paintings being copied.

But Magnus didn't know about that scandal, because he didn't read the news. Nor did he know how the KopyRight! worked at all because he didn't bother to read its instructions. He cleared out a spot in his captain's quarters for the refrigerator-sized machine, snipped off at least 100 durable-plastic zip ties, pried off the cardboard casing, removed the plastic wrapping, detached the faux Styrofoam packing material, plugged it in, hooked it up to his laptop, waited for it to warm up, calibrated the levers, installed the software, asserted that he had reviewed the End User License Agreement, told the computer to tell the KopyRight! that yes, he wished to clone the guy he had gotten a picture of from a user-generated online encyclopedia, filled up the supply tank with the sample pack of blank carbon that came free with the KopyRight!, and poured in all of the Edison DNA he had on hand, carefully, so as not to spill any of its precious genetic material, and also because it would be gross to get it on his hands or the rug.

Had Magnus bothered to glance at the KopyRight!'s LCD display at any moment, he would have seen an error message telling him that the sample blank carbon had only filled up the supply tank to a 30 percent level. Magnus was too excited at the prospect of a real, live Thomas Edison clone aboard the *Bohrs, Oars & Libertine Ladies* that when the low-tank buzzer repeatedly sounded, he just turned the machine off and back on again, which reset it and tricked it into picking up where it had left off.

Magnus, who had dozed off a couple of times during the hour or so it took the KopyRight! to do its business, was startled back to consciousness when he heard what seemed to be the unholy auditory marriage of tiny rodent shrieks with that of fur getting mangled in sophisticated machinery. He awoke just in time to look over at the KopyRight! to see a burst of koala fur and flesh come shooting out of the supply tank. As his brain comprehended that a boat koala had gone foraging inside of the KopyRight! at what was definitely the worst possible moment, Magnus heard the distinctive sound of a cute little fist and an adorably tiny claw pounding on plastic.

"I demand you release me at once!" the squeaky, obnoxious voice of a 30-percent sized Thomas Edison implored from inside the KopyRight!'s thick plastic walls. As the tiny Edison clone slammed his fists on the inner walls of the KopyRight!, Magnus noticed that just one of those fists was a fist, or really a balled-up little baby hand. The other fist was a koala paw.

16

Elements was a classy place, classier even than Angular Velocity, Half-Life, Ohm, and any number of the other upscale scientist bars in San Verguenza. It was thematic in that its vast menu of cocktails corresponded to each of the 124 entries on the Periodic Table of the Elements, which was displayed everywhere, even, appropriately enough, on the tables. The establishment had once had a standing deal where if you drank every single of those 124 themed cocktails in a night, they hung your picture on the wall and gave you a free lab coat. Albert had read about it in a fancy science magazine, *Fancy Science,* but the article had left out the part about how all three people who had completed the challenge had died immediately. But after what went down at the Product Announcement Event, Albert considered going for it.

Albert didn't go to bars very often, preferring to stay at home and enjoy his in-home vaporized alcohol tap. But his apartment didn't have what Elements did: glowing plastic ice cubes at the bottom of every glass, a bubble fountain, and HydroJim and the H2Oh Yeahs, an elegant sci-quartet featuring a Theremin player, drum machine, Moogist, and the electronically modulated vocals of a disembodied robot head.

Albert perused his individual electronic chalkboard menu, and a concoction called "The Magnesium" caught his eye, up until the bartender did the same. She was, scientifically speaking, beautiful, because her features were symmetrical and her ratio so very golden. Also, her just-past-the-shoulders length hair was dark brown, almost black, which Albert had always thought was the best kind. She was dressed in her Elements-issued novelty lab coat with embroidery that identified her as a "Doctorship Fellow of Molecular Mixology."

This woman, Albert felt, was pretty enough to be an astronaut, and Albert would give anything to go back in time and prevent himself from making that very statement the first words he ever said to her.

"You're so pretty you could be an astronaut."

To her credit, the bartender ignored or didn't hear the remark.

"Can I get you something?"

"What's in 'The Magnesium'?"

"Whiskey, house-made cherry bitters, and a crap-load of magnesium."

"Any specials?"

"A Cosmos."

"What's that?"

"It's your standard Cosmopolitan, but I sprinkle in billions and billions of stardust particles."

"That's very clever," Albert began. "But technically speaking, everything is made of star-stuff. You could put anything into that. You could empty a dustpan into the glass and call it star-stuff."

Despite Albert's absolute inability to flirt, the bartender's eyes grew large in amused surprise. Without breaking Albert's gaze, and a wry smile on her face, she reached underneath the bar and took out a dustpan full of hair, dirt, and fingernail clippings.

"Trade secret," she said.

He laughed. She laughed.

"You should probably just start with something off the regular menu. What's your favorite element?"

"Tungsten."

The bartender went to work behind the bar, filling an Erlenmeyer flask with a jigger of something, a splash of something else, then a fizzy liquid, a small solid item, and finally a spoonful of shiny, metallic flakes. It glowed brightly from within, incandescently, but not fluorescently. She then placed the drink on a small raised platform and lowered a glass dome over it. Instantly, it disappeared and then reappeared directly in front of Albert, even though the bartender could easily have just picked it up, turned around, and handed it over.

"The Tungsten."

He tasted it and was struck by the cold, hard, and undeniable taste of metal. That gave way to a sour, bracing kick that made him feel both warm and sad, which meant that the bartender had used really good liquor.

"Is there nickel in that?"

"No, but there's *a* nickel in it."

There was an awkward pause as they stared at each other, not without a little bit of attraction, probably entirely on the part of the Albert toward the bartender.

"I'm Rosalind."

"Oh, like Rosalind Franklin."

"Yes. That's...that's who they named me after, actually."

He couldn't tell if she was kidding or not. Rosalind spoke with a subtly dry tone that consistently made it difficult for people to tell if she was being sarcastic or sincere.

"My father talked about her a lot. Discovered the double helix structure of DNA, and then, like any woman who tried to make a name for herself in science in the 20th century, got completely screwed over," Albert explained.

"My parents thought having her name would propel me into the world of science, but with enough of a chip on my shoulder that I'd stay scrappy."

"And here you are," Albert said, and meaning it, because apart from Rosalind's supposed degree in "molecular mixology," Elements was pretty scientific. And the drink was quite good.

"And here I am," Rosalind responded glumly.

"I'm just shocked somebody has heard of her," Albert said, desperately trying to bring the conversation back to just before it started to go wrong.

"Most people think it's from Shakespeare."

"Who the hell is Shakespeare?" asked Albert in total seriousness. His education had been primarily science-based. Rosalind, however, thought that he was joking, and she laughed accordingly.

While Rosalind had to step away to attend to a group of wealthy-looking scientists who wanted only to smell wine corks and were willing to pay good money to do so, Albert grew dizzy on his Tungsten, as well as the second and third Tungstens Rosalind had preemptively mixed and programmed to beam over to him at regular intervals over the next half-hour, at which point Rosalind had returned to patronize him in every sense of the word.

"Bartender. Gimme 'nother Tunnsssten," Albert slurred.

"Oh, I think you've had enough," Rosalind said, placing a bill in front of Albert.

"What are you talking about? I'm fine," he said, too loudly, and not convincingly. "It's fine that they made billions off of me and didn't say thank you."

"Yep, you're perfectly okay right now."

"You wanna know what happened? *You really wanna know what happened?*"

"You totally just told me."

"Oh! So *everybody* knows! That's how it is!" He almost fell off his stool. "That's how they getcha."

Rosalind bent down on one shoulder so she could whisper to Albert, who had slumped so far down that he was basically laying atop the bar.

"Sounds like you need a little revenge. Something toothless. To make yourself feel like you've still got some power."

"What do you mean?"

Rosalind leaned down even farther, placing her own face on the bar to match Albert's. It would've been intensely romantic if one of them weren't drunk and the other one working at a job she hated.

"Once a week, I steal an Erlenmeyer flask, and then I go sell it at The Unified Theory."

HydroJim and the H2Oh Yeahs struck up an old chestnut, "I Wish I Could Store Time Up in Bottles Forever."

"They don't even know it's gone."

"How much you get for it?"

"Like two bucks. But that's not the point."

"But revenge on the people that pay me sounds...bad."

"You're weak, Albert," Rosalind joked.

"No, I'm not."

"You're weak."

"Maybe I'm weak."

"Every company expects some stealing will happen. They write it off on your taxes."

"But I can't steal. What should I steal? Let's steal something!"

"It doesn't matter. A few really nice ballpoint pens. Maybe some stamps?"

"MAYBE THEY HAVE A TIME MACHINE!" Albert shout-whispered, more shout than whisper.

"Uh, yeah. Maybe." Rosalind got up and went back to her work, filling up a glass bucket with more used wine corks.

Albert carefully pulled from his pocket and placed on the bar all four gold pieces of his "Boldness Bonus."

"The last one is for you, thanks so much."

Rosalind reflexively pointed to the wall behind the bar, where, just under the ironic, retro "fallout shelter" sign and just above the non-ironic, informative "fallout shelter" sign over a metal door was a neon sign that read, "No Gold Coins."

"You don't take gold? Is this not Northern California?"

"Some guy at Gray Labs figured out alchemy. We keep getting people in here paying for things with gold coins they'd made out of what I hope was just dirt. We start taking those and the economy is ruined."

That cinched it.

"Gray Labs is where I work at," Albert said, quite drunkenly. "Do you mind if I get a tab going and pay you after I make a real quick stop over there at the place where I work?"

"Are you going to steal something?"

"Yes."

"From the equipment shack?"

"Yes!" he answered, a little too quickly. "The Bold Barn, you mean."

"Take some of these with you." Rosalind took Albert's increasingly shaky palm and placed into it a handful of round, stainless steel bite-size candy pieces, the kind purported to melt in one's mouth rather than their hand. Albert swallowed the handful.

"I like candy," Albert slurred.

"Those are nanobots. They'll gobble up the alcohol in your stomach, and you'll be sober in five minutes."

Elements was just that fancy.

17

"Who the fuck are you?" the very small clone of Thomas Edison demanded in a sniveling, nasally tone.

"I'm Magnus Riptide," Magnus said, beaming. "And I'm honored to —"

"Are you foreign?"

"Icelandic, but American."

"Well, which is it?"

"Beg your pardon?"

"Are you Icelandic," he repeated slowly and sarcastically while rolling his eyes, "or are you American? You can't be both."

Thomas Edison was old and came from a different, less tolerant time, so Magnus assumed that he'd have a predilection for saying charmingly off-color things, i.e., be totally racist. And so he thought carefully before he delivered his answer.

"Icelandic."

"Good. If you're an American these days, you're essentially a mongrel."

Magnus was glad he somehow chose the more agreeable answer, and also that he didn't know what "mongrel" meant.

"What is this place? Why am I here?"

"Because you're my hero, Mr. Edison."

"Dr. Edison."

Magnus knew that Edison was not a doctor, and had, in fact, dropped out of elementary school.

"Because you're my hero, Dr. Edison."

"Is that kraut bastard Tesla behind this?"

Magnus silently deliberated. Would Edison have an existential crisis if he were informed of his cloneiness? Could it also trigger an existential crisis, Magnus thought, if Edison learned that he had, in fact, been dead, and then, in a way, reanimated, and in a new physical form, and with his memories of his old life intact? Rather than address any or all of these issues, Magnus went with his gut and did what he always did in delicate situations: He lied.

"No, Dr. Edison. You...*time-traveled*."

"I did?" Edison asked, astonished and thrilled.

"Um, sure! That tube you came in, it was a time machine."

"My times lorry? It worked! Huzzah, for ol' Thomas Edison!" he shouted, pumping his fist in the air. A look of confusion crossed his tiny, angry face. "But I never got my times lorry to function. It *was* that kraut bastard, Tesla! That son-of-a-bitch..." he went on, launching into a flurry of profanities, some familiar to Magnus, some specific to the early 1930s.

While Magnus had many Thomas Edison biographies, he had never heard that Thomas Edison had tried to make a time machine, or a "times lorry." And so his lie grew and rolled along to accommodate.

"Oh, well, as it turns out, you'd just left it unplugged. So they plugged it in when you were dying, and your family put you in it, and the time machine came to my time and to my house, which is great because I'm a big fan of your work."

"Ha! And where is my times lorry now?"

"Well, it came here, and then it went back to your time, and then it broke down from all the wear and tear." Magnus was quite pleased with his magnificently improvised lies.

"I see," Edison said, visually examining his entire body. "Then can you tell me why I'm so goddamn small?"

"Well," Magnus said, vamping, "you tend to lose a lot of weight during the time-travel process. Like how astronauts lose muscle if they're in space for a long time."

"Hmm, Edison seemed satisfied. "What is an astronaut?"

"The gift!" Magnus shouted, avoiding the question.

Magnus excitedly ran to his closet, and from a shelf, pulled out a sealed glass box with a book inside. He placed it into Edison's hands.

"Tesla's notebook!"

"Forty bucks at a museum's going-out-of-business sale."

"You paid too much," quipped Edison, partly out of sarcastic dismissal, and partly because in 1931, forty bucks could buy a three-bedroom house.

"Oh, money doesn't matter much to me right now."

Edison, aghast, slapped Magnus in the face, hard. A tear of pain streamed down his left cheek, while a tear of feeling at home streamed down his right cheek.

"Boy, if there isn't money, then there isn't anything!"

"Father..." Magnus muttered with a smile.

18

It was a great start to what Magnus would later realize was the best weekend of his life. But as Magnus was abundantly wealthy and thus beholden to the whims of no one but himself, weekends were a dubious concept at best, and it was really a Tuesday morning when his marvelous weekend began.

Magnus and Edison enjoyed a rollicking, hours-long conversation in which Magnus updated Edison on how the world had changed since 1931, such as how casual racism had fallen out of fashion, how reality was now in color instead of black and white, and, at Edison's prodding, the notable changes to patent law, as well as any new loopholes. Edison furiously took notes on an adorably tiny yellow legal pad.

They played a game called "catch," which Magnus had never done but was super great at anyway, while Edison dropped the strange, oblong object every time it was thrown to him. He pitched to Magnus an idea for an "Edisonball," a more streamlined, easily catchable, perfectly spherical ball that fit in his two, tiny hands, as well as a simple sports-type game, also called Edisonball, that would use the Edisonball as its ball of record.

They also made a homemade pizza. Magnus tried to get into a food fight with Edison, playfully throwing little slices of pepperoni and cheese shreds at him. Edison got so angry that he smashed a jar of tomato sauce on the floor, threw all the cheese on top of it, and kicked in the oven door, which was impressive for a such a teeny man. "Your ginzo sandwich is done!" Edison yelled and then stormed away. This delighted Magnus.

Magnus then had to take the boat ashore in southern California for a spell, to film some scenes for *The Scientist.* He thought the cast and crew of the show, ostensibly a show about science, would get a real kick out of meeting one of the most prominent scientists who ever lived.

A production assistant assumed that the "very important person" Magnus wanted everyone to meet was, owing to his advanced age and tiny stature, one of the original old-timey astronauts. Edison, who still didn't know what an astronaut was, ran with it. He ran with it so well, in fact, that he was cast in the episode as "himself": a retired space explorer who casually mentions an obscure scientific fact to Police Detective Lt. Dr. Claude Von Scientizt — that the Earth revolves around the sun — which leads to the big break in the case-of-the-week.

When he wasn't shooting his scenes, which he performed with the kind of hammy relish befitting such a project, Edison spent his time on set belittling Magnus to the latter's coworkers, grabbing and complimenting on the "capital fannies" of bit-part actresses, and grilling the director on patent law.

Magnus might have been interested to hear what the director had to say on the subject, as the guy had once been a professor of mechanical engineering at USC before giving it up for a more stable career in episodic television. But Magnus was stuck in his trailer, recording disc 7 of 15 of a "Get rich buying real estate" seminar he'd agreed to endorse and pretended to have invented, for which he'd been heartily compensated.

"I'm afraid I haven't kept up with all of the latest innovations," Edison said to the director, who sat in his personalized directing chair, scribbling phonetic spellings of all the words on an actor's copy of that week's script. "What would you say are the most important inventions since, say, 1931?" Edison pulled out his tiny yellow notepad and a golf pencil, which, in his hand, looked like a regular pencil.

"Since 1931? That's kind of a ridiculous question."

"The nerve!" shouted an agitated Edison, raising his koala claw into battle position.

"Whoa, hey, spaceman," the director said with a patronizing chuckle. "That's not what I meant. I just meant that there's been so much. Where would I even start?"

"Oh. Of course. I was...jesting," said Edison as he stuffed his quivering paw into his jacket pocket.

"Probably easier just to print you out a list."

"It shall take a fortnight to configure the linotype!"

The director ignored him, choosing instead to poke his fingers on a thin, glowing rectangle he pulled out of his pocket. This baffled Edison.

"I am baffled!" Edison gasped.

"Printer's in my trailer."

He briskly walked to his trailer, the tiny Edison desperately trying to keep up with his legs that were both small and thoroughly ravaged by diabetic neuropathy. When they got to the house on wheels, a tiny light on a desktop machine blinked red.

"Ah jeez," the director said with a sigh. He walked to the desk, opened a drawer, took out some paper, and shoved it into the desktop machine. The device soon sprung to life and shot out pieces of paper with text written upon them. Edison was confused as to why anyone would ever curse and sigh at this technological miracle.

When the printing ceased, the director picked up the stack of papers, which was as thick as a dime novel, and handed it to Edison.

"Here you go, from EncycloCheatia to your hands. Every invention patented in the U.S. since 1931. Enjoy!"

"Why, it is the size of a dime novel!" Edison said.

"I don't know what that is."

Edison held the still-hot papers up to his head and rubbed them on his face.

"Harness this heat and sell it to the local municipal government!"

"It's just warm from being printed by lasers."

"La...sers?"

"Jeremy," said a garbled and exhausted female voice from the thick black rectangle hanging on the director's belt. "Wardrobe needs you. Chris got his head stuck in an armhole again."

"Actors!" the director said as he ran off.

Edison couldn't believe how easy it had been to get a list of inventions, in both asking someone for it, and how quickly it had been procured. He was truly living in a time of wonder in which magic and science were one and the same. He felt sick over how all this innovation had happened without him to be the one to deliver it all, or at least to steal credit from those who had.

He read the list of every vital invention and technological concept and breakthrough that came along since he had died. Edison marveled at the breadth and creativity 20th- and 21st-century technology, everything except for something called a "3-D printer." Having just a few moments earlier been introduced to a

2-D printer, he assumed that this entry was a repeated listing of the same item.

The trailer's screen door banged open, and Magnus glided inside, startling Edison.

"There you are! What are you up to?"

"As if it is any of your business, you common buffoon, I am reading a list of everything invented since I left my time and I'm plotting how to steal the patents for all of them."

"Neat," Magnus replied, not listening at all. "Wanna go get something to eat?"

19

Rosalind had a bit more of her shift left, so Albert arrived at the equipment rental shack first. Located on the remote, quiet, northern end of the Gray campus, what was actually inside of "The Bold Barn," Albert could only guess. As he wasn't a senior member of staff, he didn't have rental privileges.

Before he came, he'd made a quick stop at his dorm room to change his clothes, so as better to blend into the night — dark grey pants, dark grey shirt, dark grey lab coat, and a dark grey stocking cap that was so big it covered most of his head. He'd tried to look like Eli Gray, but he wound up looking like the Eli Gray dolls they sold in the Gray Labs gift shop. Albert hoped Rosalind wouldn't notice.

"Nice outfit," said a voice from around the corner of the shack. "You look like one of those Eli Gray dolls they sell in the gift shop."

Rosalind was still dressed in her standard white shirt and black pants bartender clothes, but she'd replaced her novelty lab coat with an authentic one.

"Oh, yeah, that, that was the idea," Albert stammered. "In case we get caught. I'll just say I'm Eli Gray."

"Good plan. You ready?"

To demonstrate his readiness, he took the flashlight he'd brought and shined it up onto his face from a low angle to look mysterious, which didn't really work because it was still a little bit light out.

"Uh, I just thought of something," Albert said, glancing at the keypad and card scanner on the upper part of the thick metal entrance door to the Bold Barn.

Rosalind rifled through her pockets, and several empty astronaut ice cream packages fell to the ground.

"Should we short it out with some kind of electrical charge? We might be able to scramble the magnetic strip..."

Rosalind held up a Gray Labs ID badge with her picture on it and swiped it, opening the door immediately.

"You work here?"

"I'm an intern. Which is why I also have to work at Elements."

Expecting a wonderland of gadgets, gear, and raw scientific materials, Albert was disappointed in that it looked like most every other room at Gray Labs: tidy, white, and lined with white metal cabinets.

"So what do you think? What would you like to steal?"

"What do you have?"

"Everything.

"Won't they be able to trace all this to you?"

"There's another Bold Barn much closer to the main building where everybody goes. I haven't had a single customer in the six months I've worked here, and nobody has ever checked the inventory on anything. I'm not even sure anybody knows this place exists. Probably why an intern is guarding it."

"Have you got time travel stuff?"

"Well, what goes into a time machine?" she asked with a slightly patronizing laugh.

He tried his best to think back to the Presentation Presentation. But a shoddy neurologist or excellent psychologist will attest that the hardest memories to access are the ones a person has repressed in the name of self-preservation.

"I made one in college, but I can't remember exactly what I used."

"From what limited knowledge I have of both you and time travel, I'm going to just throw out some suggestions. How about...tungsten?"

"Yes!"

She walked over to a drawer. "Raw or pre-abyssed?"

"Abyssed."

"Small, medium, or king-size?"

"Oh, king, definitely."

From a large stack of large cardboard boxes, Rosalind grabbed one bearing the name of a California-based grocery chain's private label wine, removed the bottle separator, and threw a few large single-use abysses into it.

It all started to come back to Albert. Flashes of scientific materials popped into his brain, and he coldly stated them aloud to Rosalind as they mentally revealed themselves. With each item, Albert felt sicker and more panicked.

"Do you have any centrifuges?"

"Um, *yeah*."

"Do you have any that go up to 3,600 revolutions a second?"

She went to the "CENTRIFUGE" section, dug around, found one, and threw it into the box. Meanwhile, Albert thumbed through the atomic clocks bin but was disappointed by the results.

"Do you have any extra-large atomic clocks?"

"Do they keep more accurate time, the larger they are?"

"Um, *yeah*," Albert said, echoing Rosalind's mock sarcasm.

"Is this big enough?" She removed a dusty sheet covering an object propped against the wall. This atomic clock was the size of a table where people with more friends than Albert would sit around to play board games. It would certainly suffice.

Albert and Rosalind went through drawer after drawer, grabbing electrical tubing, safety gloves, goggles, and handfuls of wire.

"You wouldn't happen to have any potatoes, would you?"

She opened a large cabinet at the back of the shack. It contained hundreds of bags of potatoes.

"How many do you need?"

"Is it okay if we take all of them?"

"Then you're going to want to rent a van, too."

She opened another door, which gave way to a dingy garage, which contained five identical green, windowless vans adorned with the Gray Labs logo and "EXEMPT" license plates.

"What else?" she asked.

"All I can think of would be a test subject."

"We don't do test subjects. There apparently used to be a guy whose job it was to have things tested on him, but he got promoted or died or something."

"So you don't have any teacup pigs? Do you know where I could get one?"

"To refer you to another business would be a violation of my internship contract, so I will not tell you that you couldn't not get them from Joules Newton."

Albert was glad that he had a secure and durable van, for consulting with Joules Newton would require a trip to the bad part of San Verguenza.

20

The good part of San Verguenza, legally designated The Good Part, housed the legitimate scientific supply businesses and expensive bars. On the other side of the hover-train tracks was the bad part of San Verguenza, legally designated The Bad Part, where the results of local science gone wrong congregated and withered. The kind of people who lived in The Bad Part were those who'd fallen through the cracks or evaded Gray Labs' liquidation squads — vaporized alcohol enthusiasts, trepanners who hadn't trepanned correctly, and Smart Cream addicts who spent their nights spray-painting profane formulas on the walls of abandoned laserdisc factories.

This is where Joules Newton ran the scientific black market. Joules could get a scientist anything they couldn't get legally, or when they didn't want to pay full retail. Long ago, Albert would tag along with Ron on his trips to Joules' legitimate supply shop, which got shut down when Joules was caught selling bootleg copies of *Shades of Gray* and Eli Gray body pillows.

Now in The Bad Part, he conducted business as usual, if usual meant speaking entirely in binary to avoid detection. Fortunately,

Albert had taken binary as his foreign language requirement at WSI. It was either that or German, which Albert found terrifying.

"Hey, Albert, what's slappin', captain?"

"Uh, not much," Albert said nervously, with a quiver. *"What's, uh, slappin' with you?"*

"Makin' money, makin' money. How's your dad?"

"He's good, he's good."

"Then you definitely haven't talked to him. Why you gotta be like that? You can be honest with your old pal, Joules."

"Sorry, Joules. I'm having trouble remembering all my binary."

Joules turned stiff. *"Dang. This isn't a social call, is it? How come nobody ever wants to be friends with Joules? Everybody always wants something from Joules. Nobody ever wants to hear Joules' self-recorded Theremin album that would blow their minds!"*

"Wow, Joules. You're the best! No thanks, no cake for me," Albert replied because, due to his creaky binary, he'd thought Joules had just told him that he always liked him, and also offered him a freeze-dried cookie.

"You have no idea what I just said," Joules said, and then said once again, but slower. Albert shook his head yes, unconvincingly, leading Joules to take one of his rubber-gloved hands, grab Albert's face, and gently force his head to make the "no" gesture.

"Come on. What do you want?" Joules asked.

"I need a pig to test on, please," Albert said in perfect Binary, because *"I need a pig to test on, please"* is the third phrase taught in Binary 101, right after *"Where is the bathroom?"* and *"I am not a human, there is no need to kill me."*

Joules widely grinned at Albert and held open his long, leather lab coat. Inside were dozens of pockets, each one occupied by a miniature pig. While Joules had a very impressive selection, even if some of them were fakes — two or three were obviously

Chihuahuas — Albert immediately knew which one he wanted. He liked the one with sunken eyes, patchy fuzz, and a tail curled in all the wrong places: Carl, his lab partner, best friend, and test subject.

Carl leaped into Albert's hands and familiarly nuzzled his snout into Albert's ear. "*I know this one.*"

"*Yeah, everybody says they know the pig. 'I love that pig, and that pig loves me. We're gonna start a family.' But nobody's coming. And nobody's coming for Joules, either. A pig has to dream, though. A pig has to dream,*" Joules said wistfully, drifting off and then wandering away.

"*So do you want me to pay for this, or...*" Albert said, but Joules was gone, mumbling something to himself about loneliness or ham.

21

———

Not long after successfully cloning a human being, Nobel Prize-winning scientist Magnus Riptide added another item to his impressive list of achievements. He became the first person in a century to face, and walk away from, The Edison Automatic Scientist Killer, a claptrap contraption of pulleys and knives that a younger Edison kept rigged up in the doorway of his New Jersey workshop at night to thwart competitors and disgruntled scientists from whom Edison had stolen inventions. Magnus assumed that was an urban legend but learned that this feat of Edison badassery was real when a bunch of knives flew out of his underwear drawer.

"The one day I consider wearing underwear!" Magnus said, more amused than alarmed, after dodging the flying knives.

Attempted murder should've tipped him off that something was amiss, as should have the fact that nearly anything remotely resembling technology aboard the *Bohrs, Oars & Libertine Ladies* had disappeared. The food over Wi-Fi, his e-book thing, the many unopened boxes that held at least a couple of microscopes, the 30-percent-size clone of Thomas Edison — all of it was gone.

At least Edison left a note. It wasn't so much a note as it was a recording on a wax cylinder playing on repeat on an old-timey music machine once owned by the real Edison that Magnus had bought — the only technology still onboard, apart from the scientist-killing machine. In a fun bit of Edison branding, he sang his words on the message to the tune of "Mary Had a Little Lamb."

"I have stolen all your stuff, all your stuff, all your stuff. Gonna make a times lorry, and ruin all your lives."

But since it was an old-timey wax cylinder recording, the words were warped and impossible to understand. Magnus turned the machine off, sighed, and chuckled to himself. "Oh well," he said. "I suppose good experiences can't last forever," he sighed contentedly before setting out to find his old trepanning supplies. With little to do on the days when *The Scientist* wasn't filming, and especially now with Edison gone, Magnus figured he might as well drill into his brain and tickle it with a feather.

22

"It's a pretty night," Albert said, breaking the comfortable silence with Rosalind while she drove.

"It is," Rosalind agreed, "but is it as pretty as an astronaut?"

Had the boozy contents of his stomach not just been devoured by nanobots, Albert would've thrown up.

"Yeah, I heard it," Rosalind repeated, chuckling in a manner that Albert was 80 percent sure was good-natured.

Albert let out a slow sigh. "Well, it was nice of you to pretend like you hadn't. I mean, for as long as you did pretend."

"I didn't want to make things weird."

"Oh, well then," Albert said sarcastically.

"I mean, even if I weren't from an astronauting family, it's still a nice thing to say to a lady."

Albert looked at Rosalind, and even in the low light from streetlights and the moon, or perhaps because of it, Albert realized, finally, exactly who she was.

"You're Rosalind Howard."

Rosalind slammed down on the breaks. Albert, who hadn't been wearing a seatbelt, slammed into the dashboard, then immediately fell backward, hard, into his seat. Rosalind grabbed her lapel-affixed name badge and flipped it around to where she could read it. It was an especially humorous action, as, like every other intern's name badge, Rosalind's didn't have her name on it. Like every other intern's name badge, Rosalind's read, "INTERN – IF LOST, PLEASE RETURN TO GRAY LABS, S.V., CA."

"Yes, I'm Rosalind Howard," Rosalind said in mock-seriousness.

"Your father is Commander Jimmy Howard. From the Moonbounce place!" Rosalind resumed driving and at that moment they just so happened to drive past Commander Jimmy Howard's Moonbounce Emporium. Rosalind cranked her window down and waved to a silver-haired man in an astronaut costume sweeping the sidewalk out front.

"Hi, sweetie!" Jimmy Howard called out as he returned the wave.

"From the Moonbounce Emporium and also from going to space a bunch of times. Did you know that he's been to Saturn?"

"What?" Albert blurted out, impressed and astonished.

"Good. You're not supposed to know."

"Rosalind?"

"Yeah?"

"I should probably tell you something."

"Is it that I'm pretty enough to be an astronaut?"

"Yes."

"Oh, okay, then. Thanks."

"Sure."

"Oh, was there more?"

"Yes!"

"Do go on."

"Okay," he said. "Back in high school, there was this girl from an astronauting family that I was too nervous and weird to ever talk to. You reminded me of her."

"I reminded you of myself is what you're saying."

"Exactly."

"You were a senior when I was a freshman. That's creepy, Albert. I was basically a child."

"Yeah, but so was I."

"I was 15, and you were 18! That's a big difference."

"No, no. You were 15, and I was 16. I skipped kindergarten because my father thinks it's a secret German conspiracy, and I skipped the seventh grade because that was the prize for winning the sixth-grade science fair."

Albert stopped talking, and Rosalind waited for him to catch up.

"Wait. *You* remember *me*?"

"How could I forget the guy who was the son of the guy who said all that... stuff? Your dad tried to recruit my dad for his, you know, project."

"Wait, so if you're from a rich -- I mean, a family like yours, why are you working as an intern?"

"For the same reason I went to a public high school. Dad wants me to stay humble, to do things for myself. After he became a self-made millionaire, he decided that everybody needed to be the same way."

"Oh, you mean he's cheap."

"Well, he did pay for me to go to art school. And intensive martial arts training. After letting him foot the bill for the various vocational whims of my twenties, I kind of owed it to him to give science a try. It was either that or start cranking out grandkids."

"So we went to the same high school, and your dad is an astronaut. This is a lot of information to take in."

"Yeah, it's not that big of a deal. I mean, I get into the Moon-bounce for half-price on Thursdays, and I got to go to space camp. That was pretty cool."

Albert's eyes widened. He'd always wanted to go to space camp, but they had a strict rule about not admitting anyone named Malfort. "Were you there when they had an accidental launch?"

"I was there like the one year that there *wasn't* an accidental launch."

"Bummer," Albert said. "Before we attempt to travel through time, is there anything else I should know about you?" Albert asked, thinking he was flirting.

"I have a severe shellfish allergy."

For an experiment of this nature and magnitude, Albert and Rosalind would need a large, safe, and most importantly, unoccupied, and unsupervised workspace. The most unoccupied and unsupervised large space in all of San Verguenza on a Friday night in the fall was the high school football field.

Rosalind drove the van right down onto the immaculate sod. "Has this field ever even been used?" she asked rhetorically.

"I doubt it," Albert answered. "The children of scientists are generally not a sporting bunch."

And yet, per the country's many sports-boosting laws, the athletic field and its surrounding facilities had been kept in top working order: the grass was freshly mowed, the field lights burned brightly, and the scoreboard carried blank, black boxes for "Visitor" and "Solid State Amplifiers," the team name should San Verguenza High School ever form an athletic department.

"I think I forgot something," Albert remarked, surveying all the equipment he and Rosalind were in the process of scattering about the grass.

"A table?"

"Yes! Why didn't we get a table?"

The long-malnourished Carl happily grazed on the grass, eating all the way through the dark-green grass that spelled out the "SV" on the otherwise light-green field by the time Albert and Rosalind had finished setting up and connecting the necessary time travel equipment.

While this was admittedly a rehash of his previous time travel attempt, Albert could argue that this experiment was a larger-scale test. His working, private theory was that more potatoes equaled more time to work with, and bigger abysses meant more wiggle room, scientifically speaking. Albert could think of no reason why Carl shouldn't be able to travel beyond five minutes through time. If he'd used around 10 potatoes to get Carl a few minutes away the first time, it stood to reason, then, that using 200 times as many potatoes would get him 200 times as far, which worked out to 1,000 minutes. That's approximately 16 hours, enough to send Carl back to just before that morning's disastrous and humiliating Product Announcement Event. Albert had a plan.

With wide eyes and a crazed, determined stare and the other-worldly humming of a centrifuge filling the brisk, ionic fall air, Albert squatted to Carl's level.

"You guys need a moment?" Rosalind teased.

"Yes, if you don't mind," Albert replied. Rosalind rolled her eyes and took no more than three steps away and turned her back.

Carl lay on his side, breathing heavily, and moaning adorable little pig moans. He'd gorged himself on grass, and by the looks of his potato skin mustache, a few raw potatoes.

"Carl. Listen carefully. When you go back, I need you to take this and go to Gray Labs."

Snort.

Albert took off his employee work ID lanyard and put it around Carl's neck. Rosalind walked over and snapped a picture with her phone because it was adorable.

"When you're there, go to the auditorium and reserve a seat."

Snort.

"You're right. A lab coat would make you look more inconspicuous."

"Do I have to think of everything?" Rosalind asked in mock exasperation. From the pocket of her lab coat, she produced another lab coat, a tiny, white one bearing the Gray Labs logo. "Got this in the gift shop for my brother's cat."

"That's amazing!" yelled Albert. He found a felt-tip marker in his pocket, and under the Gray Labs logo, he wrote "Alpig Malpork." He wrestled Carl into the coat, and then Rosalind took about 100 smartphone photos of the little guy.

"Where were we?"

Snort.

"Right. Get into the event, and then, when Eli Gray takes the stage, just charge at him with all your might. If you hit him just so, I think you can knock him into the 2-D incarceration unit. That should immobilize him for a while."

Snort.

"I love you, too."

Carl gave Albert's face a sweet, tender lick. He trotted over to Rosalind and nudged his snout into her leg.

"I look forward to getting to know you better, too, Carl."

With Carl following, Albert walked over to his improvised command center, sat down on the ground, and flipped a switch. Everything hummed to life and got gradually louder, and then violently louder.

"Is this all going to plan?" Rosalind shouted over the noise.

"Yes!" Albert yelled back. "I mean, we're working on a much bigger scale here, so I don't know, really!"

"What?" she asked. "You don't know?"

"It's fine!"

Light shined out of the abysses. The van shook, rocking back and forth from one side of its wheels to the other. While the powerful potatoes inside had something to do with that, it was probably a side effect of the ground rocking back and forth, too.

"Are you doing this?" Rosalind shouted, even though she was sitting right next to Albert.

"What?"

"It's fine! It's just like I did it in college!"

"Really?"

"No! I have something to tell you. I didn't know what I was doing then. I thought if I did the same experiment, but bigger, with better and more sophisticated equipment, it would work out!"

"Your hypothesis needs some work!"

Albert assessed the situation. The equipment was the same. The ratios of materials were the same. The only difference, Albert surmised, was that the original experiment had taken place inside a lead-and-steel-lined room. Perhaps that acted as some kind of control function, he thought.

Just as he was about to drop Carl into the abyss, the one on the left, the ground below them ruptured. This was California, so that happened often, but this time felt different to Albert, what with the bright purple and blue ooze that shot up out of the ground. Also unique: the horse-sized lobster wearing a cowboy hat and a tin star as it surfed the purple and blue stuff out of the earth, right up onto the surface.

Albert and Rosalind sprang to their feet in curiosity and terror.

Albert held Carl, petting him softly, which soothed the animal but also himself. The lobster lurched toward Albert, a demented and unhinged look in its eyes and weird, purple-colored slobber dripping out of its mouth. As it backed Albert toward the van, it lunged forward, its mouth agape. Albert quietly and internally prepared for death. His life flashed before his eyes, but all that was so boring that he lost interest and refocused on his horrific but totally exciting current predicament.

"I always figured this was how I'd go!" Albert shouted to Rosalind.

"Me, too!" she cried out. "And I'm not okay with it!"

"Neither am I!"

Albert opened his eyes and noticed that the tater-tot watch on his wrist was gone, and the lobster was crunching on it, with his head tilted all the way back and the timepiece just kind of clanging around in his weird, narrow lobster mouth. The lobster choked on it, prompting him to hack and cough and spit, which stopped the choking. Albert's watch flew out of the giant creature's mouth and hit the top of the van with a clang.

"Carl, no!" shouted Rosalind, grabbing onto Albert for some semblance of safety and sanity. Albert broke his stare with the lobster to steal a glance of Carl, although it was too late to stop him. Fueled by adrenaline and love, Carl ran. He repaid all the kindness Albert had ever shown him by absolutely going to town on that lobster, tapping into his tiny wild boar ancestral instincts and chomping into one of the lobster's legs, which is where the good meat is. The lobster, shocked and a little offended, made a hasty departure, fleeing back into the luminescent goo from which it came. Just in time, Carl jumped off to the relative safety of the ground and squealed out the pig equivalent of "And stay out!"

Unfortunately for Albert and Rosalind, that lobster was immediately replaced by another lobster, identical to the first, from out of the primordial goo. Carl squealed a hellish piggy war cry as blue blood from his attack on the first lobster dripped down his chin, cheeks, and soaked his entire body.

He glanced over at Albert, and he actually smiled.

"Aww..." the humans uttered in unison.

Carl would've feasted on the second lobster, too, but he didn't see it. This lobster had no interest in Carl, slapping it out of its path with its claw appendage. Carl landed somewhere near the 10-yard line, scrambled to his feet, and ran back at the lobster. He leaped onto its back and tried to tear off some of its protective shell, to little avail, and to little notice by the lobster.

Rosalind grabbed a stray potato off the ground and reared back to throw it. With a precise, fast motion, the lobster lunged at Rosalind and ate the potato right out of her hand. It also ate her hand. And her arm, too. Standing so close, Albert could feel the intense heat from the lobster's breath, so hot that it seemed to have instantly cauterized Rosalind's wounded stump. That heat was cold comfort to Rosalind, screaming in pain, terror, the shock of sudden and involuntary amputation, but primarily because she'd been spirited away in the mouth of a giant lobster. As the lobster dived back into the hole, Rosalind helplessly ensnared in its mouth, and Carl gnawing at its back, Albert heard Rosalind belt out four words.

"I WILL FIND YOU!"

Albert later thought that her declaration may have been a de facto admission of romantic interest, but Rosalind had really meant it as a mock promise to get revenge on Albert for getting her mixed up in his drama.

A rocket of blinding light shot up into the air from out of the hole. Albert felt a wave of heat that was extreme, even for California. He thought that this might be one of those times in life when he should run, so he did, taking off for the bleachers. As he did, he turned around so he could trot-run backward, for while he wished to live, he also didn't want to miss anything that was going on.

He pivoted at the exact, perfect moment. The light followed the circuit of time-manipulating technology that Albert had set up. It eradicated both tungsten abysses, fried all the wires, snapped the motor of the centrifuge, and gobbled up what was left of the potatoes. As each potato traveled through the cylinder of light, through the air and back into the ground, the brightness began to recede. Finally, as Albert looked on, it retreated entirely into the ground. All that remained was a crack in the ground, and the van, which had somehow survived the ordeal with only a small dent from where the tater-tot watch had hit it. It was a very well-built vehicle.

Albert then could've sworn that the universe once again conspired to add insult to injury. The light burst out of the ground once more, spraying leftover purple and blue ooze all the way to the grandstands and all over him, then shot up into the sky, formed something not unlike a hand, and slapped Albert right across the face.

23

Magnus arrived on the set of *The Scientist* and picked up his script for that week's episode. He never actually read these, nor learned his lines. Per audience demand and network orders, the show was so formulaic and predictable that Magnus could just ad-lib from a list of keywords some production assistant stapled to the front of each script. For example, an episode about a sad-sack rank-and-file employee at an R&D firm who stole a bunch of equipment, opened up a time hole, and lost an intern, Magnus's given keywords were "loser," "time hole," and "company property." As he managed on every episode, what Magnus came up with was verbatim to the scripted dialogue. (Magnus won a Golden Globe for his work in this episode.)

As he stood on set the first night of shooting — they always shot at night; it was a crime drama — he balanced a cup of coffee in one hand and a trepanning drill in the other. A P.A. squatted in front of him and held up the list of keywords for him to memorize. Just before the cameras were about to roll, Magnus looked at the words: "legendary scientist," "disappearance," and "patent theft." These words were intriguing to Magnus, personal even, so much so that for the first time during his tenure on *The Scientist,* he read the whole script. (Actually, he had the P.A. read it to him and made the rest of the cast and the entire crew wait until they were finished.) The plot description, as it would run in *TV Tonight*: "Dr. Claude Von Scientizt tracks down a tiny version of Thomas Edison traveling through time to steal patents and rewrite history for his own glory and financial gain."

Magnus stormed into the trailer of the guy who directed most episodes and wrote the occasional one. If he were going to confront him and ask a lot of questions, he felt like he should really know his name, but he'd never bothered to learn it. Now it was far too late in the relationship to ask without it being awkward.

"Hey, chief, is this real?"

"Is our *TV show* real?" he asked, a little condescendingly. "No, Magnus. It's not. You're an actor."

"Where did you get this?" he demanded, waving the script.

"Your friend last week. The little astronaut guy. We had a great conversation about patents and time machines. Although he called it a 'times lorry.' And he was just so aggressive in a charming kind of way. I thought, *Hey, what if we have a guy like that on the show, but he was evil?*"

"Ha. Yes."

"Yeah, so I wrote about a scientist that travels through time and steals patents and reassigns them to himself and becomes a kajillionaire credited with every great invention. Like how they say Thomas Edison tried to do, back in the day."

"Sure, yeah. Like Edison."

"Your guy even looked like Thomas Edison. He's got that 'resting scowl face.'"

"Really? I never noticed..." Magnus trailed off.

"Hey, by the way, did you see that Edisonball game last night? A real buzzer-beater."

The director went on and on about some kind of sport, prompting Magnus to stop listening and turn his attention to the trepanning drill still in his hand. He scuttled away to a quiet part of the set and got his mental juices flowing.

Edison *had* asked a lot of questions about time travel and patent law.

Then Edison came back to his yacht.

And Edison obviously stole all his stuff.

Something called Edisonball was a thing now.

Edison possessed a list of every invention since 1931.

Magnus put it all together.

The worst part, besides the possibility that his own inventions had been re-patented to Edison, was that if anybody ever found out about this, he would be held responsible and get sent to one of those new two-dimensional sky jails that just creepily hovered over a city. Or he faced an even worse, and more likely scenario: Nobody would like him anymore. His fame would be gone, and so would the adulation. Charisma could only take him so far.

Magnus realized that to ensure he suffered no consequences for his actions, he'd have to time travel. Perpetually unreasonably confident, he wasn't stymied by that notion, only a little perplexed as to where to start. He'd need somebody to show him the basics but had no idea who that would be.

It wouldn't be until he began another brain-drilling session about five minutes later that he would uncover the faint memory of a qualified associate.

24

—

The hypothetical home of the San Verguenza Solid State Amplifiers had been completely sealed off. The bleachers, scoreboard, and lights had been dismantled, and the entire parcel of land covered over with a metal sheet. To mask the crime scene, brand new signs had been installed on all four sides of the field, which read, "SVHS Swimming Pool. Open Since 1948. Closed." Also erected, albeit temporarily, was a large adjudication tent, the site of Albert's disciplinary hearing. These were usually conducted on Gray Labs campus, but Albert had been banned from the premises, which was a good indicator that the disciplinary hearing wasn't going to go his way.

As two Gray goonbots dragged Albert into the tent, a third fitted him with a tight, metallic skullcap. Instantly, the white walls of the tent filled with mentally projected images from Albert's life, ones he'd consider highlights: Grade school science fair wins. Eating astronaut ice cream. Carl. The night with Rosalind, up to the moment she was kidnapped by a lobster-monster.

"You like the pictures," a helmeted Eli Gray stated coldly.

"I, I do," Albert answered unsurely.

"They're coming from your little hat there. A new thing we're working on with LockedIn."

"Oh. The prison people?" Albert asked, hoping he sounded sarcastic, because he was mad, but not too sarcastic because he was about to go on trial.

"One day I read a line in a book, some pour sap saying something to the effect of, 'they can never take away my memories.' And I, being bold, thought, well, what if we could?' We can! We take an inmate's happiest thoughts and project them onto the walls around them, literally imprisoning them with their own joy, rerunning those moments over and over again until they're both sick of them and fully aware that they're years away from making new happy memories!"

Albert could've sworn he heard the spectral echo of an Eli Gray giggle come from inside the helmet. He tried to sit down at the empty chair in front of him, but before he could, the goonbots forced him into it. It was too tall for his feet to reach the ground and offered little to no lower-back support. Eli Gray and his thought of everything.

About 10 feet away sat the Gray Labs Disciplinary Board, as the plaque on the table indicated. The entire Gray Labs front office had come out: Eli Gray, an Eli Gray hologram, a very lifelike Eli Gray robot, and an Eli Gray promotional cardboard standee, just like the ones that sold in the Gray Labs gift shop for $129.99. Because the infraction took place off-campus, but inside San Verguenza, the city was represented by Mayor Richard "Sam" Verguenza III. He was far too busy mashing the buttons of a brand new, not-yet-commercially available Gray Pocket Video Game Thingy HD to pay any attention to the hearing.

"Alan Malfort, you stand accused," asserted the Eli Gray robot.

"No..."

"*Yes.*"

"No, well, I mean yes, I do stand accused. My name is Albert."

The helmeted robot looked to the real Eli Gray for assurance. Eli Gray nodded his approval.

"*Albert.* You stand accused of knowingly committing crimes, both venal and severe, against your employer. How do you plead?"

He didn't really know what to say, and since he couldn't think of a good excuse or a lie, he told the truth. "Well, I did it. So guilty, I suppose."

"Wrong. Guilty. Case closed."

"Eli, he said he was guilty," boomed the real Eli Gray.

"He did? This never happens. I'm not really suited for..."

Faced with this logical conundrum, the Eli Gray robot silently imploded into nothingness.

"Can't even get my own robots to do anything right," Eli Gray muttered.

The hologram applauded in earnest approval. The mayor made a "whoop," but that was in response to unlocking an achievement in *Hero Mayor 2.*

Eli Gray moved out from behind the table and hunched down in front of Albert.

"Why don't you just tell me what happened," Eli Gray said, sounding alarmingly warm and open.

"Fine," Albert replied through clenched teeth. He recounted how he'd checked out a bunch of equipment, took it out to a field, and did a little after-hours scientific testing.

"Was this related to a work project?"

"Not...precisely," said Albert.

"What was the purpose of this experiment?"

"To, um, to see if time travel worked."

"And did it?"

"My hypothesis would need…more testing," Albert said, truthfully, charitably, and, he hoped, non-incriminatingly.

Eli Gray hit a few invisible buttons in the air in front of his face. He ran his finger along lines of text that only he could see.

"Albert, can you confirm that on the night to which this hearing refers, you checked out two king-sized, single-use tungsten abysses, a centrifuge, an atomic clock, a moderate amount of potatoes, a company fleet vehicle, one intern, and handfuls of wire?"

"Yes, sir."

"And did you check back in all of that equipment?"

"No, I did not."

"Why is that?"

"Because it was destroyed."

"What about the intern?"

"She has a name."

"It doesn't matter," Eli Gray said, hanging his head and doing what sounded like crying to Albert.

Albert was shocked by this uncharacteristic display of emotion. He didn't think that Eli Gray would really care about Rosalind. Albert was right.

"All of the equipment, Albert. It's all insured. We'll get it all replaced, from merchandise we make ourselves, and the good people over at Gray Insurance give us a nice little settlement for our pain and trauma at losing our stuff. But you know what we won't be reimbursed for, Albert? Our intern. That intern represented more than $100,000 in free labor over the next three months, and now it's gone."

"But, but what about insurance?" Albert felt a little dirty for bringing it up.

Eli began to frantically pace in front of Albert. He walked over to the long table, took a deep breath, and karate chopped it in the middle. The hologram applauded again; the mayor didn't notice. The cardboard standee fell over.

"Some fly-by-night, business-hating conspiracy that calls itself 'The Government' won't let companies take out secret life insurance policies on their employees anymore. I tried to argue that interns aren't really employees because they don't get paid, but no dice. Thanks a lot, Albert!"

Eli Gray walked very quickly toward Albert with his finger stuck out. As he got closer to Albert, Albert flinched and looked away.

"You're just like your father, aren't you?"

"Excuse me?" Albert yelled, taking the bait.

Eli Gray circled Albert, jabbing his gloved, yet somehow cold finger into Albert's arm with every word. "Wanted to do things *your* way. Wanted to do *your* work. Your own thing. With *my* equipment. With *my intern*. You want to go to work for yourself? Be my guest."

"Good," said Albert indignantly. Eli Gray had obviously been trying to scare and surprise him by firing him, but Albert knew that was coming.

"Albert, did you know that losing an intern is the second-worst thing you can do at Gray Labs?"

"What's the worst, then? Stealing the time bottles that keep you alive?" Albert thought that an exceptionally clever retort, but Eli Gray pretended not to hear it, or maybe he just didn't hear it at all; Albert wasn't sure entirely what penetrated the helmet.

"You're lucky you didn't hurt the van. You wouldn't *believe* how much fleet vehicles cost. Unconscionable mark-up."

Albert started laughing a little. And then he started laughing a lot. And then he couldn't stop laughing. He freaked himself out.

"For the crime of misplacement of an intern, you are sentenced to…"

The word "sentenced" is what got Albert to stop laughing. But before he could finish bringing down the hammer, the hologram Eli Gray raced over to Eli Gray — it had wheels instead of feet — and whispered to the real Eli Gray.

"Oh, oh, that's a good idea! Way to be bold, Eli Gray!"

The Eli Gray hologram saluted Eli Gray and sauntered back to his seat and folded his gloved hands in his lap.

"I keep all my extra ideas in my hologram. This brain isn't big enough for the one of us!"

"Get on with it."

"I'm getting there. *This is just so good!* Okay. Okay," he said, tittering. "Albert, for the crime of misplacement of an intern, your punishment is…a choice."

Albert's heart sank into his stomach, which held Albert's heart more often than it had held food when he had been a college student.

"You resign, and we don't have to give you benefits. Well, except your COBRA. I'm not a monster. I won an award from the Gray Human Resources Foundation. Did you know that?"

"What's the other choice?"

"You keep working here, but for only 20 hours a week, and we double your salary and expunge this whole thing from your record."

"I imagine there's a huge catch to that."

"Oh, absolutely. You see, you'd have the worst job in the entire Gray Labs complex."

"The gift shop." Albert and Eli Gray said at the same time.

And that's how Albert lost his job.

But while he sat there in what he figured was about five

seconds before the robots dragged him out of the tent, he heard a ruckus, inasmuch as the sound of a tent flap whipping open can constitute a ruckus.

"Eli Gray, Eli Gray! How many time bottles did you drink today?" screamed Ron Malfort, his mouth agape, hair askew, and eyes sunken. Ron was clad in just a pair of red bikini briefs along with dozens of potatoes he'd wired to his arms, legs, and torso, which fed into a detonator with a clock flashing "12:00" that rested atop his protruding belly.

"I came here to give you the truth!" Ron Malfort screamed as the robots extended their grippy claws and speedily rolled toward the intruder. Eli Gray, for his part, went back to his seat and folded his hands.

"Run, boy, you're free!" Ron shouted at Albert. "There's enough electricity in these potatoes to blow up the block! Git!"

Before Albert could git as instructed, Ron took the little black box in his hand, a modified 1980s video game joystick, and pushed the big red button on it, which was the exact same shade as his bikini briefs. Nothing happened.

"I guess I needed more handfuls of wire," Ron said to himself before a robot's hand gripped around his throat, diminishing his ability to speak and breathe. As the robots dragged Ron away, Eli Gray stood up calmly, chuckled, and shook his head.

"Parents can be *so* embarrassing."

25

———

The original Thomas Edison's body succumbed to the ravages of diabetes in 1931, leaving him bedridden with terrible pain for a couple of weeks before he actually died. It was just enough time to settle his financial affairs, preserve his semen so that he may sire more children over the coming years, and ponder why he'd invented diabetes in the first place.

His final project, what he had been up to when his kidneys respectfully resigned, was what Edison thought would be the crowning achievement of an already remarkable career: a time machine.

"*This Times Lorry,*" as Edison wrote in his journal in 1930, employing the era's parlance for time machine, "*will make me a giant of Science, one so big and lofty so as to slap the Almighty himself in the face and guffaw at the laws of His Universe.*"

Edison's primary professional goals had always been twofold. The first: Invent amazing things. The second: Manipulate his contemporaries, via the nascent and incompetent U.S. Patent Office, to obtain ownership and legal rights of all the amazing things that he didn't invent. When Edison first got the idea for a times lorry, brazenly lifted from H.G. Wells, he realized that such a device was a way to accomplish both goals at the same time. *"Creating a Times Lorry would, in fact, be a remarkable achievement in its own right,"* Edison wrote in his diary. *"It may also be used to procure and claim for myself ownership of things I would know to be soon invented by others."*

A network of electric streetcars in New Jersey bearing the Edison name was a repurposed, secret Edison experiment. It had once been an elaborate device that Edison used to attempt to electrically jolt himself through time. Not only did it not work in the way Edison intended, but it also gave him diabetes. From the moment he was reborn anew as a tiny, unnatural, imperfect facsimile of himself, Edison conspired to pick up where he'd left off.

He didn't make an ad hoc times lorry in one night from various scientific gadgets stolen from the yacht of Magnus Riptide. Even a guy dead for decades knew that. That's not to say that Edison didn't try that. He connected all the random gear he found on Magnus's yacht together with handfuls of wire, plugged it in, and stood in the middle of the powerful magnetic field it produced. No time travel occurred.

But then Edison got the idea to put some wheels on it. It was, in fact, Thomas Edison who coined the aphorism, "Science is 90 percent putting wheels on things." He spied two thick, rubber roundies on Magnus's seafoam-green Italian motorbike that the young scientist kept onboard for brief land excursions.

As Edison pried the tires off the motorbike with a steak knife he found in the boat's galley, he started to feel just the teensiest bit guilty about exploiting and abandoning the person who had been his guide to the world of the future and made his whole scheme possible again. Then he remembered that this person had also forced him to appear in a lousy two-reeler called *The Scientist,* which Edison felt was an affront to what he claimed was his legacy as the inventor of recorded images. The guilt instantly dissipated.

The wheels made all the difference. Edison would have no way of knowing how to do this on purpose, but he inadvertently turned the large pile of stuff into a compact piece of machinery that to the modern, naked eye would resemble one of those gyroscope-powered stand-up scooters that resemble lecterns, the kind favored by mall security guards, gated community security guards, and amusement park security guards. Unlike those low-speed objects of derision, however, Edison's contraption was capable of land speeds of more than 200 miles per hour, which felt 70 percent faster to Edison because he was 30 percent the size of a regular human.

That was fast, but not fast enough to propel Edison into the past. It was fast enough, though, to propel him through most of California, from the greater Los Angeles area, through the Inland Empire, Stockton, Fisherman's Wharf, and all the way up into the hills of the northern part of the state.

Edison made it from Los Angeles to San Verguenza so fast that he, reasonably, thought he was about to cross over from three dimensions into the fourth at any time. And then, he did, although it wasn't because of anything he did. As he rounded a school and some grandstands, he plowed headlong into a purple and blue river shooting high beams of light into the air. The waves of heat threw him from his brand new times lorry and consumed it. Edison landed atop what appeared to be an extra-gigantic lobster in a cowboy hat, making a retreat from what the tiny Edison could've sworn was a regular-sized pig. The lobster jumped into the source of the bi-colored river, and Edison grabbed onto its thick back-shell as it did.

After a downward fall through a dark tunnel, Edison, the lobster, and some rogue pieces of breakaway gadgetry from the times lorry fell, hard, onto dirty, faded floor tiles, which were white with little flecks of gold in them.

"What in all of damnation is this?" asked Edison to nobody, because nobody was there, while grabbing all the broken future-tech pieces he'd inadvertently brought with him, clutching them to his tiny chest as best he could.

The grand, soulless cathedral reminded Edison of the many outdoor shopping promenades on the boardwalks of coastal New Jersey. This particular boardwalk promenade was different, in that it was enclosed in a massive, rectangular, windowless building in which the rafters of white metal tubes were visible. Cold air, a little too cold for an old man like Edison, blew all around. Unflattering, artificial light emanated from the interior heavens.

This all left Edison with the desire to spend hours in this building, going into each one of the many little storefronts that lined the sides of the corridor, and from what Edison could tell, on another level above that one, too. And even more above that one. Edison had no idea which of these storefronts to enter first, until he spotted, just a few yards away, a three-sided landmark. This triangular obelisk bore a list of points of interest, a map depicting each point of interest's relative location to one another, and a large red arrow indicating that Edison was, in fact," here."

Edison examined the listings on the obelisk and noticed that they were mostly four-digit numbers. "2005." "1994." "1979." "1877." "1929." He frowned disapprovingly, feeling that it was unhelpful to list the mailing addresses of shops but not the names of the shops. He glanced around and saw that one of the storefronts was labeled "1931."

"Why does that number seem important to me?" Edison wondered aloud.

Edison sauntered over to 1931 and looked inside. There was no merchandise on display, no mannequins showing an inappropriate amount of faux flesh. As he looked in, moving images swirled around. He spotted a few things he vaguely recognized — a terrible earthquake, baseball games, and fast-dancing. One, in particular, spooked him: a procession of people filing into a church bearing the signage: "EDISON FUNERAL."

"Aha, it's not a store at all. It's a year!"

Because Thomas Edison was a relatively smart guy, he'd finally figured it out.

"I was in my time, the light of life flickering to its end, and then I was in another time that I was told I'd time-traveled to, a process of which I had no memory. And yet here I lie in this year of 1931, dead as the prospects of Nikola Tesla. Certainly, this can mean but one thing, from the scientific perspective," Edison said to himself. "I am unable to be killed! I am resurrected, bound not to the laws of time, space, or biology! As was my intent all along. Huzzah!"

As for why he had a marsupial's paw instead of a hand, Edison decided that it was the result of a poorly-remembered experimental limb replacement procedure from 1931. A diabetic losing an appendage and having it replaced with that of an animal seemed entirely plausible for 1931, Edison reasoned.

Having finally invented time travel, or stumbling on it, as it were, Edison realized he could finally make good on his plans to travel through time and steal patents as he did so. And it would require far less effort than he'd initially intended. Now, he'd simply:

1. Go to 1931. Inform a world in deep mourning that he wasn't dead.
2. Immediately patent everything that he'd learned about that had been invented since his "death."
3. Popularize Edisonball.

With a confident chuckle, Edison strode into the realm of 1931, only to be knocked back by a powerful unseen force, which threw the tiny little scientist to the cold, hard ground. He also could have sworn he heard his lobster companion snicker.

"Are you laughing at me?"

"1-2-3-4-5-6-7-8-9-10-11-12!" the lobster grunted out through what sounded like a century's worth of shellfish phlegm.

"Are you speaking in base 12?"

He repeated the number sequence.

"Say, you're a *time lobster*, aren't you? I've got your number!"

The lobster grunted in sarcastic approval.

"Come now," Edison said firmly. The lobster refused to budge, sitting down, turning his back to Edison, and harrumphing in base 12.

"Beast, did I offend thee?"

"1-2-3-4-5-6-7-8-9-10-11...12!" the lobster squealed.

"Oh, well, as the case may be, I shall give you a name then."

"1-2-3-4-5-6-7-8-9-10-11-12?"

"Indeed, yes. You remind me of an old friend. He was also a monster blessed with powers and deserving of much renown. I shall name you in his honor! Now come along, Topsy Too."

The lobster roared.

"No, no, not like Topsy the second. Topsy *Too*. Topsy *the also*."

So, the gigantic lobster, named for an elephant Edison had once electrocuted to death to discredit a rival's form of electricity, skittered over to the inventor, slipping here and there on time goo. Edison, who'd dreamed of being a cowboy ever since they were invented when he was in his forties, mounted Topsy Too, and loosely tied two of its antennae together to create a rein.

"Yah!" he shouted, slapping the lobster's back. Together they moseyed on yonder through a thick layer of protective radioactive time jelly right into the storefront and year of 1931, all of it in glorious black and white.

26

———

Following his termination, the only place Albert could afford to drink was Phrendly's, a bar so sketchy that it accepted checks from Joules Newton. Also unsavory was that it was a theme bar, and the theme was phrenology, the favorite discipline of Gus, its owner and bartender. Vintage brain maps covered the walls and ceramic phrenology model skulls were bolted down to the bar and the ceiling, giving the bar an innate ghoulishness. Albert drank for free because he let Gus read the bumps on his head.

Albert had often fetched his father from this bar when he was a child, back when it was a 1940s-themed place called The Manhattan Project. These days he'd spend an hour or two at Phrendly's, drinking some swill like Sir Isaac's Extra-High Gravity Ale, which accordingly picked him up and then brought him down. He preferred to sit at the end of the bar because that's where he could best see the TV. The volume was usually down, which was unnecessary because the patrons of Phrendly's were a sad bunch who never spoke to each other. The only sounds in the place came from clinking glasses and the introduction screen of a *Theremin Hero* arcade game that nobody ever played.

An ad came on the TV for one of those sleazy art sales at a hotel near the airport. Albert noticed that the quality of the art was not bad; the KopyRight! had really revolutionized that industry. These art sales didn't just offer Van Gogh prints, for example, they sold what were ostensibly Van Goghs, recreated down to the last stroke. When the commercial ended, the image cut to a bunch of rapid-fire images: cops running around, firing Tesla coils at bank robbers, and smacking thugs with microscopes.

"Hey, *The Scientist* is on!" Gus shouted, reaching up to the TV to turn up the volume.

Albert had never heard of this show, and he was intrigued because as a scientist, he was likely within its target demographic.

"*The Scientist*?" Albert yelled, moderately drunk and nursing a tender scalp. "I'm one of that!"

"You've never seen this? Oh man, it's the best! Detective Lt. Dr. Claude Von Scientizt is a genius ex-NASA scientist who now works as a police consultant," Gus enthusiastically explained. "He solves crimes using only the power of science!"

Albert's interest dissipated when the credits told him the show featured probably his least favorite actor in the world.

"*STARRING MAGNUS RIPTIDE AS DETECTIVE LT. DR. CLAUDE VON SCIENTIZT.*"

"Yeah, that Magnus Riptide is in it. Only man in history to get the Nobel for Chemistry *and* a Teen's Choice Award."

"I'm...familiar," Albert said. And then he involuntarily crushed his beer bottle with his hand in a bit of that momentary superhuman strength that comes during exceptional moments of blinding rage.

On the screen, Magnus, clad in a long, white lab coat, and a blonde woman wearing a midriff-baring lab coat, stood in a muddy field. It was night; they were lit by the red-and-blue lights of a parked police car. They shone their flashlights around the ground below them in a bit of pointless stage business.

"Amber-Melissa, it's obvious what's happening here. This is a time travel experiment. One gone horribly awry."

"How can you tell?

"This purple and blue stuff," Magnus explained as he dipped a test tube into a puddle of two-colored waste. "Radioactive goo most closely associated with time lobsters."

"Gasp!" Amber-Melissa said rather than did.

"I wish these mad scientists would learn that the real time machine is in...here," Magnus said, pointing to his heart, and then his brain, and then his groin. Then he pulled "Amber-Melissa" close and kissed her.

"Why, Dr. Von Scientizt, whatever was that for?"

"Because love," he said, "is the enemy of time."

She swooned, and he released her, and she straightened her lab coat, smoothed out her hair, and puffed on an e-cigarette.

"Let's run some science tests on him. Detective Amber-Melissa, hand me those test tubes."

Amber-Melissa handed him some test tubes. Using tongs, he picked up a glob of goo from the ground, placed some in a test tube, and put the test tube into an old-fashioned supercomputer that was just sitting there.

"Just as I thought," he said, authoritatively.

"How can you tell?"

"Science never lies," Magnus said, before turning to the camera. "Now then. Let's make a science guess!"

Gus said the line, too.

"I love it when he says that!" Gus enthused.

"I helped put a man on the moon, but I still don't know why

man is so inhumane," Magnus as Dr. Von Scientizt lamented. And then he and Amber-Melissa kissed again.

As the episode wore on, Dr. Von Scientizt and Amber-Melissa investigated the disappearance of an intern from a respected research-and-development firm, eventually catching the very guilty "Alan Mulfort," who they finally found in the woods, dressed only in filthy underwear, and eating astronaut ice cream. When the detectives cornered him, he cried like a baby.

"Don't shoot me!" he whined. "I am a science man!" The sounds of rapid-fire flatulence then emanated from the TV for a solid minute and a half. Gus thought this was the most hilarious thing in the world.

"He pooped his pants!"

Albert didn't really remember what happened next, but when he tried to go back to Phrendly's the next day, Gus told him that he wasn't allowed in anymore, on account of how the previous night he'd jumped up onto the bar, ripped the TV off the wall during *The Scientist*, and tossed it through the window.

27

Traveling through time was one thing; traveling through space was quite another. That's what Edison thought, at least. Following the images of his own memorial led him directly to 1931 East Orange, New Jersey, site of a patent office, his workshop, business offices, to a lesser extent his family and friends, but most importantly in that moment, that memorial service. He tied Topsy Too up to one of the horse hitches that were still in use at the time, and, to limit suspicion, concealed the beast with some of the many pieces of loose garbage littering the streets of this typical East Coast city.

Edison entered the church, walked through the lobby, and tried his darndest with his small hand and paw to open the big doors to the worship room. After he threw a shoulder into it, he was inside, where he screamed, "Behold, that I am alive!"

He thrust his arms upward, opened his eyes that he'd closed while enduring the pain of opening the door, and found that the room was completely empty. Well, there was one person there: Thomas Edison. The real one, the original one, only dead and lying in an open casket. The newer, clone Thomas Edison thought his original version looked beautiful, scowling even in death.

A fun idea occurred to the mischievous, emboldened Edison, as will happen when one bears witness to his own funeral. He quickly ran outside, unattached Topsy Too, and quietly brought it into the church, having the lobster open the door this time by smashing through it as if it were no firmer than a bowl of melted butter. Edison directed Topsy Too toward the front of the church, where, knowing he would be unable to lift his own lifeless corpse out of the coffin, he had the lobster do it. Topsy Too deftly used a pincer to reach in and pull out the body, all in one piece, not unlike the lucky seafood restaurant patron who gets a crab leg out of the shell all at once. Similarly, the lobster ate the previous iteration of Thomas Edison in one big bite.

"Bully, Topsy Too! Now hide, you, hide!"

The lobster scuttled over to one of the church's confessional booths and closed the door behind itself. Edison climbed into the empty coffin, closed the lid, and waited. About 30 minutes later, when he heard voices, the somber strains of an organ, and photographers' flashbulbs firing, he decided the time was right. In one motion, he pushed the lid off, sat up, jumped out, and shouted, "Behold, that I am alive!"

The crowd gasped.

"The Shrinking Edison trick. I fooled you all!"

"Topsy Too, come!" Edison shouted, and then he whistled with his fingers. Topsy Too burst out of the confessional room, destroying it.

Thus began something of a mass public freak-out when this very famous figure thought dead emerged from his own coffin at his own funeral, but 30 percent his size, only to ride a gigantic, drooling lobster out of the church and onto the streets of New

Jersey. This would not be the first time that the presumed threat of an alien invasion would lead to frenzied mass hysteria and subsequent exodus in New Jersey. In anticipation of such an event, Edison wrote down in the margins on his printout of inventions, "New Jersey-based frenzied mass hysteria and subsequent exodus."

He would patent that, as well as the Shrinking Edison Trick and the two-fingered Edison Whistling Technique. And then everything else on his list. He and Topsy Too confidently set out on their four-mile walk to the closest branch of the U.S. Patent Office.

28

Fired from Gray Labs, and living in a house suddenly and conveniently vacated by his recently re-imprisoned father, Albert finally had the time and space to pursue his own independent research into the nature of time and space. He didn't, however, have the financial resources by which to do so; after he missed a few payments, the walruses that looked after his finances vacated his accounts. Forced to earn a living and blacklisted by Eli Gray, Albert converted his father's old sperm bank into Malfort Labs, "a private scientific consulting and research concern," which was what he called doing freelance work out of his garage. He attracted business by charging rock-bottom rates and not requiring clients to use their real names. It would be safe to categorize his customers as disreputable.

Albert usually woke up around 11:00 a.m. and savored his favorite part of the day: the half-second before he remembered that his life had completely gone to hell. Then he'd force himself out of bed, fall to the floor, fight depression and hangover to get to his feet, trip over an empty Spazzatura box, snort some powdered Smart Cream, and start the 16-hour workday necessary to barely make ends meet. To do that, he just had to shuffle from one end of the garage to the other — his lab occupied one side, and his living space the other. He couldn't step foot in the rest of the house; it was quite full of the bad kind of mold.

On this day, he'd just turned on the lights when there was a knock on the garage's side door, the one marked with a sign that read "Malfort Labs." While searching his lab coat pockets for any loose granules of Smart Cream, Albert opened the door. There stood a middle-aged townie in a dirty plaid shirt and a mesh cap grinning widely, but not as widely as the little girl he'd brought along.

"Hey. Y'all got puppies?" the man asked.

"No, I don't. It's a common mistake."

"Y'all got the black ones or the little yellow ones?"

"I want a little yellow one, Daddy!" the little girl jubilantly declared.

"She wants one of the little yellow ones."

"I don't have puppies!"

"It says Malfort Labs, don't it?" he asked, pointing at the plaque. "Y'all sold out?"

"You're confused. 'Labs' means 'laboratory.'"

"Oh, like a bathroom."

"Daddy, I have to pee."

"Can my girl use your laboratory?"

Albert slammed the door. He realized once more that if he was going to call his freelance, home-based company "Malfort Labs," he probably should've gone with a simple sign bearing only the company name, and not one with a picture of a Labrador retriever wearing a lab coat and goggles. He thought it would be cute and attract a mainstream audience. But since having this exchange with a walk-up customer literally every single day, it had obviously been a lot more trouble than it was worth.

The return of silence made Albert do something he didn't like to do: think about Rosalind. In moments like this, he'd consider how she was kind of sort of maybe dead and how it was his kind of sort of maybe his fault. This made him feel uncomfortable, and sad, and panicked. Avoiding those feelings-filled periods is why Albert filled up his life as much as possible, with work, sleep, and alcohol.

Another time he was forced to think about Rosalind was when her father, Commander Jimmy Howard, would try to firebomb his garage, which was every other day. The damage was minimal; the Molotov cocktails would self-extinguish by the time they hit the window glass. There wasn't enough oxygen in the air for them to burn, as this part of San Verguenza was choked out by precisely directed air pollution from Gray Labs.

There was another knock on the garage door.

"Hello, Alvin."

Albert sighed and pretended to smile nervously through gritted teeth, trying his best to look scared for the sake of the two short and ancient men in crew-cuts and NASA bathrobes who he found at his door on the mornings when Commander Jimmy Howard didn't toss a firebomb.

"Hey, Chet. Morning, Mike."

"Find Commander Howard's daughter," Chet proclaimed robotically through his electro-larynx held up to his neck.

"Or else!" Mike added before a coughing fit took hold.

"Or else what?" Albert asked, bored, as he'd said these lines so many times.

"Or we'll dust you!" Mike said.

Chet, his hands quaking, slowly reached into the pocket of his bathrobe, pulled out a handful of what he wanted Albert to think was volatile moon dust, and blew it, aiming for Albert's face but depositing it on Albert's socks. Mike shook his fist at Albert, and then both astronauts scurried off, back to the idling San Verguenza Home for Retired Scientists and Astronauts shuttle van.

"See you guys on Thursday."

Albert brushed the cat litter off his feet and staggered over to his lab bench to get to work. He was about 90 percent finished with a mind-controlled robotic arm that gave superhuman strength to whoever wore it, which he's pretty sure was a long-serving warlord from a failed state in South America.

As he attached the robotic arm to his own arm and the electrodes to his bald spot, the garage door started to rise. It rose creakily and with the moaning churn of the old electric automatic door opener. Albert grew concerned, as nobody could possibly possess the handheld, clip-backed device necessary to open the door; Ron had destroyed it with a hammer many years earlier, convinced it was a spying tool of Eli Gray.

He rushed to get the robotic arm in place and thought the nasty thoughts required to make it work, which made the transparent, inch-wide orb at its end fire three times, striking underneath the door twice and the door itself once. As the green smoke cleared, he could see somebody moving around, so, apparently, he'd missed.

"I have a forcefield!"

To secure his lab, Albert had juiced up an invisible dog fence on that door, set to deliver 400,000 volts of vengeful electricity. The only thing that could defeat such a forcefield was, obviously, a stronger forcefield, one with a higher electrical charge that superseded or absorbed the electrical charge from *his* forcefield.

"My forcefield eats other forcefields," the voice proclaimed.

Magnus always packed a personal forcefield generator when traveling to hostile environments, such as neighborhoods that the *CIA World Factbook* noted were upper middle class or lower.

"Well, I have two forcefields, and the second forcefield can destroy other people's forcefields."

That time Albert was lying, and it's also when he finally realized that Magnus was the figure he'd failed to shoot and kill, and who had also evaded the equivalent of 200 simultaneous deaths in an electric chair. Albert picked up an old can of paint (the converted garage was still a garage) and threw it at Magnus. It sailed through Albert's own forcefield, but bounced off Magnus's forcefield and clanged loudly to the ground.

"Hey!" Magnus jumped to the side to avoid the paint can's bounces; he didn't want to get paint on his narwhal leather shoes. "Knock it off! No more paint cans. No forcefields. It's okay!" he cheerfully called out. "Albert, old friend, it's me, Magnus! Magnus Riptide, from television! And college!"

Albert simply did what he had done many times before, and entertained the thought of what it might feel like to grip Magnus Riptide around the neck, lift him off the ground, and just *squeeze*. Since he was wearing a thought-controlled robotic arm, that particular dark fantasy immediately came to fruition.

Magnus didn't lose his cool. Sure, he was scared, but he was Scandinavian, and so he was unable to physically express any of that fear.

Albert had little to no intention of actually killing Magnus — he'd been a blight on his life, but he didn't want him to be a blight on his soul, too, even if he didn't believe in all that nonsense. He was about to set him down when the robot arm overheated and melted right off his arm into a puddle of liquid metal. Magnus straightened his sport-length lab coat and patiently waited for Albert to wipe the remaining metallic liquid from his arm with a laboratory rag. "Ask General X for more time," he said into a hand-held device. "And while I'm thinking of it, take down the sign with the dog on it, and murder Magnus Riptide."

"Hey, you remember me!"

This comment re-excited Albert's mental rage center. Constant testing of the robot arm had synced his brain, body, and robotic arm. Even though the robot arm was so longer attached or even functional, Albert's brain instantly responded to the anger cue by extending Albert's biological arm outward in a shooting motion. No laser came out, of course, but Magnus still flinched. Albert enjoyed that.

"Oh, Albert. You always were quite the prankster!"

"Would you like to see the undetectable water-borne poison I've been contracted to make for a guy that the global political community thinks died in 1993?"

"Hey, come on. I came all the way from L.A., and on non-private transportation."

"You had to take a regular flight? Boo-hoo."

"A helicopter lifted my yacht and me up here. And I just know that it had been rented out previously because someone had crudely fingered the words 'wash me' on its exterior. The first thing I did when I landed was purchase the company and have their booking agent put on a week of paid suspension."

"How magnanimous of you."

"I'm a changed man, Albert."

"That means you need something from me, doesn't it?"

"Why would you think that?"

"Because you're a horrible person."

"So, only horrible people ask for favors?"

"They do if the person they're asking is someone whose life they ruined."

"How did *I* ruin your life?"

Albert thought he was being teased, but he looked at Magnus, who seemed genuinely confused. Albert realized that Magnus honestly had no idea of the influence he'd had on Albert's existence.

"Do you...do you not remember at all?"

"I know that you know something about time travel. And I know that I knew you in college. Details about either? It's been a long time, and I've done a lot of trepanning, so you could say that there are some cracks in the foundation of my memory palace."

From Albert's left hand came a sound that sounded like glass breaking; he'd squeezed a stray clump of stem cells so hard that it shattered and splattered all over his Malfort Labs lab coat, which was an N-monogrammed terrycloth bathrobe he'd gotten at a thrift store for a dollar.

"I'm guessing that we did not part on good terms," Magnus said. He noticed what Albert had done to his stem cells, and he subtly took a few steps backward. "Whatever happened, it's ancient history."

"Ten years isn't ancient history."

"Time can be very tricky to the memory."

"Not really. You don't remember at all, and I remember exactly."

"Let's just leave the past in the past!"

"You don't get to say that!"

"Why can't you just let it go? Be free of this burden, Albert!"

"It's pretty hard to let go of some guy destroying your life's work and then shrugging it off because he's too entitled to care."

"Sure, but I don't *remember* doing it. Doesn't that count for something?"

"Get out of my house."

"Fine." Magnus turned around and headed for the garage door. "It's just that all of the past, present, and future of science depends on you helping me."

"What, you need me to help you crash that party that Stephen Hawking supposedly held for time travelers? Well, when you get there, say hi to my mother for me!"

"Wait, your — your mom is with Hawking?"

"Yeah? So what. Lots of people drop out of society, abandon their families, and follow around a famous scientist."

"No, it's just that –- my mom was involved with Hawking, too."

Albert's demeanor notably softened. That was exactly the reaction Magnus was hoping for when he'd decided to tell Albert that his mother had also left him and his father to follow Stephen Hawking. He was lying because Karolinka Wakimovich-Riptide had never done that. However, after seeing her photo in a magazine, Stephen Hawking named a singularity theorem after her.

"It's fine, I'll go. I hope you can live with yourself knowing you've abandoned the profession that's given you so much."

"Given me so much? Look around you!"

Magnus did, surveying at the garage. Albert had a point, Magnus thought, because Magnus felt unclean.

"I finally come up with something good, and it's swiped away from me, and I fight back a little and, after being humiliated on national TV..."

"What? Where? Who would do such a thing?"

"Some show called *The Scientist.*"

Magnus realized at that exact moment that the Albert Malfort of reality and the Alan Mulfort of *The Scientist* might be connected somehow.

"Now I work out of a garage on projects for seedy and dangerous clients who can get away with paying me less for questionably legal and very expensive projects, for which I have to buy all of my own equipment, also from questionably-legal channels. It's all so below the board and gross that I have to do all my business on a cell phone."

"Hey, those things will give you cancer."

"I'm a scientist. Don't you think I know that?"

Magnus jumped suddenly off his stool, disturbing and knocking over a large stack of canned hams.

"And I have to use canned hams for test subjects instead of pigs."

Magnus started to pick them up, thinking it might make him appear "nice," but Albert waved him off.

"But you're still making science, at least," Magnus offered.

"Barely."

Albert went to his mini-fridge and removed a vaporized alcohol canister. He broke off the transparent glass part, which contained the alcohol, and he slurped its contents through a crack. Then he grabbed a screwdriver off the ground and punctured the metallic base, then sucked out the Freon inside. Magnus, who got his head changes by drilling into his brain, winced.

"Albert, what's the most important thing in science?"

"I don't know."

"Okay, what's the second most important thing in science?"

Albert thought for a moment. "Innovation, I guess."

"I'll ask you again. What's *the* most important thing in science?"

"Credit!"

"Why didn't you say that the first time?"

"I didn't want to sound like a jerk. I'm not a jerk. You're the jerk."

"I'm also a good scientist."

"Are you?" Albert asked skeptically and rhetorically.

"Yes!"

"What have you done?"

"I won the Nobel Prize!"

"You're Scandinavian. That's basically a participation trophy."

"Yeah, but I've won it, like, more than once." He honestly couldn't remember exactly how many times it had been.

"What did you do with the prize money?"

"I don't keep track of every *kall* I spend, but I do believe that I spent it on a cocaine party."

"Unbelievable!"

"A cocaine party for underprivileged teenagers, Albert."

"You're the *worst.*"

"I sent food over the Internet."

"If you can call that food."

"I discovered a natural reserve of pure charisma in my brain!"

"Doesn't count."

"Sure it does!"

"No. That was in college, and it was an accident."

"Most science is an accident!"

"It sure is. My time travel was an accident. Your charisma fountain was an accident. You know how I know?"

"How?"

"Because we're really defensive about those things. Had those been legitimate discoveries, we both would've freely shared the science with others, because that's what science is about. And because we'd have already received the awards and the money and the credit."

"Exactly!" Magnus has pleased he'd caught Albert in a word trap. "Credit. This is all about credit. You don't even understand. If you'd just let me talk, I could tell you what you'd be –- "

"I'm willing to venture that your food over the Internet was an accident, too."

"So?"

"So what?"

"Was it an accident?"

"Why should I tell you?"

"Yep. It was an accident. What have you ever done on purpose, Magnus? How have you ever actually used your brain for good? When did you ever, just once, come up with a great idea and follow through with it, on your own, and see its development through?"

"Well, when have you?"

"Not relevant!" That struck a nerve with Albert. "Name one real act of science you've done in the past year."

"I cloned Thomas Edison with a KopyRight!"

Albert paused. Once again, he figured, Magnus was teasing; a KopyRight! just didn't work that way.

"That's the reason I'm here. I think we both know I didn't come to apologize."

"You should probably explain what's going on then."

"In short," Magnus said, pausing to laugh because the word "short" reminded him that the Thomas Edison clone he'd unleashed was very small, "I cloned him, and then I think he escaped into time somehow to take credit for every invention that was ever invented."

"Oh, like how he tried to do that the first time around?"

"Precisely."

"Why do you think that's what happened?"

"He's gone. Also, my director on *The Scientist* gave him a list of every invention patented since the year he died."

"Okay," Albert said, trying to process all of this information.

"I'm also starting to notice that random objects suddenly have Edison's name all over them."

"Oh, come on. That's impossible."

"Well. What's that coat made of?"

"No idea."

"I'm guessing it's a woven poly-cotton blend, a fair amount of stretch. Patented, if I recall correctly, in 1966, by Thomaston Cotton Mills of Georgia. Patent number 3290752?"

"You know the patent number of a poly-cotton blend?"

"I'm not merely a man of science, Albert. I'm also a man of fashion."

Magnus acted like he was going to move left, and Albert tried to block him. Magnus got around Albert and yanked his collar backward. As he restrained him with his left arm around the neck, Magnus grabbed and ripped out the care tag from the inner collar of Albert's lab robe. Magnus flicked the paper tag to Albert, which fluttered down directly into his hand.

"Polyester-cotton blend with stretch characteristics. Patent number 3290752. In 1931...by Thomas Edison."

"So, are you going to let life keep happening to you, or are you going to make a choice and actually do something?"

Magnus's blunt assessment surprised Albert. Yes, it was true, and it hurt to hear, but he had no idea Magnus could be so psychologically insightful.

29

"She was a beautiful and majestic beast, but a beast nonetheless, and it took a million volts to bring her down."

The lobster grunted in response as Edison rode it down some hardscrabble urban New Jersey street.

"*Direct* current! How dare you?"

The lobster grunted again, in exasperation.

"Well, it wasn't a very good joke."

"The day I electrocuted Topsy — Topsy the first — was the proudest day of my life. Science is 90 percent sending a powerful current of electricity through something just to see what happens."

The lobster grunted.

"Topsy Too, you wouldn't believe the way they've tarnished my legacy. When I was in the time of that preening sissy who calls himself a scientist, do you know what I saw? Household devices powered by alternating current. Newfangled coiled light bulbs which cast a weak and pallid glow. My design was perfect, Topsy Too. Tungsten filament, a vacuum tube..."

Seeing a group of children approach, Edison pulled on Topsy

Too's antennae to direct it to cross the street immediately. Edison hated children. They were always coming up to him. "Please give me a job, Mr. Edison!" they'd say, or "Please let me return home to my family's filthy tenement apartment because I've been working in your factory for 20 hours, Mr. Edison!"

The small mob of children followed him and Topsy Too to the other side of the street. Seeing them up close, these weren't just children, Edison noticed — they were common street urchins. *Ragamuffins*, he thought. *Orphans, even.* Edison stiffened and sneered extra hard, belying his fear of this mob of tots.

"Hey kid, where'd ya get that dog?" asked the one who was apparently the mob's leader by virtue that he spoke first. That set him apart from the utterly interchangeable gang of a dozen children, none over the age of 8, but all with the exhausted, harried, world-weary appearance of a man of 17, which was considered middle-aged in 1930s New Jersey. All of them were filthy, dressed in filthy paperboy caps and filthy, ill-fitting wool pants held up with frayed bits of filthy rope. Edison was aghast that none wore a waist jacket, let alone a bow tie.

"You wanna be in our gang?"

"Quiet, Harry," the leader said, throwing a handful of jacks in Harry's face, making him whimper and scurry to the back of the pack. "He can't be in our gang. He's not a tough kid."

"Yeah, we're tough kids!" called out one of the other children.

Edison dismissively looked up and away from the gang, refusing to meet the leader's sallow-eyed gaze. He gently pulled on Topsy Too's reins to signal that it was time to move along.

"Off you go, street toughs," Edison said, aggressively shaking his koala paw at them. "Go see to your game of stickball or whatever waste of time children occupy themselves with these days."

"Hey, you ain't no kid," the leader realized.

"Yeah, Honus, he's some kinda tiny grown-up!" another street orphan offered.

"What's your name, tiny grown-up?" asked Honus.

"I don't have to answer that." Edison pulled the reins a little more anxiously. Breathing rapidly now, Topsy Too couldn't, or wouldn't, budge.

An exceptionally large child pushed his way through the crowd, incidentally knocking down some of his cohorts. This one was not only the largest of the ragamuffins but also the dirtiest. His face was covered in soot, and instead of clothes, he wore a garment fashioned out of a bag of Mickey O'Mulligan's Potato-Shaped Nutritional Rocks.

"Tell me your name, or I'll sock ya good!" the fearsome child screamed, shaking his first in Edison's direction.

Edison did not want to get socked.

"I'll have you know that I am Thomas Alva Edison."

The children frowned in a collective display of non-recognition.

"The Wizard of Menlo Park!" Edison added.

Silence. A few shrugged.

"The World's Greatest Inventor!"

More silence, except for some sighs. One of the children growled like a dog.

"The Tungsten Marvel!" At the time of his first death, Edison had been trying hard to get that one to catch on.

"You're boring. We're bored now," the one called Honus said. "Let's get to it, gang!"

Topsy Too cried out in terror and mild annoyance and then in pain as the orphans clubbed at it with makeshift shell-crackers and hammers, primarily discarded auto parts, horse bridles, and garbage can lids, all of which were in abundance on the street.

"Topsy!" Edison called out in vain, as the wicked children effortlessly freed the lobster meat from the shell. They ravenously devoured the flesh of the still-living beast, the stronger and bigger children helping themselves to the succulent claw and tail meat. The scrawnier children honored the hierarchy and feasted on the shells and unidentifiable lobster muck. The animal was wholly consumed in less time than it takes a prominent inventor to file a patent, which is to say, not very long at all.

Lacking the time or inclination to mourn, Edison held on tight as long as he could with his one human hand and one koala paw, retaining the only evidence of Topsy Too's presence, a single antenna he had used as a rein. The children scurried off.

"See ya later, Alva!" Honus shouted.

"Yeah, you got a girl's name!" the gigantic and angry child added.

Edison sat alone on the cobblestone street. His thoughts turned to those of self-preservation and the execution of his goals. Both, it seemed, were in jeopardy. Topsy Too, whatever he was, provided safe passage. Without Topsy Too, Edison reasoned, he was stuck in 1931 forever. There would be no way to carefully go to each year and patent each invention separately. The only way out was if he invented a times lorry, or stole a times lorry. Neither option seemed terribly probable.

As he sat on the ground and felt sorry for himself, he was inspired to try out an old creativity ritual. He reached into the pocket of his jacket with his human hand, pulled out a light bulb, and held it aloft over his head. This, Edison believed, caused particles in the tungsten filament to dissipate out of the bulb and slowly fall, where they would then embed themselves in the brain and facilitate thinking.

It worked. Edison realized that he didn't *have* to travel through time; he could just patent everything from where he was. Why go to 1960 to beat a 1961 patent, when he could just as easily patent the entire list of inventions in 1931, where he was, and also probably couldn't leave?

"Paradoxes are nothing but a load of applesauce," he screamed into the empty streets. "I'm Thomas Alva goddamn Edison!"

30

The proposal was irresistible: Save science from a tiny but formidable menace while figuring out time travel, and somebody else would pay for it. It's everything that Albert had ever wanted, more or less, and he was fully committed as soon as Magnus explained the situation to him. But, Albert reasoned, Magnus didn't need to know that.

"I may help you. I may not," Albert said while sitting in a heated, vibrating lounge chair onboard the *Bohrs, Oars & Libertine Ladies*. Magnus had tried hard to ensure Albert's participation. They continually dined on the finest molecular gastronomy creations prepared by El Robót, flown to the boat from Spain. "¿Desean algo para comer?" the waist-high robot chef in a matador costume asked in a robotic voice as he emerged from the ship's galley carrying a tray.

"Muchas gracias El Robót," Magnus replied, immediately digging in.

"What is this, exactly?" Albert asked enthusiastically. He'd enjoyed the field greens syrup and translucent croutons, as well as the duck confit flatbread foam served in a comically oversized syringe. He appreciated how each selection had been paired with artisanal whippets, presented in little metal cartridges that had been molded into the shape of Whippets.

"Patatas bravas."

In front of Albert sat a plate of what appeared to be nothing.

"Translate please," Albert said.

"I'm not going to translate Spanish for somebody from California," Magnus replied.

Albert felt a vibration in his pocket. He reached into his pocket and pulled out his flip phone, which, for the first time ever, was glowing with the alert of a new text message. He discovered that he had been sent a photograph of a plate cubed, fried potatoes, topped with a red sauce. He also suddenly felt full and could feel the residual effects of spicy red peppers on his tongue.

"Wow!"

"Buen provecho," the robot said as it scooted out of the room.

"What do you think he's going to make for dessert?" Albert asked.

"Shut up."

"What?" he gasped, feigning righteous indignation.

"Albert, I understand this is a difficult decision for you," Magnus said, his impatience palpable, "but you can't keep doing this. What can I do to force your hand once?"

"Nothing. I'm in."

"Really?"

"Nope. See what that feels like?"

"What *what* feels like?"

"To have somebody be nice to you and then betray you."

He sighed as he stood up. "Come on. What do you want? I can give you anything."

Albert hadn't thought about what, exactly, he'd want from Magnus, merely the idea of trying to take as much as possible from Magnus. He tried to think of specific, tangible things that he desired, but he couldn't come up with anything. He wanted Rosalind, or at least he wanted to know she was safe, but it hurt too much to think about that, and not even Magnus could bring her back. What he most wanted now was what he had always wanted, to research time travel and get paid for it. And Magnus was offering exactly that, but Albert still felt entitled to a sign-on bonus.

Albert did all this thinking silently and slowly, which made Magnus get really antsy; as far as he was concerned, the longer Edison was out there, the more patents he'd file and wealth he'd consume, and leave more evidence that the whole debacle was Magnus's fault. Moreover, Magnus was not used to having to work so hard to manipulate another person. His natural stores of charisma just weren't working.

And that's why Magnus knocked Albert out of his lounge chair to the ground, held him down, and crammed a drill with a feather on it into his skull.

"Hey, relax. It's good for you. 90 percent of science is drilling into skulls."

Albert couldn't come up with a witty rejoinder as he'd been suddenly plunged into a trancelike state, the kind he figured religious people must be in all the time, except that this came from an extrinsic stimulus that actually existed. Despite the pleasure, he held out a hint of resistance as the drill's actions flooded his brain with delightful wishes.

Albert was no longer on Magnus's grand yacht. His essence had traveled far, far away, but really far, far closer — into his own brain, specifically the dark, dangerously ignored place where his dreams lived, the ones both too pathetic to give voice to, or too grand and unattainable to acknowledge.

Albert stood onstage in the Gray Labs arena. He looked behind himself, and he saw his Presentation Presentation project, but shinier, less crude, and with the words "Malfort Labs" written on it, along with a little picture of a dog. The arena sat empty, except for the front row, occupied by his mother, his sane-seeming father, Eli Gray sitting up straight and eagerly, Carl in an adorable white tuxedo and propped up in a chair, and Rosalind, with both of her arms.

"So that's how time travel works. I figured it out," Albert heard himself say. "Any questions?"

"I have one," Rosalind asked, raising her hand. "Why am I here among all these important people in your life? We'd known each other for literally hours before I disappeared."

"What about high school?"

"That doesn't count. I don't belong in this hallucination."

Rosalind stood up and walked out of the arena.

"Don't listen to her, my friend. You do what you need to do."

It was a voice he had never heard before, as he had known preciously few men with thick Spanish accents in his life, and yet he knew that voice.

"Yes, it is I who has said these things to you," said Carl, his lips moving while human, English words in a Catalan dialect coming out of them.

"It's time to let all of this go. To let all of *us* go. Be easier on yourself. You have worked very hard, and it's time to get all the things you've always wanted. Do you deserve them all? Some of them. Also, you probably got that girl killed."

"At least maimed!" Rosalind shouted from the exit.

"He's so desperate for your help that he drugged you to find out exactly what you want so he can give it to you, so then you can get on with it."

"But I'm faking my disinterest."

"So what? Keep gaming him. The system has gamed you for your entire life. It's time to game it back. What do you like?"

"Science."

"Great. Obviously. What would you get in science if money were no object?"

"I'd go on a shopping spree at Orange East," the hallucinatory version of Albert blurted out.

The auditorium faded away. Carl, standing fully upright and walking with a cane and a top hat to match his tuxedo, guided Albert through the aisles and mannequin-populated tableaus of Orange East, the science supply store for people with money and the taste that money can buy.

"Ooh, a fur-lined lab coat. I could wear that to Science Day!"

And then he was wearing that coat at Science Day, in San Verguenza, feeling the cold sting of tungsten flakes fall from the sky. He and Carl held out their arms and trotters, respectively, and bathed in the cascade. An astronaut, in full space-gear floated by and waved his gloved hand at Albert and Carl.

"Howdy, fellas. Can I get y'all some ice cream?" the astronaut asked in a Texas accent.

"Yes, sir!" Carl responded, also in a Texas accent.

The astronaut zoomed high up into the sky and then burst into three clouds of chocolate-brown, vanilla-white, and straw-berry-pink mists, which then reassembled according to color and flavor and coalesced into a perfect dodecahedron of astronaut ice cream. It floated through the sky erratically and irregularly, bumping into the sun, the moon, and various planets, which kicked off space-dust flakes that Albert and Carl tried to catch on their tongues. It was hard to do because they were giggling so much.

Carl caught some, and he started to convulse. Albert leaned down and put his hand on Carl's shoulder, which on a pig is called the butt, to see if he was okay.

"GO AWAY!" he screamed and then hog-squealed. Carl horrifyingly melted into a puddle of pink goo with a curly tail sticking up out of it. The puddle then reshaped itself as it grew into a menacingly smiling Ron Malfort. He was huge, but only slightly huge — not a giant, but still intimidating. Albert looked around and realized he was back in his childhood home, which was his current home, only it wasn't full of garbage and decay.

He sat on the living room floor reading a book called *Silly Science!* "Hey, Mom," he called out to her over the din of *Ask Dr. Science* blaring from the TV. His mother sat on the couch, drinking a vaporized martini, and doing the "Heretofore Unsolved Equation of the Week" from *Science Beat* in pen. "Did you know that Stephen Hawking once announced a party for time travelers," Albert parroted from the program, "just to see if anybody from the future would show up?"

"Yes, Albert, I did know that," she replied.

The front door slammed open against the wall. Albert, startled, looked up to find his father, who had hauled in an unwieldy black cabinet with lots of vector shapes painted on its sides.

"Who wants to play *Vectorquest*?"

"I didn't think that was even real! How did you get it?" Albert asked, jumping up and down.

"Just a little perk for working for Gray Labs. Let's fire it up."

Albert remembered this. This had all really happened. Ron plugged in the video game, and each took their place behind their controls, which consisted of twelve buttons of many colors, a joystick, a spiked joystick, a heat-sensitive rod, a sealed clear box that pulsed light at irregular intervals, and a numerical keyboard.

The screen displayed the message, "PUSH ANY BUTTON TO START."

"Go it for it, Albert."

"Okay, Dad!" Albert said, and did.

And then he had a massive seizure, which is why, he realized, he didn't remember this life event. The seizure in the drug fantasy was also apparently so intense that it triggered a real one in real-world Albert. He woke up to find Magnus slapping him in the face with a dried fish.

"Hi."

"That was...strange," Albert said, trying to not give away too much about his very exciting dreams.

"The first time? Sure. I bet it was. So. Tell me. Any ideas?"

Albert realized it was time to get on board.

"I want to go to Orange East. And get anything I want."

"Sure, we can get around to that. I've got a white card there."

"White card?" Albert muttered. His head was throbbing.

"It's three steps above the black card. And technically, it's not white. It's absent of all color. It's very exclusive."

"I'd also like a fur-lined lab coat."

Magnus admired Albert's taste, even if it was repressed.

"Narwhal leather-lined okay? I've got a bunch of those already."

"I thought they were extinct."

"They are. But Iceland is cold and full of scientists. What size do you wear?"

"No idea."

"What else?"

"I want a lifetime supply of astronaut ice cream, like you'd win on a game show."

"Leave this room, two doors down on the left. It's full of astronaut ice cream."

"Why do you have so much?"

"I won a lifetime supply on *Celebrity Science Bowl*."

"What flavor?"

"I don't recall, exactly. I think half of it is Neapolitan, and half of it is Strawberry-and-Vanilla-Free Neapolitan."

"My two favorite flavors."

"Perfect." He was getting a little exasperated.

"Oh, I want VIP passes for Science Day. I want to see the tungsten dump from the highest possible vantage point."

"Are we done yet?"

Albert still had a shred of free will remaining in his swirly, poked brain, which he struggled to grasp onto to make clear that he was holding out, even though he wasn't. It's tough to be duplicitous while trepanning.

"You must defeat me in the arena of my choosing."

"Ha, fine."

This one made Magnus worry, but only a little. He was marvelous at absolutely everything he'd ever tried, with only one exception: video games. He was just terrible at them, and there was no way around it. For example, when he was 11, his parents took off for their fourth honeymoon and had given him the equivalent of a thousand dollars' worth of Icelandic money and sent him to Reykjavik's first arcade. That money was supposed to last a week, and also cover snacks. Magnus blew through it all at the arcade in an hour. This being his one weakness, Magnus hoped his hopes that Albert would challenge him to anything other than video games, and, if he did, whatever showdown he picked would be a breeze, and they'd soon be on their way to find Edison, wherever and whenever he was.

"You have to beat me at *Vectorquest.*"

"What's *Vectorquest*?"

"It's a video game!"

Andskottin, Magnus swore quietly to himself.

"Tell me, which one is *Vectorquest*? I play so many video games and complete them so quickly that I have a hard time remembering them and telling them apart, you see," Magnus lied.

Albert told Magnus the creepy and mysterious saga of *Vectorquest,* that its weird, 3-D-simulating line graphics reportedly made some teenagers back in the '80s completely lose their minds. Apart from the conventional wisdom that it was all an urban legend, the going theory was that the government contracted Gray Labs to make a video game to brainwash kids to become hypnotized killing machines, or to condition employees against unionizing. The story went that Gray Labs had set up the game without fanfare in some obscure arcades around California to test it out and recruit the victims, but that the whole project backfired and gave everybody who played it seizures in the short term and sleep disorders in the long term.

"So I have to find a copy of this game, and beat you at it?"

"Yep. If you can find it. It might not even be real."

Albert knew this was an impossible task, but he was impressed that it seemed, on the surface, to not faze Magnus in the least. He kind of just wanted to see if he'd do it. If he said no, he wouldn't press him on it, and he'd suggest a pie-eating contest, or some other competitive event in which he'd have the upper hand over Magnus.

"I just want to make things clear. If I beat you on *Vectorquest,* you will help me?"

"Absolutely."

"Cool.

"Well, let's get on this. How are you going to find an arcade cabinet of *Vectorquest*?"

"If it's anywhere, Cold Storage."

"Bohrie," Magnus said, addressing the ship's voice-activated navigation and steering system, "set a course for San Verguenza."

The ship lurched forward suddenly, and then immediately stopped.

"San Verguenza, California, Captain."

"Thank you, Bohrie."

"It's here?"

"Right. Cold Storage."

When Magnus had first said the words, Albert had thought he had meant "cold storage," a phrase that means the long-term filing away of objects. But then he realized that since Magnus was a fancy person, he was referring to Cold Storage, a San Verguenza nightclub as mysterious and weird as *Vectorquest*.

31

———

"Being young and fabulously wealthy inevitably culminates in one dumb action, Albert," Magnus said as he carefully felt around an empty wall in The Good Part. When he apparently found what he was looking for, he pressed down hard, and a portion of the wall opened. He walked into the darkness within and signaled for Albert to follow him.

"Investing in a nightclub."

Magnus and Albert, each clad in a floor-length narwhal leather coat with pockets stuffed with packages of astronaut ice cream in the likely event that *Vectorquest* made their blood sugars drop precipitously low, walked down a staircase of at least 300 steps (Albert lost count), lit by blue-glowing black lights and hot pink fluorescent bulbs. Magnus and Albert reached the end of the stairs, walked back up a stairway of equal length, then down a short hallway, until they reached a thick metal door.

"Do you know how many nightclubs have ever made money for their investors, Albert?"

"None?"

Magnus gently rapped on the door exactly *M* times until he

heard a loud click. Magnus opened the door and held it open, allowing Albert to enter first and take it all in. Cold Storage was a cyberpunk hellhole, so then cyberpunk heaven. Albert likened it to a post-apocalyptic pizza parlor, what with the rusted animatronic animal musician heads and the addition of passed-out junkies, bored gigolos poking around on their phones, and a lot of stray dogs wearing bandanas decorated with anarchy symbols.

Faux, individual cryogenic chambers filled with mannequin parts lined the walls, alternating with video game cabinets. Some worked, some didn't, and all were marked not with enticing graphics but their vague, presumed titles in simple block letters, such as "*Night*" and "*Game Set in Space.*"

"You think *Vectorquest* is here?"

"It could be anywhere," Magnus teased. "It could be in some guy's garage by now. Somebody could have stolen it. It could be in the Gray Labs executive lounge. Or it could be right over there."

Magnus pointed to a particularly dark corner where a *Vectorquest* video game cabinet stood with wide berths on all sides. Its screen flashed blue and purple lines at random intervals.

They approached, and the game launched its pre-play sequence, asking unfortunate passersby to "INSERT KOIN." Albert felt a minor electrical jolt go through his brain, and the same one went through Magnus's brain.

"Let's play," Magnus said, his forced enthusiasm betraying, he hoped, his fear that he was going to lose badly. Each stood in front of their controls, which consisted of twelve buttons of many colors, a joystick, a spiked joystick, a heat-sensitive rod, a sealed box that pulsed light at irregular intervals, and a numerical keyboard. Albert motioned for Magnus to put in some coins, and he did.

An indeterminate period of time later — somewhere between five minutes and four days — Albert and Magnus regained consciousness, along with the worst headaches either of them would ever have. As they slowly rose to their feet, both bracing themselves against the video game cabinet, Magnus and Albert glanced at the *Vectorquest* screen, which displayed a static "GAME ØVER" message along with the scores. Player one, Albert, had 0. Player two, Magnus, had 1.

Magnus smiled a grin so big and goofy it reminded Albert of his nonexistent college friend, Magnus Bigfaker.

"Alright, you win," Albert said to Magnus, and meant it, for the first time, with almost no animosity. "What now?"

"What do you mean?"

"We've got to stop Edison."

"Yeah, that's where you come in."

"Oh, well..." Albert said. "I don't really know how we'd do that."

32

As Magnus and Albert hung out aboard the *Bohrs, Oars & Libertine Ladies,* trying to think of some way they could stop Edison, piece by piece every item on the yacht dropped its old signage and logos in favor of a large, red, "E," the official emblem of Edison Labs. Each gadget was further burdened with a small plaque that read, "THIS IS A THOMAS EDISON'S EDISON CORPORATION PATENTED MACHINE IN THE UNITED STATES OF AMERICA IN THE YEAR OF OUR LORD AND THOMAS EDISON 1931."

These were constant, urgent reminders to Albert and Magnus that Edison was succeeding and quickly changing the future via the past. And their efforts to locate Edison had been entirely unfruitful.

• They'd tried to pass Magnus's boat as rapidly as possible back and forth over the International Date Line during a Daylight Saving Time switchover, but no time travel occurred.

• Albert read an article about a millisecond lag between what happens in reality and the brain processing the information, roughly the blink of an eye. That inspired Magnus to gather

20,000 viewers of *The Scientist* for a "fan convention," but which was really just an excuse for he and Albert to place diodes on all of their eyelids, and then connect those diodes to a supercomputer, in the hopes that they could capture those milliseconds, put them together, and use them. No time travel occurred.

• Magnus made a PSA asking viewers of *The Scientist* to set their clocks back a few years, "as a favor to him." More than 30 million people did so, but no time travel occurred.

• Magnus collected soil samples from every time zone on earth, and Albert threw them into a big pile. No time travel occurred.

• They checked out a book called *Time Travel and You* from the San Verguenza Public Library, but it turned out to be a bunch of nonsense about lucid dreaming and astral projection, and so no time travel occurred.

These unsuccessful attempts left Albert and Magnus feeling defeated and frustrated.

"Albert, I think this might be it," Magnus said, briefly brightening Albert's pallid face. "Have you ever heard of *hypothetical time manipulation theory*?" Albert nodded in the negative, and so Magnus demonstrated, shoving a rotten potato into the battery compartment of a suddenly-Edison-branded clock radio. Then he threw it all on the ground.

No time travel occurred, but right after it smashed into various chunks of plastic, metal, and starch, Albert glanced up at a wall clock just as the time shifted from 5:59 to 6:00. Magnus followed his gaze, and an expression of mock triumph filled his face.

"I did it!" Magnus shouted in jest. "Afternoon to evening. Just like that! We'll be in 1931 in no time!" He paused and then laughed. "Ha! I made a time joke!"

Scientists are only as good as their ideas, and they didn't have any of those at that moment, which would suggest that they were not very good scientists.

"Music," Magnus stated rather than asked, impatiently. "Bohrie, music."

Wishy-washy 1970s style folk music flooded the boat from dozens of hidden speakers. The music made Albert feel comforted and then paranoid and alarmed, indicating that the tune strongly reminded him of childhood.

"I know this song! Bohrie, what's the name of this song?" Albert asked.

"Magnus, tell your friend I don't answer to him."

An interlude of a maudlin string section ended, replaced by gentle guitar strumming and the emotionally pitiful wailing of a male singer. The wimpy lyrics matched the mealy-mouthed performance.

"I wish I could store time up in bottles forever," Albert dueted with the man on the radio. "Because then I could keep my memories safely locked up inside."

Magnus looked on in fascination with Albert's display of emotional vulnerability, and also disgust because the song was just really terrible.

"Yeah, what *is* this garbage?" Magnus asked.

"This garbage is called..." Albert trailed off, waiting for his brain to find the information. "'I Wish I Could Store Time Up in Bottles Forever.'"

The song being the worst thing ever was the first time that Albert and Magnus had agreed on something.

"Hey, I *do* know this song. I spun a remix of this one night in a club in *Ibiza*," Magnus said, obnoxiously pronouncing it *ib-eeth-ah*. "That version was *much* better than this one. It had a thumping beat on it. That always makes everything better. Albert, did you know I sometimes D.J.?"

Of course you do, Albert thought.

"Who is this singing, though?"

Albert thought hard, and an image popped into his mind of a very earnest-looking man, with a large mound of curly hair, and a hairy chest to match. It was an album cover he'd seen hundreds of times.

"That's my father's favorite singer. His name is...John Knitty!"

"Seriously? *That's* John Knitty?"

"You've heard of him?"

"This is the first time I've heard his emasculated claptrap, but I've heard what some bonkers American scientist said about him, and how he supposedly left secret messages in his songs detailing how Gray Labs keeps time bottles stored somewhere on the premises to keep Eli Gray alive indefinitely."

"Okay, that of course was the late, great John Knitty," the on-air personality rattled off. "Go ahead and give us a call because if you're the 14th caller and can tell us the name of the wackjob who destroyed his career by accusing the dear and honorable Eli Gray of being an immortal monster kept alive by Linus Pauling because the song you just heard contained *secret messages* that told him as much, we're gonna hook you up with two free tickets to tomorrow night's sold-out Monsters of Theremin show down at the Gray Center!"

"Oooooooooh," Magnus said, processing everything he'd just heard and connecting the fact that Magnus's father was, in fact, both the "bonkers American scientist" and "the wackjob who destroyed his career."

"Oh!"

"Yeah."

"Should we call in?"

Perhaps it was a lack of sleep, or perhaps it was years of exposure to radiation, chemicals, and working in a section of Gray Labs that had no ventilation, or perhaps his toxic genetics finally kicked in. But for the first time in Albert's life, Ron Malfort's assertions about Eli Gray made sense.

Eli Gray *could be* short for "Elisha Gray."

Elisha Gray had never quite gotten over missing out on the telephone, and phones hadn't been allowed at Gray Labs for decades.

Eli Gray encased himself in jumpsuits and helmets, which seems like the kind of thing an extremely biologically delicate person and/or somebody with a big secret would do.

Also, Linus Pauling was a genius. Up until the day he died, he claimed Vitamin C could cure anything. Death qualified as an anything.

"Magnus…" Albert said softly, but acutely aware that his declaration was going to be mind-blowing.

"Yes, hi, what caller am I?" Magnus said into his phone. "Alright! Yes, I do. The name of the man is Ron Malfort! Oh, wow, this is wonderful!" He paused. "No, I've never won anything off the radio before, but you could say that I'm just a very lucky person." Another pause. "Just repeat it? Okay. 'Easy101, where winning is easy!'" He hung up. "Albert, guess what I just won?"

"Magnus. I have an idea. About my dad."

"Is it to send him a big basket of *kartoflur* to thank him for helping me to win third-row tickets to Monsters of Theremin?"

"Magnus. What if…he's right?"

"About what?"

"All of it. Everything he said that made him a laughingstock.

What if he wasn't crazy, and he was just blowing the whistle on something that Eli Gray did?"

"So then you think that Linus Pauling really is somewhere in Gray Labs, keeping time in bottles?"

"I don't know. Maybe?"

"And I assume that we can use those bottles for time travel?"

"If we have time in its physical form, we can manipulate it to help us travel back in time."

"What other option do we have?"

"Can we stop by my walrus vault on the way?" Albert asked. "They accidentally gave away my savings, and I need to head out there and try to make things right."

"Nooooo!" Bohrie replied, no longer in the sweet feminine voice, but rather the preemptively hostile and gravelly growl of Thomas Edison, indicating Edison had just patented navigational software.

"You heard the boat," Magnus replied, having just made a connection between the Malfort money he took from a walrus vault and the Malfort with whom he was now maybe friends.

33

"What kind of car is this?" Albert asked of what looked like a papier-mâché volcano on wheels, not unlike the one he'd made for a science fair as a child, but with wheels.

"Thanks, it's new!" Magnus replied, ignoring the question.

"Is this a papier-mâché volcano on wheels?"

"That would be very impractical," Magnus chuffed. "This is a *real* volcano."

Albert couldn't tell if Magnus was messing with him or not.

"Well, it's *powered* by volcanoes. Our main source of energy in Iceland is geothermal power, and that comes from simmering volcanoes. We figured out how to make it portable long ago."

"So, this car runs on lava?"

"Pretty much, yeah."

"How do you store lava?"

"Tungsten cans."

Albert was thawing to the man from Iceland.

"Tungsten is entirely heat resistant. In Icelandic, it means 'best metal.' That's no accident."

"You know, I used tungsten in all my botched time travel experiments."

"And I thought we had nothing in common!"

"Well, both of liking what's objectively the best element is a stretch," Albert said, trying not to show his emotions, which was futile. They were having a real moment.

"So you just poor in the lava, and it goes?"

"6,000 miles to the gallon. I won't have to buy gas until I'm, perish the thought, 50."

The car buckled and resisted under the influence of the turbulent, five-mile-per-hour Northern California winds. Magnus had a hard time keeping the car going in one direction because as the car swayed in the wind, it kept hitting the inflatable bumpers on the roadsides, installed after a Gray employee had crashed and died attempting to drive off campus after a 60-hour shift.

The unpredictability of the car only exacerbated Albert's nerves over attempting to get into Gray Labs.

"They have tight security," Albert warbled as Magnus rounded a curve and spun the car all the way around before correcting. "Particularly to keep out those whom they've publicly fired."

"It'll be fine," Magnus said confidently, in the manner of a maddeningly smug person who has never not gotten his way.

"You think we can just stroll in there, and they won't notice me or question me because *you're* Magnus Riptide?"

The car spun out, hit an inflatable bumper, sailed across the road, and hit another road bumper, which gave Magnus enough time to look deeply into Albert's eyes.

"That is *exactly* what is going to happen."

"Maybe we could just stop in the gift shop and get a L'il Eli Gray Officially Licensed Eli Gray-Style Helmet, and I can wear that?"

"Albert, please. I'm not going to say 'trust me' because asking someone to trust you carries with it a tacit admission that things may not or could not turn out exactly the way you expect them to. But things will go exactly as I expect them to."

"Do you still have one of those privacy helmets?" Albert asked, referring to the head-blocking headgear Magnus wore before the Presentation Presentation. "We could flatten it out, and I could maybe wear it, like, all over my body. Do you think that could work?"

Magnus rolled his eyes.

Albert had already done his best to disguise himself with the assistance of appearance-blocking technology, some of which he'd developed himself at Gray Labs. The Mustache Generator had produced upon Albert a dainty handlebar but had also left a thick rash over a lot of his face when it had done what it was supposed to do, which was yank out the hair follicles from deep inside his face. He'd paired this with some green contact lenses he found in a box of his work stuff; these were a sample of the ones that purported to display the time of the wearer's death, but as these were from the beta testing period, they consistently displayed a distracting "NOT SURE ASK AGAIN LATER" across his line of vision. Capping off his disguise was an official Dr. Claude Von Scientizt wig, modeled after Magnus's own head of immaculate blond hair. Albert hoped he wouldn't have to wear it for long, because it was burning his scalp.

Magnus swerved into the Gray Labs parking lot, doing so at just the right time to avoid hitting an intern engrossed in a thick textbook. The volcanic car took up only one and a half scooter parking spots. They got out and started the short walk to the security post.

"You could play the Nobel card!" Albert quietly suggested to

Magnus, who stared straight ahead and strode along confidently. "They used to bring laureates on tours here all the time. Never down to where I worked, but one time in the cafeteria, I saw Albert Fert."

"Ha! *Fert.*" Magnus laughed, and then Magnus made a fart sound with his mouth, and then, involuntarily, with his bowels. Magnus surprised himself, and he laughed uproariously.

"Yeah, Nobel. Mention those. But whatever you do, don't mention the Fields Medal. Well, okay, *maybe* mention the Fields Medal. You know, it really depends on the guard."

"Albert," he said, farting once more. "Stop."

"I can't stop, I'm worr —" Albert stopped talking because he had walked into the guard station's robotic arm.

"Can we help you?" the guard asked, moving into the road.

"Hi," Magnus said, shaking the hand of a guard who had at least six inches and 100 pounds on him. "I'm on TV."

"Hell! I know exactly who you are!" the guard slapped Magnus on the back. "Me and my wife never miss it!"

"Thank you very much," he said coolly if disingenuously.

"I mean, I'm a fan, but she's the real deal. After we watch it, she makes me pretend I'm you," he said, before adding with a wink, "If you know what I mean."

"I do know what you mean. Please do not go into detail."

"What I mean to say," the guard went on, ignoring Magnus's request, "is that when we have our weekly maritals, I wear a Dr. Claude Von Scientizt wig. It burns the living daylights out of my scalp, but we do what we do to keep our women happy, am I right?"

"I've never spent more than five hours with the same woman, so I have no idea what you mean."

"Yeah, you get it," the guard said. He had, so far as Magnus had predicted, failed to notice anyone standing there but Magnus. "So what are you doing at Gray Labs? Here to see Eli Gray, I bet, a big shot like you. Let me call up, let him know you're here."

"No," Magnus said, without a hint of urgency. "That's not necessary. He knows I'm coming. I know my way around the place."

"Oh, doing some research for an episode?"

"Sure."

"You want to know what my favorite episode of *The Scientist* is?"

"Not really."

"It's the one where the guy messes up the time travel thing, and he loses the girl, and then you arrest him in his underwear when he's eating the astronaut ice cream. So great!"

"Thank you," Magnus said to the guard. "Follow my lead," he said directly to Albert, even touching him on the shoulder for emphasis. Still, the guard did not avert his gaze away from Magnus.

"You know, the man that inspired that episode is here with me today."

"What? Aw, you're pulling my leg!"

Albert looked to Magnus for approval. He nodded.

"That's right," Albert said. "I am literally standing right here. My name is Albert Malfort. I used to work here."

"He's talking right now," Magnus added. "His name is Albert Malfort, and he's standing right next to me, in front of you, right now, and he just said words out loud to you."

The guard's adoring gaze did not divert from Magnus. He didn't even blink.

"You're hilarious! You ever think about giving comedy a shot?"

"No, I've got some dignity. And if you don't mind, I'd like to be on my way."

"You want a guided tour?"

"Like I said, I know where I'm going."

"Ah, well, let me know if you need anything." He stuck a hand inside the kiosk and, without breaking his eye hold on Magnus, raised the robotic arm; Albert walked right in.

"Okay, I will. Say, do you have a skeleton key?"

"Of course!"

The guard walked back into the kiosk, unlocked a safe, and from it pulled out not a key or keycard, but a key cube, embedded with the most beautiful synthetic eyeball with a rainbow-colored retina Albert had ever seen.

"Modeled after Eli Gray's real eye, you know."

"Thanks so much. Well, I'm off. Lots of research to do."

Magnus and Albert began to walk off through the security gate. Then Albert felt himself being tackled by the guard. It was all over now.

"It's fine," Magnus whispered, sensing Albert's anxiety.

"Let me get your coat!" he shouted, holding Albert down to the pavement.

"Ow!" Albert shouted.

"No, no, I've got it. Come along...coat," Magnus said, improvising.

Albert staggered to his feet and walked along.

"Oh, one of those new Float Coats. Very neat. I've got to get me one of those."

Magnus and Albert scurried away, almost running.

"Wait!" the guard shouted.

"That's it," Albert mumbled without moving his lips. "*Now* we're sunk."

"We're fine," Magnus assured.

"Can I get an autograph?" the guard shouted.

Without turning around, Magnus reached into a pocket, pulled out a crumpled bit of paper, and sky-hooked it over his back. It landed in the guard's hands, where it instantly unfolded and smoothed itself out into a black-and-white publicity shot of Magnus, pointing a microscope like a gun. It had been stamped with Magnus's signature and the inscription, "Let's make a science guess together some time!"

And then, they were inside Gray Labs. Presently, they were in a wing with which Albert was not familiar: the floors were metal, the walls were white, and the doors made from tempered, opaque glass.

"Well, here it is," Albert said, unjustifiably proud of the sector he'd never seen in the place where he was once an anonymous, underpaid cog.

"Yeah," Magnus said, shutting his mouth tight and while his eyes went wide, stifling a yawn. "I've seen a lab facility before."

"Well," Albert said, immune to the social cue, "have you ever seen *this* lab facility before?"

"Yes," Magnus said, now halfway down the hall and indiscriminately pulling on doorknobs to see if they would lead to the room he was looking for. "Many times."

"Then you'd know that all the doorknobs are for show. Eli Gray is terrified of germs, so everything opens electronically."

"Yeah. I know," Magnus said, rolling his eyes as he pulled the key cube out of his pocket and threw it to Albert, who miraculously caught it. "How do we get to the sub-basement?"

"Well, I know it's not through the basement, because I worked in the basement, and some parts of the floor were just dirt. Asking somebody would arouse suspicion, I think."

"*I* could ask somebody."

It was very lucky for them then, when, at that exact moment, a kindish-looking employee in a Gray Labs lab coat walked by.

"Excuse me," Magnus said, attempting to be charming, "can you tell me where the sub-basement is?"

"Why, what's down there?"

"Just meeting somebody."

"Why would anybody want to go to the human resources department?"

Albert chuckled, because of the idea that if Linus Pauling really were hidden away, he'd be in a subterranean basement, and that the basement was also where the human resources department was located, to be as inaccessible as possible. It was a decent, if deeply cynical joke on the part of Eli Gray.

"I'm sorry, is something funny?" the scientist asked.

"No, no, I'm sorry. I have allergies."

"We all have allergies. It's not funny."

"What if somebody actually needed to ask a question from someone in the human resources department?"

"And risk losing their job?

She hurried away.

"She was rude," Magnus said, checking his breath in a subtle show of hurt and confusion over his charm not working on a member of the opposite, or any, sex.

"So, how are we going to get down there?"

"I think it's time we tried the Scientific Method."

"We don't have time for that. A hypothesis? Testing? Peer review?"

"I've never heard any of those phrases in my life."

Albert then explained to Magnus, a world-famous scientist, the actual steps of the Scientific Method.

"Oh, *that's* the Scientific Method? I was talking about the one I learned from my show. Episode 205, 'The Scientific Method.'"

Magnus explained to Albert the plot of "The Scientific Method," in which his character was scientifically blocked and locked himself up in his mansion, unwilling to see guests or take on any new cases, which were building up. He made himself so sick that he couldn't eat anything but noodles. He got so angry while eating that he couldn't think of any good "science thoughts," and so he threw the whole plate against the wall, where it stuck. That was his *aha*, "eureka!" revelatory moment, throwing something against the wall to see what sticks, and then pulling a case-solving piece of evidence out of thin air.

"I did have a, what did you call it, a *hypothesis*? Yes, a hypothesis that there would have to be a door into the sub-basement for Eli Gray to access, but he would not want anyone else to see it. So it would be invisible. But we have a key that will allegedly open any door in the complex."

Magnus took the key cube back from Albert and wound up his arm and threw it straight down the hallway, very quickly, reminding Albert of a professional sports guy. Albert ducked and cowered as the key cube ricocheted off the walls, floors, and ceiling, curiously, silently. The cube then hit a wall once more, generating an audible click as a heretofore invisible door swung open. The key cube bounced off the ground, and Albert tentatively reached out a hand to try and catch it. He did, but then the key cube melted into freezing liquid all over his hands.

They walked through the door, down exactly 100 steps, and found another door marked "Human Resources." Probably because of the other safeguards in place to prevent anybody from getting to this far, this door was unlocked and it opened with no trouble at all.

Inside was yet another laboratory room like dozens of others at Gray Labs, just like the ones Albert had worked in, only much, much nicer, and much, much larger, like the ones he'd seen in Gray Labs corporate training videos. But there did not appear to be any time bottles, although they could have been in there because Albert wasn't sure what they would look like.

The walls of this lab, about the size of Albert's house or Magnus's auxiliary shoe closet, were lined with transparent plastic hoppers, all filled with lemons, each of which pulsed in unison at a rate commensurate with that of a human heart at rest. Each time they pulsed, they'd glow a little. Mechanical arms steadily picked a few dozen lemons at a time from a hopper. They placed them on a high-positioned conveyor belt, carrying the fruits to a refrigerator-sized juicer, which collected gallons of liquid from the strange, pulsing lemons in just seconds. The spent lemon husks were unceremoniously discarded by another mechanical arm into a colossal metal waste receptacle, which Albert recognized was tungsten-based.

The juice then flowed directly from the bottom of the juicer into thin tubes, over to an array of metal bowls carefully arranged on a paper-lined surgical cart. In those bowls were many human organs, the lemon juice giving each kidney, liver, and such a nice soak for a few seconds, after which the liquids were drained and replaced with more fresh lemon juice from the industrial juicer. Albert and Magnus witnessed a few of these cycles, all of which took scarcely under a minute, before they even noticed that the organs were still tenuously attached via blood vessels to the comatose, gurney-prone body of Eli Gray. The only part of Eli Gray not being treated to a lemon juice bath was his head; the helmet, as always, was firmly in place. That's how they knew the laid-out man was Eli Gray.

Albert looked to Magnus, expecting to engage in a silent, wide-eyed, "This is crazy!" moment, but Magnus was still looking up at the lemon-juicing equipment, not yet aware of the body of Eli Gray, still trying to make sense of it all.

"Aw, those aren't time bottles. Let's get out of here," Magnus said, turning around and pushing the door.

"Yeah, but..." Albert grunted out.

"Hmm?" Magnus looked to Albert, and then past him, where he finally caught a glimpse of Eli Gray, laying on a gurney, in a medical sleep, having all his organs soaking in the juice of pulsing lemons. Magnus's facial expression slowly changed from blank to confusion to horror to realization.

"Albert, your dad was right!"

"Who's talkin' about time bottles?" they heard a male voice say. "*If I could store time up in bottles forever...*" the same voice sang.

Magnus ran back to Albert and tried to hide behind him, instinctively defending himself, even though Albert was much shorter than he was. Albert, for his part, also tried to hide behind Magnus. They ran around in a little circle like that before they both tripped and fell.

Then they saw the source of the voice, which came from the giant, red, boxy, retro-styled robot standing in front of them.

"A robot!" Magnus whispered excitedly.

"A cyborg, man."

From the short distance away, the cyborg (not a robot) extended both of its metal, telescoping arms and gently embraced Magnus and Albert all at once. Another hand extended from the back of its body and stroked their heads.

"I'm so psyched to have you here. I don't get many guests."

It released Albert and Magnus from its incredibly tight if friendly grip and rolled backward on its triangular tread.

Albert instantly recognized the robot, or cyborg, or the human element of the human/robot combination. Encased in a transparent dome atop the 10-foot-tall series of red tin boxes was the bushy-haired head of Linus Pauling.

"What's up, guys?" Linus Pauling breezily drawled, the sound muffled only by the glass dome that encased his head, "I'm Linus Pauling, man."

"Whoa, Albert! Your dad was like, *super* right!"

Amidst the robotic enhancements, the only original, biological parts of Linus that remained visible inside of the robotic exoskeleton were his head, of course, and his genitals, which bobbed up and down in clear view inside of the robot body's inner chamber of preserving liquid, visible through a little Plexiglas window. Once those caught Magnus's eye, their gentle, jellyfish-like swaying kept him completely transfixed.

"His *drjóli*," Magnus muttered. "It's like a *marglyttur*."

Albert, however, kept glancing down at Eli Gray's body, and back up at Linus. He was having trouble making sense of both concepts, and how he now had proof that his father's career-ending and life-changing conspiratorial dementia had, in fact, been at least somewhat accurate.

"Oh, Eli Gray over there? I should probably explain."

"Okay," Albert croaked.

"Uuuuuuunnnngh..." Magnus murmured, still entranced by the delicate dance of the cyborg's waterborne genitals.

"Science is 90 percent soaking."

Albert continued to silently freak out.

"Just a joke, man. Relax," Linus said, again extended a telescoping arm, which he used to pat Albert on the back. His words and actions indicated that this Nobel Prize winner for Chemistry had evolved into a lovey-dovey, Nobel Peace Prize-winning hippie.

"I have proven, with real laboratory results, that lemons can cure, like, anything. And everything. Even death, man. Everything except facial aging," he said, rapping his robot claw three times on Eli Gray's helmet. "That's all moisturizing and, like, avoiding processed foods."

34

Rosalind had endured plenty of unpleasant situations in her life. She'd been through NASA boot camp, accidentally stowed away on one of her father's space missions and fought aliens on the moon, competed on the mixed martial arts circuit to pay for art school, and attended art school. While all that wasn't nearly as tough as fighting a giant lobster while surfing a hot wave through a time tunnel, it had undoubtedly prepared her.

Rosalind held tight to the lobster as it fell infinitely downward through the black emptiness of time. This was especially difficult because 1) Rosalind only had one arm, and 2) the lobster violently thrashed around, irritated as it was by a human simultaneously trying to cling on to it and to bring it pain, assisted by a surprisingly viciously miniature pig.

The delicate dance continued, human and pig working independently but toward the same end, the end of that lobster, and the lobster looking to end the retaliation for the attack it wishes it hadn't started, as they fell, and fell until the darkness abetted. That was right before the cold, dingy, linoleum floor greeted them.

Rosalind wisely maneuvered so that she'd be on top of the

lobster as it landed first and broke her fall. Carl, devoted to trying to break through that lobster's same hard shell to eat whatever sweetmeats lay within, noticed that he was about to hit the ground a fraction of a second before everybody else hit the ground. Carl jumped off as the lobster struck the surface, and the pig bound into the air, flipping around 360 degrees snout-to-tail-to-snout mid-air before landing feet-first on the lobster's head. Then he got right back to trying to eat that lobster.

Rosalind let Carl do that while she got up and looked around. She thought the area looked like a mall, but a crummy mall, with greyish floors made from what looked like cheap tiles. Unflattering artificial light poured down uniformly to complete that mall vibe.

It was also set up like a mall, with storefronts extending in every direction, to the left, to the right, and upward, seemingly forever. But instead of peddling the wares that a regular, terrible mall in decline would — the hottest fashions of six years earlier, cell phone cases — none of the storefronts sold anything, like a main street shopping area put out of business by a mall. Instead, the rooms held moving images, each an infinite loop of curvy, angular shapes depicting vaguely recognizable historical events. Above each store, and there were *lots* of them, was a neon sign listing a year: 1865, 1931, 1987, 1595, etc.

Rosalind had some notion on where she was and what those numbers and loops of historical holograms represented, namely that those were years; she did, after all, just participate in a time travel experiment. It was then that the other piece of time travel fallout, whom she thought dead upon arrival with the impact of the ground after a fall of indeterminate length and time, suddenly sprang to life and tried to quietly scurry away. She ran after and tried to dive on top of that lobster, but she missed. Lobsters are slimy, and her balance was off, as she'd recently fallen from a great height and lost an arm. The lobster, caught off-guard, picked up the pace into a rapid gallop. Carl managed to tear off cleanly one of its giant, delectable legs but regretted that he didn't have a tub of melted garlic butter in the pocket of his novelty lab coat, or that one of these mall storefronts didn't stock flavored butters.

Still, the lobster was quite fast, and it had almost escaped Rosalind's reach and orbit of violence when she grabbed a tight hold of the tail. It squeezed and pulled forward, dragging a resolute Rosalind a few feet before it could break free and seek shelter in the nearest storefront, which happened to be a gateway into the year 1936. As it ran through the ephemeral wall of time, or whatever it was, Rosalind grabbed the lobster's tail again, and she was pulled into 1936, too.

The world itself was black and white, as Rosalind had always assumed the past would be, but the crowd was entirely white. Very white. So white that there were scores of Nazi troops breathlessly listening to incomprehensible German barking by a short, angry, farting man standing behind a lectern a few feet in front of her. He didn't need to turn around for her to know that it was Hitler, history's worst vegan. (Hence the farts.) But she was too distracted by the task of pursuing the lobster to take the time to really feel the rage and disgust that bubble up when a person meets Hitler. She went where the lobster went, and the lobster went scurrying toward Hitler. And then the lobster was eating Hitler, for Hitler was very small and easy to catch, particularly for a giant lobster.

"Helpen der Führer!" Hitler screamed as the lobster in a cowboy hat chomped and swallowed his legs, then worked its way up. "Der cowboy lobster est munchen Hitler!"

Many Nazis with many guns sprang into action, but the lobster had devoured Hitler so quickly that there wasn't much they could do. Nevertheless, they shot at the lobster as it scuttled back to the spot where it had entered 1936. Rosalind hopped on its back and ducked down to avoid Nazi gunfire and held on as the lobster jumped back into the time mall and then threw her off its back with an annoyed grunt.

Rosalind didn't think that they had settled their dispute yet, and chased after the lobster and dived, grasping its tail as she hit the ground. The lobster swayed its tail wildly back and forth as it scuttled off, trying to lose Rosalind once and for all. But it couldn't decide where to go and hesitated before running into another storefront time-spot, 1620, giving one more unsuccessful shake-off attempt as it went. Rosalind was very strong.

"You ate my non-dominant arm, you dick!"

Now they were in shallow water, like that of a bay, overlooking a lovely but cold and rocky beach where a group of perplexed Native Americans stood. The confusion had nothing to do with Rosalind and the lobster; coming into the bay was a tiny boat filled with way too many somber people in black hats adorned with stylish although altogether nonfunctional buckles.

A woman on the boat was the first to see the time travelers, and she shrieked. A Native American on the beach raised a bow and arrow. The lobster turned on its heel, back from where it came and into the time mall once again. It stopped, breathed heavily, and looked back to see if Rosalind was still following. She was. The lobster squealed.

"Hi," she said. "Where we going next? You already killed Hitler, so what now? Gay '90s? Medieval times? The golden age of disco?"

The lobster nervously hobbled into another yearfront, looking back over its shoulder in terror at Rosalind, who casually grabbed its tail once more and pulled her way onto its back. The lobster didn't notice that it had gone into 1937. Once again, they were on a black-and-white stage in Berlin. But this time, all the Nazi stuff was gone, replaced with giant banners depicting the silhouettes of a monster-sized lobster and a one-armed woman engaged in fisticuffs. The assembled masses were equally delighted and terrified when their new gods returned. The lobster finally managed to shake off Rosalind, who rolled off into a wrestling stance. The lobster sighed dramatically, and its head slumped down in exhaustion.

After a grunt that obviously meant, "Let's get this over with," the lobster made the first move, lunging at Rosalind. She easily deflected the blow, not only blocking its pincer with a well-placed kick but getting her foot underneath the lobster, striking it hard in its soft underbelly. The monster screamed in agony (as did the empathetic crowd), and it writhed around on the ground for a few seconds.

"We're done here," Rosalind declared.

The lobster let out a massive groan, and then its stomach started to roll visibly, like concrete during an earthquake. The lobster gagged, then dry heaved, and then vomited up a quaking, shocked, and still alive Hitler.

"*Ich bin am leben!*" Hitler rejoiced at his survival. "*Hurra!*"

Sometimes throwing up makes everything all better, and that's what happened to the lobster, instantly revitalized without the burden of Hitler rolling around in its stomach. Rosalind, however, was as strong as ever, if not stronger, bolstered by the adrenaline pumping through her system, not to mention her body clock getting super-jazzed from all the time jumping.

The chase continued, with the lobster popping into years to escape his punisher. Rosalind had to do the same, following the lobster into wherever it went to deliver a series of hearty beatdowns.

- She saw the signing of the Magna Carta in 1215 and punched the lobster in the face, which detached a retina, much to the delight of King John *and* the serfs.

• She witnessed the beheading of Marie Antoinette in 1793, and then she ripped off one of the lobster's antennae (which some hungry peasants fought over).

• She got to go back to the 1990s and drink some of that discontinued transparent cola the older scientists were always going on about, and she used the glass bottle it came in to crack a whole bunch of the lobster's remaining shell.

Finally, after a few more jumps through dozens of years, the lobster crawled out from the kidnapping of Helen of Troy, into the time station, and collapsed. It eked out a single pitiful moan as it lay on the ground, missing an antenna, a leg, most of its shell, and then its other leg. Carl helped himself to another round of delicious lobster meat.

Rosalind coldly kicked the lobster in the stomach. Once again, it started to spasm and heave, and once more threw up the contents of its stomach. Having rid its body of all traces of Hitler a few minutes and/or years earlier, the lobster's digestive system had to dig a little deeper to find something to regurgitate, and fortunately, for Rosalind, its vomited up Rosalind's severed arm. Stomach acid had already disintegrated most of the fingers, but it otherwise maintained its structural integrity.

Rosalind was pleased to have it back and made tentative plans to preserve and reattach it later. Perhaps this mall-like place was like other malls, she thought, and it would have one of those snack bars that sold frothy orange drinks, and they would give her an extra-large cup of ice to store her arm. All of that would have to come later; Rosalind grabbed the arm with her extant arm, wiped it off on her lab coat, and then used it to beat the lobster until it wasn't moving anymore.

Exhausted, Rosalind sank to the ground and lay there for a second to catch her breath. Improbably, the lobster lurched back to life and started crawling away, one last attempt to abscond with his life. Rosalind just couldn't let that happen. With her one hand, she reached into her front pocket and pulled out the preloaded syringe full of emergency allergy medicine she always kept on her person. Tossing the plastic case aside, she held the syringe with two fingers while using her thumb to pull back the plunger as far as it would go. She got up on her feet and blocked the lobster's path.

"We all only get one shot," she said aloud, aware of how cheesy it sounded but also thinking it was totally badass, as she took the anti-shellfish allergy pen and stabbed the lobster in the eye. *Now* it stopped moving. Finally.

Satisfied, Rosalind smiled, bent down, and picked up Carl, who nuzzled her neck. She giggled, but then quickly put him down because he reeked of raw shellfish. It was then that she got the feeling that she was being watched. Sure enough, surrounding her in a circle on the faded linoleum floor of the time station were dozens of other lobsters, identical to both each other and the lobster to whom Rosalind had just laid waste, whom Carl continued to snack upon. All wore little tin stars with clocks on them, and cowboy hats, of course.

"Uh, hello," Rosalind said with as little intonation as possible to avoid upsetting anyone.

"Thank you kindly for dispatching with Terry, ma'am," said the lobster wearing the tallest cowboy hat and the biggest tin star with a clock on it. She spoke with a feminine voice and a Western drawl. "I can't tell you how happy we are that he's gone."

"You're...not mad?"

"Because Terry is as cold as a wagon tire? Nah, he was a hard case, through and through."

All the other lobsters buzzed with excitement, rapidly repeating the sequence of numbers from 1 to 12 and back again and clicking their claws.

"Oh, okay," Rosalind processed. "Hey, but aren't lobsters immortal?"

"We are, unless somebody up and kills one of us. Plus, this job as a time lobster, protecting the sanctity of time and whatnot, is for life, which makes it pretty hard to get rid of somebody that you just don't git along with very well."

Rosalind was glad that she wasn't going to be punished for killing what was, as she had suspected but not yet coined a name for, a time lobster. Then, the shock from losing an arm and traveling through time disappeared for a second, and the absurdity of the situation finally hit her.

"You can *talk*?"

"Well, ma'am, *I* can talk. Most of us just drone on in base 12. Just 1-2-3-4-5-6-7-8-9-10-11-12, and back again, *blah blah blah*. But I can speak human speak. That's why I'm the sheriff. I guess you could say around these parts, I'm the...main lobster."

Carl squealed a delighted squeal, approximating laughter as best he could. The talking lobster gave him an appreciative hat tip.

"I'm Susan. What's your name, pardner?"

Snort.

"Oh, after Carl Sagan?"

Snort.

"Oh, sure, we're big Sagan fans in the time community."

All the other lobsters happily recited some numbers and clicked their claws together a bit more.

"Alright, alright, let's all settle down," Susan said. "It's time for the medals."

"Medals?" Rosalind whispered to herself. She loved medals.

One of the many lobsters sauntered over to Susan and handed her a small velvet bag. Susan reached in and pulled out two tin stars with clocks on them, much like the one she and other lobsters wore, but these were made of plastic instead of tin.

"I hereby deputize thee..." Susan asked expectantly as she pinned the clock star on Rosalind's lobster bloodstained lab coat.

"Rosalind."

Susan stayed silent, still prompting.

"Howard."

"I, Time Sheriff Susan Darden Cangrejo hereby deputize thee, Rosalind Howard, an Official Junior Deputy Time Lobster."

Carl snorted in mock indignation.

"You're next, Carl!" Susan said playfully, and all the other lobsters made a weird sound that was their version of laughing. She pinned the second medal onto Carl's coat. He snorted proudly.

The rest of the lobsters scurried away, all into various year storefronts where Rosalind noticed they instantly turned into timepieces befitting the era to which they entered, such as a gorgeous grandfather clock for in 1684, or a shiny, boxy, computer-ized wrist-phone for the lobster that hit 2015. Left alone with Susan, in silence, Rosalind felt it would be polite to make conservation.

"So, time sheriff, huh?"

"That's right," Susan said.

"I suppose that's why you dress like a cowboy."

"I suppose that's why cowboys dress like *me*."

"So," Rosalind fished, "could you maybe explain all this?"

"Ma'am, I'm head of the time lobsters. Time is wild and untamed, and it needs order to pass by peacefully and to make sure that nobody comes in and wrecks it up, real bad-like. My kind has been keeping time together since my daddy's daddy invented time."

"I hope we didn't mess things up too much."

"Only thing it did was create new legends. Replaced the old ones. No more Mothman, no more Bigfoot. Only major cryptid now is the big lobster, plus his constant companion, the One-Armed Warrior Queen. And Carl, her faithful pig steed."

Rosalind thought that was cool. Carl snorted.

"Woulda even been okay if y'all had left Hitler dead, though."

"But wouldn't that mess up time?"

"You would think, but nah. However, I do need your help."

"Well, we're deputies, aren't we?"

"Junior deputies."

"Okay, well..."

"I need y'all to get into 1931 as soon as possible."

35

"It's just so good to see you again, Albert. Wow, man!" Linus said, his robotics-enclosed face absolutely beaming.

"How do you know who I am?"

"I don't figure you'd remember me because you were a little man, man. Me and your dad. We were friends. I'm your godfather, or whatever you want to call that. I got you a My L'il Juicer for your third birthday."

Albert vague recalled being very, very young, happily playing in his bedroom with a plastic grocery cart full of plastic lemons, and pretending to squeeze them with a play juicer. It was a happy memory, so he'd kept it safely repressed where nobody could ruin it.

"I...remember that!"

"Far out!"

Albert was more confused than ever.

"So here you are," Albert said, sort of to Linus, but also to Eli Gray.

"So here I am," Linus answered. Eli Gray didn't respond; he just laid there, continuing to soak up precious lemon juice.

"The lemons, they...they work?"

"Heck yeah, man."

"Vitamin C. You were right." He looked down at Eli Gray. "My father was right?"

"Not exactly. "I *am* keeping Eli Gray alive indefinitely."

"Okay."

"Yeah, but I'm not doing it with time bottles. I'm doing it with lemons."

"With Vitamin C."

"Nah."

"Are you here against your will?"

"Oh, absolutely, man."

Linus looked over at Magnus, still catatonically staring at the cyborg's bobbing genitals.

"This suit is pretty top-notch, but that design flaw is a real killer," he said, tapping a mechanical claw on the view window. Then he grabbed the top portion of Eli Gray's jumpsuit, since he wasn't wearing it, and wrapped it around his boxy waist to hide his floating genitals and allow himself a modicum of modesty. Instantly, it broke the spell over Magnus.

"Great exoskeleton!" Magnus shouted. "Very chic. Futuristic, but also retro."

"Retro? Nah, man, this is vintage."

36

Despite having kept himself alive through various and increasingly difficult means for somewhere around 190 years — he'd lost exact count — Elisha Gray was still waiting for his name recognition to eclipse that of Alexander Graham Bell. He was at a loss as to what else he could do. He'd developed Gray Labs into the world's most scientifically important and lucrative corporation, and he had introduced thousands of world-changing products, but there would always be the one that got away. He'd invented the telephone at literally the exact same time as Alexander Graham Bell, but Bell beat him to the Patent Office by a few minutes. He'd always kick himself for taking a pit stop; subsequently, thanks to a series of medical devices developed at Gray Labs, he hadn't urinated in decades.

But despite his voluminous achievements, he never achieved the fame or wealth afforded to Bell, who invented just the one thing. So, Elisha Gray employed a combination of science and will to keep himself alive until he reached his vague and lofty goal of one day surpassing Bell in the collective consciousness.

Being a man of the 19th-century, he began by utilizing the health crazes from his era. He chewed each bite of food 200 times. He engineered a private oxygen supply, so he didn't have to breathe the air of Industrial Age America. He drank the blood of Irish immigrant children. He'd eat only breakfast cereals. Then only meat. Then only organ meat. Then he went vegetarian, back when that was considered weird. He carried a medicine ball around all day. And then there were the enemas; so many enemas.

These activities merely prolonged the inevitable, albeit for a remarkably long time, as Elisha Gray stayed in his original body for well over a century. Fortuitously, around the same time that his organs finally dissolved and his bones permanently splintered, robotics technology had improved to the point where he could preserve and lock what was left of his organic meat-husk into a boxy robot. Developed by the Soviet space program to fly cosmonauts into space and then spy over America from above, Elisha Gray improved on the design, but left two body parts fully visible in the cyborgian shell: his head, encased in glass, and his genitals, which floated in a saline solution. He believed that having one's testicles on display was a power move.

The irony was not lost on Elisha Gray that in his quest to increase his profile and mystique, he couldn't go out in public because the world feared both robots and Soviets. Instead, Elisha Gray, who started going by Eli in 1970 because it sounded cool, spent his days and nights in classic shut-in billionaire style, exiled to his luxurious San Verguenza mansion. His body may have been floating in pickling salts inside an airtight chamber in a robotic shell, but his mind remained sharp enough to allow him to run Gray Labs from home. Eli Gray actually invented the wonderful concept of working from home, which still somehow didn't make him more famous than Alexander Graham Bell.

Eli Gray rolled his tread over to a large picture window one morning and looked down into San Verguenza to observe preparations for his favorite time of year, Science Day, or Gray Labs Presents Science Day as it was known because he'd recently purchased the naming rights. As he gazed down at the demonstration stages and exploding candy stands being erected, the latest issue of *Science Beat* shot through the communications slot in his office door. As he was quite old, he got all of his news from traditional print media, and he excitedly rolled over and used one of his telescoping grippers to grab the magazine.

Instead of the usual issue, it was a supplement, and a supplement to the "What Gray Labs Presents Science Day Means to Me" supplement. It seemed that some random Gray Labs geneticist had made a rambling attack on Eli Gray. He appreciated that this man, Ron something, had reminded the public that he, Eli Gray, had been the true inventor of the telephone, along with some rambling hostility.

This guy preposterously suggested that Nobel Prize winner and widely maligned Vitamin C obsessive Linus Pauling was in Eli Gray's employ, helping him stay alive indefinitely. While this wasn't true, it was a fantastic idea.

Eli Gray remembered the gist of Pauling's research from years earlier, which suggested that consuming a metric shit ton of lemon extracts could cause cancer to retreat just a tad. So, Eli Gray set out to recruit Linus Pauling. He theorized that with the unlimited resources that he alone could provide, Linus Pauling could scale up his Vitamin C research and unlock its full potential. And he could use that potential to cure the many ailments that Eli Gray still faced, such as assorted cancers, a condition called "living corpse rot," and the constant possibility of death. He quickly dictated a letter that emerged from the dot-matrix printer on the back of his robotic suit.

37

Intimidated and inundated by the hundreds of mocking postcards, letters, and hurled rocks he'd received each day since his Vitamin C advocacy was met with widespread resistance, Linus Pauling had to move around a lot. Squatting in an industrial citrus grove in a treehouse that an acclaimed Depression-era novelist had used to spy on itinerant California fruit pickers helped gave him a sense of safety and anonymity. He had no idea how the letter had reached him, as he didn't have a mailbox or even an address. It read:

Dr. Pauling,

It is with humbling respect in which I write to you today. Unfortunately, your name has now been linked to a new pariah of the scientific community, one Ron Malfort, when it was not so long ago that you were enduring the brunt of a community of peers that turned on you for daring to, as we like to say at Gray Labs, "be bold."

At any rate, hearing your name for the first time in years led me to revisit your research on the curative potentiality of Vitamin

C. While the mainstream scientific world has dismissed your findings as both "circumstantial" and "hogwash," and despite your positive results being nominal, I believe there is a possibility that, in a high volume of high concentration, the powers of Vitamin C are endless.

Therefore I am offering you a fellowship at the flagship Gray Labs facility in San Verguenza, California. You will have a fully-equipped workspace, the supplies you need, and the freedom to research unimpeded and without criticism, comment, judgment, or the need to publish.

I anxiously await your response.

Eli Gray

The letter gave Linus what he had long sought: appreciation and redemption. He decided to take Eli Gray up on the offer, especially since his only other prospect was the chance to appear in a bunch of self-deprecating TV commercials for a mall-based frothy orange drink chain. After celebrating alone with a few glasses of lemonade that had fermented after being left out in the sun, Linus hitchhiked the five miles from his grove to San Verguenza, California.

Each day, Linus received a truckload of lemons from a Gray Labs facility, where they'd been genetically modified to be packed with extra Vitamin C, and, as it were, other biological compounds. After just three months of research and tests of those pulsing and glowing super-lemons, Linus discovered that all his theories were, for the most part, legitimate. Repeated soaks of diseased body tissue in the juice of heavily modified lemons made psoriasis go away. And asthma, arthritis, Crohn's disease, fibromyalgia, male-pattern baldness, dandruff, typhoid, typhus, measles, mumps, rubella, malaria, fruit allergies...everything. Every lab pig Linus tested was cured of its malady, although he was a little concerned about how and why there were so many incredibly sick pigs wandering around Gray Labs. In the end, the only thing he had left to crack was cancer.

He took the worst-looking pig he could find, a sorry little fellow named Taft, and gave it a few scans with a Gray-produced That's Sick! Digital Diagnostic Wand. A quick pass-over revealed that Taft suffered from every possible type of porcine cancer, including tail cancer. Linus sedated Taft, which didn't take much owing to his age and health, and cut open the pig's abdomen. Indecisive about which cancerous organ to test first, Linus played a scientifically reasonable game of "Eeeny-Meeny-Miney-Moe" and went with the spleen, which, according to the Wand, consisted of 84 percent cancer and just 6 percent spleen tissue. Linus carefully dislodged the organ from the pig and transferred it to a bowl of lemon juice, taking care to not detach it from the blood vessels.

Then he went outside — he had a door that opened out near Gray Labs' loading docks — and smoked an L-cigarette (a rolled-up lemon peel), and then returned to Taft. He took a deep breath and waved the Wand over Taft's spleen in the bowl, which had soaked up all the lemon juice. Total percentage of cancer in the spleen: 73 percent. It had healed by 11 percent in just a few minutes. Linus had been right: The curative effects of Vitamin C were, it would appear, not a crazy idea that his own fevered mind had once concocted and made the mistake of sharing with a world that hostile to the notion of helping itself.

Emboldened by the results, Linus sought to isolate which compound in the lemons was the most curative, hoping that the answer was Vitamin C. He grabbed another test pig, a sleepy guy named Duckworth with pancreatitis, and, picking totally at random from the three lemon-borne compounds (Vitamin C, chronolytes, electrolytes) to test first, he somehow decided to start with Vitamin C.

He repeated the previous procedure, for the most part: cancer scan, surgical incision, soaking of the affected organ (this time in pure Vitamin C), killing some time with an L-cigarette, and another scan. The result before the procedure, as seen on the Wand's LCD screen: "SO MUCH PANCREATITIS!" The result after the procedure, troublingly: "SO MUCH PANCREATITIS!" A soak in a concentrated amount of Vitamin C, quite plainly, did nothing. His long-held theory, his life's work even, was nonsense. Discovering this completely ruined his day.

With nothing to lose, Linus figured he might as well test the other compounds. Linus procured two more pigs, knocked them out, and cut them open. They could've been twins: They looked alike, as all pigs do, and they each had, according to the Wand, stage 4 prostate cancer. Isolated, lemon-derived electrolytes did nothing; if anything, they made things worse for the pigs, which after that treatment had stage 4.2 prostate cancer. This did not surprise Linus. Like most scientists, he knew that the effects of electrolytes had long been exaggerated by sketchy rogues in the well-funded but suspect science of sportsdrinkology.

By process of elimination, a hallmark of scientific query, this could only mean that chronolytes were responsible for the reduction in the first pig's spleen cancer. Much like the God particle, the discovery of chronolytes years earlier had been breathlessly reported by major scientific and regular news outlets that theorized that the chemical represented time in a physical form, and which could someday be harnessed and directed to manipulate time itself. It ultimately proved much ado about nothing, because they were only ever located in small quantities in potatoes and lemons. Chronolytes ultimately revolutionized the potato clock industry, and that was it.

After isolating and extracting them from lemon juice, Linus took a peek at a few chronolytes under the microscope, something he'd never had the opportunity to do, as the centrifuge needed to isolate them cost upwards of $70. Before he put his eye to the glass, he amusingly wondered if chronolytes, as per their reputation for being physical chunks of time, would look like tiny clocks. He was shocked, but also not all that surprised then, when he looked under the microscope to see dozens of blue and purple circles with two rapidly spinning rods in their middles, and little black specs notched around the circle's edge in 12 equal intervals.

One cancerous pig, the de facto control group, received three successive soaks in chronolytes. The other, far luckier cancerous pig, endured 25 chronolytic soaks. The results: The control group pig's cancer reduced to stage 4. The aggressively treated one went all the way down to stage 2. Linus realized, or in scientific parlance, hypothesized, what had happened: Chronolytes didn't cure disease —they sent the treated organ back in time to where the disease didn't exist, or at least to where it didn't exist as much.

The only thing to do now was to test it on humans. But for that, he'd need his boss's approval. He picked up the handset on his Graybox, which provided a direct line of communication to Eli Gray.

"Do you have something for me?" asked the raspy voice of Eli Gray.

"Oh, I've got something for you. Something astounding!" Linus enthusiastically replied.

The line clicked dead, and a few minutes later, there was a loud banging at the lab door. Then it swung open.

"I forgot I can open any door in here," Eli Gray said as he

rolled in. At least, Linus was pretty sure that the figure before him was Eli Gray, or what was left of Eli Gray. This was the first time they'd been in the same room together, and Linus was a little taken aback that Eli Gray was not a man, but a body encased inside a 10-foot-tall Soviet robot. The only parts of Eli Gray visible were his head, encased in glass, and his genitals, which swayed in a liquid solution in the center of the apparatus. Linus found their movements both hypnotic and intimidating.

"Snap out of it, Pauling."

"Hmm? Oh! Sir! I've done it."

"It?"

"What you brought me here to do. Lemons can cure anything!"

"Anything?"

"*Everything.*"

Linus explained that he'd been wrong about Vitamin C, but right about lemons, and that he'd isolated chronolytes from lemons and used them to reverse time and therefore reverse the effects of cancer.

"Extracted chronolytes, scaled up, with regular doses, could mean permanently staving off cancer," Linus explained, "by staving off *time*."

"But it's just lemon juice, right?"

"No, it's chronolytes. It all looks like lemon juice, and it's sour, but it's not lemon juice. Fun fact: Lemons get their sourness from chronolytes."

"'For the passage of time is sour.'"

"Is that from a poem? Walt Whitman?"

"He was a good friend of mine. A real miserable bastard."

"So, then, we can go ahead and start some trials on humans? I'm thinking very small, very cautious, over ten, 15 years. Don't wanna harsh anybody, you know?"

Eli Gray balled up his grabber claw and slammed it into a table, crushing the table. "You haven't tested it on humans yet?"

"To do so before now would've been monstrous."

Eli Gray realized how monstrous *he* appeared, crushing tables and whatnot, and he knew he had to cool it, at least for the moment. He retracted his telescoping arms and placed them across his heart to appear caring. That would direct Linus's eyes toward where his heart was — somewhere in there.

"Dr. Pauling, we've got to get this out as quickly as possible. People could die from diseases tomorrow, hell, they could be dying right now. And we've got their cure right here. Think of how many people will equate the words 'Linus Pauling' with 'hero' and 'cure for cancer.' Test this on humans *now*."

"But who would possibly submit themselves to experimental research from a known quack?"

Eli Gray extended his arms, embracing Linus in a fatherly, impenetrable hug.

"I'll do it."

Pauling was so moved by this act of selflessness and generosity in the name of science, nay, friendship, that he had no choice but to allow it.

"But we've got to go all the way. No organs one-by-one. I want you to soak all my organs. All at once."

The next morning, Pauling set up a small surgical center in his laboratory in the Gray Labs sub-basement. It took most of the day, but he carefully sedated Eli Gray with a special Gray Labs sedative, cut him open, and extracted each of his organs, placing them in bowls where they were both soaked with and injected with lemon-extracted chronolytes. If nothing else, the room smelled fantastic.

Linus then replaced the organs, sewed up his patient, and Eli

Gray woke up a few hours later, a little sore, but incredibly energetic and flexible, and most importantly, totally free of his robotic exoskeleton. There was also a bag on his face, with holes cut out for the eyes, mouth, nose, and ears.

"How did it go?"

"You're cancer-free."

"Cancer...free?"

"I went ahead and cleared up the living corpse rot, too," Linus said. "No extra charge, man!"

Eli Gray felt around his various body parts, crudely and bluntly poking around his organs, and he couldn't feel any hard tumors. He felt like a teenager again, full of pep and inexplicable rage.

"Why is this bag on my face?"

"It's the weirdest thing. The chronolytes don't help the face. I think that's why your face puckers when you eat a lemon. The human face just hates lemons. Science is weird, right?"

Eli Gray sighed. "What do you suggest I do?"

"Sunscreen, moisturizer. You could put that dome back on. Oh, or you could get yourself a helmet. I hear helmets are all the rage these days!" Linus was referring to the black-helmeted villain from a space movie he'd seen a few minutes of on TV a few years before he'd come to Gray Labs. He found the villain terrifying, almost as terrifying as Eli Gray.

"At any rate, well done."

"My pleasure. What now?"

"We tell the world."

"We should also get you some clothes. A jumpsuit. Oh, how about a *grey* jumpsuit?" Linus suggested. "Get it? Because your *name* is Gray!"

Later that day, all Gray Lab employees, and more importantly, the media, were summoned to the auditorium on the top floor of the main campus building via tungsten-paper invitations laser-etched with the words "Product Announcement Event. 7 p.m." By the time Linus made his way across campus to the auditorium about 3 p.m. (in disguise, as Grace Hopper), absolutely no seats were available, so he sat on the floor, in the back, next to some reporters who could barely contain their excitement.

"I heard it's a new kind of computer mouse. It moves on its own."

"I heard it's an electric carving knife that you control with your brain."

Linus eavesdropped as they continued to toss wild rumors back and forth for the better part of four hours, up until the moment that all the lights went out and the auditorium was in complete darkness, except for a tiny white flame from the far wall of the stage. The flame grew larger and larger, as whoever or whatever was carrying it got closer. Finally, the house lights brightened to reveal a single figure, dressed in a grey, one-piece jumpsuit, and a helmet.

In came the most athletically fit person anyone in attendance had ever seen, running in slow motion through every aisle and carrying his torch, which upon closer inspection was a That's Sick! Diagnostic Wand symbolically lit aflame.

The crowd cheered and screamed. As the figure took center stage and touched a button on the side of his helmet, many passed out. "My coworkers. My team. My *friends*," the voice of Eli Gray boomed over the thousands of speakers in the auditorium. "I am Eli Gray. And the newest offering from Gray Labs...is me."

The crowd went completely fucking apeshit.

"Be bold!" the crowd, unprompted, yelled in unison three times.

"You'll be seeing a lot more of me around here. I look forward to being bold with all of you!"

And then he gave a long speech about believing in oneself, and why one should always be bold, and that sometimes being bold meant having to make the right decisions, even if they were tough decisions. He also projected some doctored images of himself looking morbidly obese, and attributed his long stint of agoraphobia to that. His transformation, he claimed, came from taking vitamins.

"But not," he added, "too much Vitamin C."

The joke was subtle, but it absolutely killed. The audience of scientists and science nerds certainly understood, and also thought it was a needlessly cruel reference to the maligned and exiled Linus Pauling. This was Eli Gray's way of letting Linus know that the world would not be learning of the great scientist's lemon-based research. Of course, Linus didn't understand that, and he happily, obliviously laughed along with the crowd.

38

"So, what happened next?" Albert asked breathlessly.

"A couple days later, he came down for more treatments, and I refused," Linus explained. "I threatened to expose him, he said nobody would believe me because I was a widely discredited kook. I threatened to quit, he threatened to kill me. You know, the usual workplace dispute stuff."

Albert understood. As Magnus had never had a boss, he didn't.

"But we both knew he couldn't *actually* kill me, because only I knew how to extract the compounds from the lemons and properly use them."

"So then you told the world, and Eli Gray suppressed the news?" Albert theorized.

"Nope. I gave Eli Gray his lemon treatments, and he shook my hand and thanked me for being bold, and the next morning I woke up in this robot suit."

"Which means you'll never die," Albert realized.

"And neither will he, man."

"So Ron was right, but, like retroactively?" Magnus asked.

"Yes. All except for the time bottles part."

"Where did he even get that idea?" Magnus asked.

"Probably got his wires crossed. He and I were in a band together!"

"Really?" Albert didn't buy it. "How come I never knew that?"

"We never practiced at your house. Your mom said our music was, and I quote, 'a pathetic attempt to recapture long-gone youth resulting in deep embarrassment to the musicians and those in their orbit.' We were called the Time Bottles."

"Ohhhhhh," Albert and Magnus simultaneously realized.

"For a time, we were San Verguenza's third-most-popular John Knitty cover band."

Magnus dry-heaved a little.

"He talked about you all the time," Albert said. "I didn't know you were friends. He just completely idolized you."

"Hey, man, if you can't idolize your friends, you need better friends."

Albert was briefly stunned by the moderate profundity of the quote until a few seconds later, when he spotted the words on a coffee mug sitting on a table behind Linus.

"Yeah, Albert. You're my hero." Magnus said sarcastically, batting his eyelashes.

"Yeah, so what I think happened is that in his brain, 'time bottles' got mixed up with this idea that Eli Gray had been on the scene for way too long."

"Also, he's profoundly mentally ill," Albert accidentally said out loud.

"Let's not discount the many fumes and chemicals that guy ingested," Magnus suggested.

"Preach," Linus said. "Back in our prime, we didn't really think about that stuff. Ventilation and masks and gloves were optional. So, yeah, he definitely inhaled a lot of fumes. Accidentally drank a lot of weird stuff, too. Hey, speaking of which, you guys thirsty?"

Albert and Magnus nodded in the affirmative because despite their different upbringings, they were both raised to always politely accept a host's offer of a beverage.

"What can I get you? I've got lemonade, orange juice, and unsweetened nonalcoholic lemon liqueur."

"Lemon juice?" Magnus asked.

"Oh yeah, *that's* what it's called!" Linus replied. "Or I can mix them all of those up together. It's a drink I invented. You know what I named it?"

Albert and Linus looked at each other, then looked back at Linus.

"A Linus Pauling?" they asked in unison.

"You guys are my *dudes!*"

With his left arm, he unscrewed a cap on the side of his robot body, revealing a spout. With his other arm, he grabbed two Erlenmeyer flasks from a table in the back of the room and put them under the spout, which dispensed two citrusy drinks impressively layered in yellow, orange, and green sections.

Suddenly, Linus jerked, shut his eyes, and his entire body shook and shot off a spray of sparks that gently singed off some of Albert's arm hair. He managed not to spill a drop of the drinks, and he handed them off.

"Here you go, two Thomas Edisons." He seemed momentarily confused. "Weird!"

Magnus and Albert took their drinks and gave each other very concerned looks, silently communicating a thought akin to "I am very concerned."

"You want to explain why we're here?" Albert whispered to Magnus. "It's kind of your fault."

"I heard that. Robot hearing and all," Linus said. "Does this have anything to do with why you needed time bottles?"

Magnus explained the Thomas Edison situation.

"That's why my drink was called a Thomas Edison all of a sudden."

"Exactly."

"And why all my stuff around here suddenly has Edison logos." Linus turned his head around 180 degrees to look at his own back. "That used to be a hammer and sickle, man." Albert and Magnus walked around to the rear of Linus to see the telltale "E" on the back of Linus's robot shell.

"Yeah, a lot of things around here have changed, man. Like seven or *E* things just today alone.

"*E* things? Oh man, now he's stealing from *me*!"

Eli Gray's leg twitched, just a little. Albert jumped.

"You guys, we gotta get out of here," Albert sputtered. "He's gonna wake up soon."

"Albert, what's he gonna do? Fire you?" Magnus quipped, dipping his fingers into some of the extracted chronolytes on their way to Eli Gray. He tasted it, and his face puckered so much it made his dimples extra deep and, Albert lamented, extra attractive.

"He could have me arrested," Albert shouted, his brain racing with all of the horrible punishments that he could face.

"He could put you in one of those 3-D sky prisons!" Magnus helpfully suggested.

"Or you could take, like, as many chronolytes as you need to get yourselves back to 1931 and stop, uh, what's his name," Linus said, glancing down at the gurney, and seeing an E-branded scalpel. "Edison. Yeah."

"You think that would work?" Albert asked.

"Of course it will," Magnus replied. "The only question is how."

"You see that big container over there, where all the lemons go after they've been drained of chronolytes?" Linus asked, pointing, and then extending his arm to rap on the side of the tungsten depository. "Once drained, the husks become highly volatile."

He reached into the box of spent lemons and pulled out one. No longer recognizable as a lemon, it had been taken over by a swarm of purple fungus that pulsed and flashed with tiny blue bolts of lightning. "Modifying them to be that powerful, and then draining them of that power, it unnerves them."

"They become unstable." Albert clarified.

"No, *unnerved*. That's the word *they* use," Linus explained.

"Um, they?" asked Magnus.

"Yeah, the lemons."

"Right, the lemons," Magnus said, struggling to not make a sideways glance at Albert.

"Of course lemons talk to me. I am but their humble servant, their consort to the human realm."

Linus was exaggerating. They didn't really talk to him; it was more of a series of vague grunts and squeaks that he interpreted liberally.

"See, modifying the lemons to have all of that incredibly powerful stuff in them means they have to be handled correctly. You drain all of that out, the universe immediately replaces it all with an electrical time fungus, to maintain the chemical weight and structure of the lemon. But that fungus is extremely unstable.

Too many spent lemons in one place get disturbed, and you could seriously mess up the very balance of time.

"I discovered this after Eli Gray had already started his treatments and begged him to dump the husks someplace safe, where they won't be hassled. He's not the best dude, but he kept his word on this one."

They stared down at the exposed body cavity of Eli Gray. Albert thought about spitting into it but decided to be the bigger man. Magnus took out a fingernail clipper and absent-mindedly trimmed his nails, and the shards landed directly in Eli Gray's guts. Albert smiled.

"Where did he dump them?" Magnus asked.

"Underneath the unused Edisonball field behind the high school."

Albert suddenly realized why his first time travel experiment in a secure room had worked, and why his second, atop a field loaded with unstable lemon husks, had not.

"So really, just don't go there. I know it seems like the ideal place for a time travel experiment because it doesn't get a lot of foot traffic, but trust me, do not do anything there, or you could open up a very nasty time hole. You don't want to get on the bad side of those time lobsters."

"Then, uh, where should we go?" Albert asked.

"Some place that Eli Gray doesn't own."

"Gonna have to get pretty far out of town then," Albert added.

"Just take the chronolytes and go. He'll be awake soon. He likes to watch his last few rounds of gall bladder treatments. He's a sicko."

"How much do you think we'll need?"

"To create a stable hole in time? Probably only a few hundred bags of lemons should do it."

"Can't we just take the extract?"

"Just the extract? No, no, no guys, you've got to have them fresh!"

Less than five minutes later, Albert and Magnus were behind the wheel of a Gray Labs truck that Linus Pauling had used his telescoping robotic arms to place on the loading dock and fill up with lemons, chronolyte-extracting equipment, and because it was so compact, Magnus's volcano car.

39
_____

After a quick stop at The Unified Theory for time machine supplies, which Magnus paid for by tossing onto the floor as they left a bunch of $100 bills with Edison's scowling face on them, Albert and Magnus ventured to the rolling hills about 50 miles outside of San Verguenza, the closest place untouched by Gray Labs in deed or toxic waste. The spot was free of any chronolytic material, according to the proprietary measuring device that Linus had made for them, which consisted of an activated carbon rod shoved into a grapefruit husk.

Albert dutifully recreated his time travel set-up, changing out the potatoes for lemons and remembering to bring a table this time. Magnus wasn't needed quite yet, so he watched funny videos on EdisonTube on his Edison Phone.

"Can you put that away and come help me?"

"Have you ever watched an elephant get electrocuted?"

"Alright, well, I get to go first."

"Wait!" Magnus called out, reluctantly pocketing his phone. "If this opens up a time hole, and we jump into it, how do we get back?"

Albert was quite peeved that Magnus had made such an astute, potentially lifesaving observation, especially an obvious one that he had failed to make himself.

"I guess you're right. We need something to tether ourselves."

"Tungsten," they said together.

Of course it was going to be tungsten. It retained its ironclad (so to speak) tenacity and strength even as it helped absorb and eliminate the third dimension. It was simply a must-have for the time-traveler's toolbox. Except that they didn't have any tungsten.

"We don't have any tungsten."

"Albert. Please."

Magnus went to the van and pushed out his volcano car. From its trunk, he pulled out a substantial length of thin tungsten rope. He kept pulling more out, and more rope came. A massive, messy pile of it collected on the ground and yet a seemingly endless reserve of it remained in the trunk.

"How does that work?"

"The trunk utilizes the same dimension-shrinking technology that a particular company uses in other avenues, such as hover prisons."

"You know I invented that, right?"

"Well, according to the patent information stamped right here," Magnus said, pointing to the inside of the trunk, "it's, and I quote, 'another great invention by the great Thomas Edison.'"

Magnus chuckled nervously; Albert sighed.

"Will it be enough rope? How long is it, anyway?" Albert asked.

"I'm pretty sure it's infinite. You know, Albert, I don't always understand how science works, but I sure do enjoy it!"

Magnus carefully continued hauling out more slack of tungsten rope while Albert made one last check of every element of his time travel setup, assuring that each thing was attached to the right thing. This was the third time he'd experimented with the same setup, which had to be some kind of record. Albert felt a twinge of sadness in his heart when a thought of Rosalind snuck into his brain and traveled down to his heart, totally ruining the bit of pleasure he'd felt when he realized how much easier everything had been to set up with a table. He quickly buried the feelings, for feelings were the enemy of science. He flipped the appropriate switches and pressed the right buttons to get the whole operation in motion.

Everything hummed along nicely. Albert smiled and laughed to himself as he realized that he was already time traveling, in a sense, to when before his life went to hell, specifically the moment just before he had met Magnus, when he seemed to be on the cusp of greatness, when he had successfully shot Carl through time a few minutes. Then he felt bad again because he missed Carl.

"Does this tungsten make me look fat?" Magnus asked of the rope he'd securely tied around his waist. It didn't. *This industrial-grade metal rope actually looks good on you*, Albert thought, fitting it around his own waist like a well-worn belt that was a size too small.

"You don't mind if I do this, do you?" Magnus said, referring to the trepanning drill in his hand. "I mean, it could be, like negative 100 years before I get to do this again, and that's a really long time."

"Fine."

Albert waited patiently while Magnus carefully pushed the whirring drill bit into his own skull. After an orgasmic shake and a succession of sighs, he opened his eyes and smiled at Albert.

"I've got a little something for you, too!"

Magnus reached into his pocket and handed a small red pill to Albert.

"Take it."

Albert hesitated. "What is this? Another weird drug that will make me fall into my own brain and make me reveal my private feelings and thoughts?"

"No, Albert," Magnus said, laughing. "It's an antidepressant."

Albert tried to formulate a nasty comeback, but instead, he just took the pill.

With all of the equipment still encouragingly not bursting into flames or causing a rupture in the earth to release monster lobsters, Magnus and Albert walked over to a welcoming abyss, the one on the left. They stared down at the nothing beyond nothing.

And with that, Magnus fell into the promising darkness. A few seconds later, despite not being ready, Albert also plunged into the abyss, a bit before he was totally ready, but because he was tied to the same rope as Magnus, he had little say in the matter.

"Don't worry," Albert thought he heard Magnus say. "I'm almost entirely certain I left the car in park."

40

Mostly because it was just too hard to talk under the circumstances, Albert and Magnus remained silent as they careened downward through the black emptiness of time. Additionally, neither felt much like talking, preoccupied with worry over what would happen when they stopped falling. The answer came soon enough when they landed hard on a cold, smooth surface.

"That didn't hurt as much as I feared it would," Magnus said, pulling himself to his feet. "Of course, I just pushed in pretty hard, so all of that may have hurt tremendously, and I won't know for a while."

"Feels like linoleum." Albert looked down at the inoffensive, bland, pale "This *is* linoleum."

"What's linoleum?" Magnus asked. "Is it like marble?"

Albert surveyed what resembled a rambling, multi-story shopping mall. But instead of stores selling stuff that Albert wanted but couldn't afford, they displayed years. Events that corresponded to the year played on what was an infinite loop, projected into curvy, angular shapes in the middle of the air. He looked over at the 1963 shop and saw a handsome guy in a convertible get shot. In the 1968 shop, a slightly less handsome guy in a hotel got shot. Next-door was the 1969 store, which showed a loop of a not remotely handsome guy and a lovely woman crash a car into a pond. It was like some sort of time marketplace, or, as he had once correctly guessed while setting up his time machine in college, a time switching station.

"I was right!"

"That Linus Pauling makes time bottles?" Magnus was a little too high from the trepanning to understand what was going on. "No, wait, *that's not true.*"

As Albert walked around noticing different years, he dragged a stumbling, giggling Magnus with him, thanks to the tungsten tether. Magnus looked at all the years, but was way more interested in an area far down the main corridor marked with a simple, hand-painted sign that said, "TIME TRAVELERS PARTY: TODAY (OR WHATEVER THAT MEANS TO YOU)."

"Party!" Magnus shouted, hoisting his arms very, very slowly up in the air due to the effects of his brain stimulation.

"Not now. We've got to find Edison. Help me look for 1931."

"No! Party! Me want party!" Magnus shouted like a petulant 19-year-old.

"There it is!" Albert said, locating 1931, and with its projections of a tiny Thomas Edison showing off technology that had once been well past his time. Albert caught a glimpse of him handing what looked like a gigantic 8-track player to King George V, who, upon taking it into his normal-sized hands, revealed that it was a regular 8-track player.

"No. Party!"

Albert walked toward 1931, and Magnus toward the party. They both fell to the ground, and each rubbed at their hips where the sudden extreme friction of the tungsten rope on clothing chafed their skin.

"No, Magnus," Albert said with a tone of patience that came across as deeply condescending. "*Edison. Time machine. Very bad. Remember?*"

"Look!"

Magnus pointed toward the sign, or at least to the best of his abilities, all things considered. His pointing was way off, and he actually gestured at 1982, where a crowd laughed at Linus Pauling and also some young men with bad haircuts played keyboards like guitars.

"'Time travelers party. Today, or whatever that means to you,'" Albert said, reading the sign aloud.

Magnus hated when people did that; he thought the whole point of putting words on signs was so that people didn't have to say stuff. He tried to say as much, but all that came out was an annoyed, "Ugh. Party!"

Albert didn't want to go to the party, even one for a club as exclusive as time travelers, of which he was a member. He hated parties, or at least that's what he told himself because he'd never actually been to one, not counting the children's birthday parties where he'd dress up as Eli Gray.

"You know, Magnus, I've always hated parties," Albert said, oddly dazed. "I feel compelled to go to this one."

"*Party!*" Magnus said again, more insistently and urgently, and through gritted teeth, dancing in place a little bit in what was excitement but looked like he needed an immediate bathroom break.

"I suppose we're invited."

"Party!" Magnus said defiantly and definitively as he marched toward this party. Albert, his mind ultimately made up for him by the tungsten rope that bound him to Magnus, trotted along.

When they got closer, Albert could see that it promised everything he'd ever dreamed would be at a party. There was a snack table with soda and candy; balloons tied to colorful ribbons; a couple of cool, red beanbag chairs in the corner; and best of all, the people at this party seemingly wanted him to be there. Magnus, meanwhile, chanted "party" under his breath.

Albert paused before entering. He wasn't sure what would happen to him when he did, for a weird mist separated the corridor from the interior of the party room. His decision, once again, was made for him by Magnus, who just barged in and brought him along.

More details about the party became clear. They had a record player, for example, and there were two people in attendance. One of them was Stephen Hawking, whom Albert recognized as 1) One of the most famous scientists ever, 2) The guy who lured his mother away, 3) The guy who had discovered black holes, and 4) The guy who had once been rumored to have thrown a party for time travelers to see if anyone, at some point in time, ever figured out time travel.

The other person at the party was Barbara Banting Malfort, Albert's mother.

Magnus didn't recognize either person right away. He certainly didn't know who Barbara Banting Malfort was, but his shred of humanity helped him figure it out. When he saw Albert hug the woman, he figured that she must have been his mother. As for the famous male scientist, Magnus unabashedly gushed.

"Wow, Carl Sagan! What are you doing here?"

"HELLO, MAGNUS." Stephen Hawking said through his electronic voice synthesizer. "I AM STEPHEN HAWKING."

"Oh, sorry, I thought you were someone else," Magnus said, desperately trying to not seem super high. "It's very nice to meet you, Stephen. What do you do?"

"I AM THE MOST FAMOUS SCIENTIST OF ALL TIME."

"Really?" Magnus was pleased, not sarcastic. "*I'm* the most famous scientist of all time! Samesies!"

"YOU DO NOT KNOW WHO I AM?"

"Should I?"

"I WAS YOUR PRIVATE TUTOR FOR FOUR YEARS, MAGNUS, YOU SPOILED BRAT."

Magnus shrugged.

"AND YOU, ALBERT, I HAVE WAITED FOR THIS DAY FOR A VERY LONG TIME."

"Believe me, Dr. Hawking, so have I."

"YOU SEE, ALBERT," Dr. Hawking continued, "IT IS TIME YOU KNEW THE TRUTH."

"About what?" he asked, genuinely curious and a little concerned.

"THERE IS A REASON YOU DO NOT RELATE TO RON MALFORT VERY WELL."

"There...there is?" Albert asked with heartbreaking earnestness.

"IT IS BECAUSE HE IS NOT YOUR FATHER. IT IS I WHO AM YOUR FATHER."

Right after Dr. Hawking had told Albert he needed to know "the truth," Albert had hoped that this was where he was going with his speech, but he had also been working hard on not paying mind to his dreams and wishes. But then it happened. Dr. Hawking said the two thing things Albert had long wanted to hear: that Ron Malfort was not his father and that somebody like Stephen Hawking was.

"HA HA HA. I AM JUST KIDDING," Dr. Hawking said. "HA HA HA."

"Wait, so, you're not…"

"Good one!" yelled Magnus.

"Stephen, don't tease my boy like that."

"I AM SORRY, ALBERT. I AM NOT YOUR FATHER," Dr. Hawking explained. "BUT I WISH I WAS. BECAUSE THAT WOULD MEAN I WOULD HAVE BEEN INTIMATE WITH YOUR MOM. PROBABLY A WHOLE BUNCH OF TIMES."

"Stephen. That is extremely unprofessional."

"OH, BARB. I AM SO SORRY."

"Stephen, in situations like this, it is more appropriate if you refer to me as Dr. Banting."

"YES, DOCTOR BANTING."

Albert noticed that she'd dropped the "Malfort" from her professional name, which he appreciated.

"Two minutes, Dr. Hawking."

Dr. Hawking didn't say anything and scooted away on his chair until it was facing into a corner.

"He's in a time-out," Dr. Banting said. "Now then. Albert. My son. It's so good to see you! And you're a time traveler! I always knew you would do something truly exceptional."

"This is…this is where you've been the whole time?"

"Where are we?" Magnus asked, helping himself to a plastic cup of transparent cola from the well-appointed snack table.

"In the macro, you're in a time-switching station. In the micro, you're at a time traveler party. So far, you're the only ones to show up. I suspect you will be the last."

"It's been years. I have so much to say to you. I don't know where to start."

"Albert, concepts like 'years' are meaningless to me at this stage of my research. Be more specific."

"What do you mean your 'research'? You left my father and me to follow that guy around," he said, pointing to Dr. Hawking.

"What? Certainly not. Did your father tell you that?"

"Well, yes."

Albert remembered the day very clearly. His father took him out for astronaut ice cream, wearing a disguise to avoid getting recognized. Ron delivered the news about Albert's mother, and several bricks of ice cream softened the blow of what he had assumed was accurate news. Albert sobbed, which his father was convinced were time bottles he had eaten leaking out of his eyes. He dropped Albert off at a hospital; two days later, he was discharged and walked home.

A digital timer beeped.

"ALLOW ME TO EXPLAIN," Dr. Hawking said as he returned to the group. "YOUR MOTHER LEFT YOU VERY SHORTLY AFTER MY TEAM AT CAMBRIDGE UNCOVERED AN ENTRY INTO WHAT WE NOW CALL TIME SWITCHING STATIONS. AS ONE OF THE FOREMOST THINKERS IN THEORETICAL PHYSICS, WE HAD BEEN TRYING TO GET HER TO HEAD OUR DEPARTMENT FOR YEARS, BUT SHE HAD QUIT TO RAISE A FAMILY. WHEN WE CAME AT HER WITH THE OFFER THAT TIME, SHE COULD NOT REFUSE."

"That is a significantly more accurate account," Dr. Banting added.

"YOUR MOTHER AND I HAVE BEEN EXPLORING THE NATURE OF TIME FOR YEARS, WITH FREE ACCESS TO AND FROM THE CHANNELS BY WHICH ONE CAN TRAVEL THROUGH TIME. ONLY OBSERVING, NEVER INTERFERING."

"I hated to leave you, Albert, but I had to. For science."

"I understand," Albert lied.

"I wish I could change the way things transpired, Albert. I really do."

"I HAVE THE NEXT BEST THING," Dr. Hawking said. He blinked three times, and a compartment automatically opened at the bottom of his wheelchair. A robotic arm folded out and placed a bottle of clear liquid in Dr. Hawking's lap.

"I CALL THIS 'THE FORGETTER.' NO TIME TRAVEL OR SURGERY REQUIRED. TRY IT."

Albert grabbed the bottle, screwed off the cap, and sniffed its contents.

"This is just vodka."

"GRAIN ALCOHOL, ACTUALLY," Dr. Hawking said. "IT IS HOW I GOT OVER HOW DOCTOR BANTING WOULD NEVER LOVE ME THE WAY THAT I LOVE HER."

Among everything else, Albert was peeved by his mother's lack of passion. He resented her, for he could think of several times he wished he could have used her to intervene and make his life better. At the very least, it would have been nice to know even a fraction of what she knew about time travel, or to have used nepotism to get ahead in the field.

"I'm sure you're wondering why I didn't use my mastery of time manipulation to interfere with your life, Albert."

"Not at all," he lied. "It's scientifically sound."

"Because it was crucial to observe now and change later. I figured that once I returned to the present day, whenever in the future that was, I would explain the situation, and we could go back and fix things together. It would be an act of what scientists call 'maternal protection.'"

"THERE WAS THAT ONE THING WE TRIED TO CHANGE," Dr. Hawking interrupted.

"Don't interrupt me, Dr. Hawking."

"I THINK HE SHOULD KNOW THAT WE WERE NOT ENTIRELY PURE IN OUR INTENTIONS."

"Very well. I will busy myself with some popcorn," Dr. Banting said and went to the snack table to very slowly fill up a bowl with popcorn.

"WE WERE ABLE TO DO MOST OF OUR RESEARCH THROUGH TEMPORAL OBSERVATION EQUIPMENT IN CAMBRIDGE, BUT WE HAD TO COME DOWN HERE TO TRY AND DIRECTLY STOP WHAT APPEARS TO BE A MENACE TO THE TIME-SPACE CONTINUUM. SOMETHING THAT IS OR LOOKS LIKE THOMAS EDISON HAS BEEN MANIPULATING TIME FOR ITS OWN FINANCIAL GAIN AND PERSONAL GLORIFICATION. BUT THEN OUR EDISON-BRANDED TEMPORAL OBSERVATION EQUIPMENT SAID WE WERE WRONG AND SHOULD JUST FORGET ABOUT IT."

"That seemed a bit suspicious," Dr. Banting said through a mouthful of popcorn.

"The actual equipment told you that?" Albert asked.

"YES, IT WAS A LITTLE ERROR MESSAGE BOX, LIKE ON THE COMPUTER," Dr. Hawking explained.

Magnus, who was still tethered to Albert and had spent the last few minutes holding his transparent cup of transparent cola up to his eye to see how funny everybody looked when viewed through such a filter, finally had something to contribute to the conversation.

"Are you guys talking about Edison? Whoa, we were *just* talking about Edison, remember Albert? Remember how Edison did all the stuff?"

"What does he mean, Albert?"

"Do I have to call you Dr. Banting?"

"I suppose you can call me 'Mom' if you prefer."

"Mom, we're down here trying to find Thomas Edison."

"And then what?" she asked.

"What do you mean?" Magnus replied. "We're going to stop him is what!"

"YES, BUT HOW?"

Albert and Magnus looked at each other and shrugged.

"You know," Albert said, "our goal has just been to get into the fabric of time, so we could find him. We kind of didn't think about how we would actually stop him when he got to him."

"Oh! Albert!" Magnus whispered, but at full volume. "When we get Edison, we should stop him!"

"MY SUGGESTION," Dr. Hawking suggested. "STREET JUSTICE."

"Dr. Hawking, that joke isn't funny anymore."

"I AM SORRY, MY LOVE."

"Please don't say that."

"I LOVE YOU, YOU KNOW."

"I know, Dr. Hawking."

"WHY DON'T YOU LOVE ME?"

"I love science, Dr. Hawking."

"AS DO I. MAYBE WE COULD GET SOME SORT OF THREE-WAY THING GOING?"

"What does that mean?" Dr. Banting was both disgusted and confused.

"I DO NOT KNOW EITHER. I AM THROWING EVERY-THING TO THE WALL TO SEE WHAT STICKS."

"Now *that's* science!" yelled out Magnus, helping himself to another cup of transparent cola.

"Okay, okay, but seriously, how are we going to stop him?"

Albert asked. "We're dealing with a guy who is, pardon the phrase, very inventive."

"Oh, I get that joke!" Magnus said.

"Can he escape through time?" Albert wondered. "Or he could run away."

"He's also very small and fast and is probably expecting us," Magnus added.

"I think I understand," Dr. Banting said, smiling warmly and maternally at Albert. "You just have to use the power of science, Albert."

The moment of warmth was over for Albert. The remark put him off, as he assumed it was a command to figure it out for himself at best or a poorly-executed reference to Magnus's TV show at worst. Then she pointed to the snack table.

"Science is all around us."

Magnus also tried to figure out what Dr. Banting meant and looked down at his soda. It was an "aha!" moment, like something out of his TV show. "The soda, Albert!"

He walked over to the snack table and grabbed an unopened two-liter bottle of the transparent cola. Albert noticed that next to the soda were several big bowls of brightly colored jagged rocks.

"Brightly Colored Fizzy Candy Rocks!" Albert called out.

"Are those the kind that sizzle and pop in your mouth?" Magnus asked. "Have you ever heard that urban legend about how I died after I ate those and then drank a bunch of sodas? As if I'd ever consume carbs."

Unfortunately, Albert thought, Magnus hadn't died from mixing Brightly Colored Fizzy Candy Rocks and soda. But it *was* a scientifically possible and probable way to die. He knew what he must do.

"I know what I must do."

"Well, you can't," Dr. Banting instructed.

"YOU JUST CAN'T GET INTO EDISON'S TIME PERIOD BY YOURSELF," Dr. Hawking explained. "YOU HAVE TO HAVE AN ESCORT."

"Mary!" "Louise!" shouted Dr. Banting.

The cool red beanbag chairs in the corner sprang to life, stood up, and took the form of horse-sized lobsters. They dutifully if sleepily trotted over to where Barbara stood and sat at her feet.

"Agh! Lobsters!" screamed Albert, who hid behind Magnus.

"It's okay, Albert. These ones won't hurt you."

"THESE ARE TIME LOBSTERS, ALBERT, Dr. Hawking said. "THEY PATROL TIME."

Dr. Banting grabbed a couple of cowboy hats and handed them to the lobsters, who put them on their heads. "Treat them well, and they'll usher you through to any year you want," Dr. Banting added.

Albert and Magnus mounted the lobsters and left the party, their pockets full of Brightly Colored Fizzy Candy Rocks and two bottles of soda strapped to each of their backs. They bid farewell, and as Albert held his arms out for a hug, his mother carefully avoided eye contact and turned away to avoid the embrace. Albert and Magnus rode out into the time station, and on over and through into the year 1931. Conveniently they were dumped right onto the black-and-white streets of New Jersey.

"Hey," Albert said. "Where should we look for him?"

"No idea!" Magnus admitted. "Where do Thomas Edisons hang out?"

They both thought for a moment and then said to each other, flatly: "Patent Office."

"Great, now we have to find a patent office," Albert observed.

"Hmmm," Magnus said, looking around. "Hey, there's one!"

Sure enough, half a block away in front of them stood a United States Patent Office.

"So...then we wait?" Magnus asked.

"Yep."

Magnus sighed, anticipating both boredom and anxiety. But he needn't have worried because they only had to wait for about five minutes before tiny Thomas Edison exited the building in a determined huff.

41

———

In his first run at human life, Thomas Edison worked tirelessly to achieve global prominence, sleeping four hours a night, and usually in his workshop. Since he now stood 30 percent of his original size, he figured that he needed 30 percent as much as he used to, or about 72 minutes. That left slightly under 23 hours a day for Edison to toil.

But he didn't need that much time, nor did he need to work so hard. In possession of an extensive list of inventions from the future he could patent and pass off as his own, the most prominent thing he'd out-and-out devised and built upon his return was the Edison Patent-Filing Machine, which he called his patent-patenter. It could file patents in .001 percent of the time it took a file clerk, which adds up to real savings when thousands of patents must get processed at once, a need held only by tiny Thomas Edison. And because of his machinations that made him the only person in the country patenting anything, Edison and his patent-patenter put the Patent Office out of business mere days after its invention. After having dealt so much with that agency during his original lifetime, it was very sweet for Edison indeed when he purchased the now abandoned Patent Office building for a pittance and made it the site of the new-and-improved Edison Labs.

Left with lots of time to consider his legacy, Edison found the perfect way to pay tribute to himself and his own greatness: producing, directing, and starring as himself in a film about his rise as an inventor, the minor hurdle of his own death, his rebirth, the destruction of his own corpse, and his triumphant return to life and the simultaneous invention of thousands of labor-saving devices and astounding conveyances which injected so much cash into Great Depression-era America that it instantly ended the Great Depression. This film, *The Greatest Man of Science,* swept the 1st annual Edison Motion Picture Awards.

America fell hard into the biggest fad since shooting arch-dukes: "Edisonmania," a word coined by President Hoover when presenting Edison with a Congressional Medal of Honor for ending the Great Depression. On the streets, it was all the rage to dress like Edison: a little black jacket, a string tie, and a koala paw. Most koala paws were artificial, held by a hand hidden in the sleeve of the black jacket. The most hardcore of Edison acolytes chopped off their own hand and then had a koala paw surgically attached at one of the country's countless Edison Hand Surgery and Taxidermy Clinics.

Edison was feeling pretty good about himself then when he awoke on a concrete slab in his basement workshop of the former Patent Office. He rubbed his eyes, careful not to scratch them with the sharp points of his koala claw, carefully scaled down the tall table so he wouldn't fall and crack his head open, and strolled through a vast private museum of his own inventions and up to the ground-floor manufacturing facility. It was 6 a.m., and he had to make sure all of the workers were present. If late, consequences were severe. If they weren't able to be in their seats, in their Thomas Edison outfits and ready to start their 20-hour shifts, Mr. Edison would replace them with seven-year-olds who could.

After making a quick headcount and not acknowledging them any further, Edison made his way to the front doors and tried, and tried, and tried, and finally, got the very big door open. He went outside to do his morning calisthenics and to look for spies from Westinghouse, such were his morning habits.

From about 20 feet away, he saw them, two lab-coated men astride the backs of lobsters. One was the soft, blonde, girl-pretty scientist who had brought him to the 21st century. The other was some slovenly sad sack.

Edison froze. The scientists froze. Edison knew they were here for him. So, he did what he had always done when he felt threatened, like when an employee talked about unions, or when a patent clerk made him fill out an additional form. He reached into his pockets, took out two light bulbs, and threw them at these men from the future.

"It's happening!" Edison screamed. "Activate security protocols!"

Then he very slowly pushed the door open and dashed back inside.

42

———

"Back away from the labs!" called out the high-pitched, New Jersey-accented voice of a child.

"Yeah, you ain't gettin' in to see Mr. Edison, no way, no how, see?" said the similar voice of another child.

Several 1930s street urchins — homeless children, really — popped out from the street's alleys, behind trash cans, from inside trash cans, through manholes, and underneath the piles of garbage that just always lay on the streets in New Jersey. Together, they formed a blockade in front of the doors to the Patent Office.

Then they all gasped...and then took off running.

"Aw, jeez, there's *three* of 'em!" the first voice called out.

"It's come to avenge the death of its brother!"

"Mr. Edison don't pay us enough for this!"

"Go on in, do whatever you want to Mr. Edison!"

"Thank you, orphans!" Magnus called out. "Three?" he whispered to Albert? "Three what? Three of us? Because there's me, and you, and our lobsters. That's either two humans or four living things in total. Those filthy homeless children are so uneducated!"

Albert didn't hear anything Magnus had said, nor anything the intimidating children had said, because who had just sidled up next to him and Magnus astride time lobsters but Rosalind herself, astride a time lobster and wearing a brand-new cowboy hat. Carl was there, too, nestled firmly on the saddle in front of Rosalind.

"Hey, Albert," Rosalind said. "What's up?"

He was overjoyed, but he successfully read the moment, and kept his cool, because Rosalind was keeping hers. He sure was glad she was alive, albeit missing an arm. But that hardly mattered; she had kept her promise.

"I told you I'd find you."

It was especially hard for Albert to keep his macho, laid-back resolve when Carl jumped off of Rosalind's time lobster and onto his shoulder, where he immediately licked Albert's face. Carl also had on a cowboy hat, which was unbelievably adorable.

"So," Rosalind asked, witnessing the tender reunion of Albert and Carl. "Who's your friend?"

"Who?" Magnus asked with a righteous indignation that he unsuccessfully tried to present as faux righteous indignation. "Uh, 'let's make a science guess.' Ring any bells?"

"Nope," Rosalind said.

Whether she really hadn't heard of Magnus, or whether she was just pretending to get under Magnus's skin, Albert liked Rosalind just a little bit more than he already did.

"Hi, I'm Rosalind. Albert's my friend. We used to work together."

"Hi. Magnus," Magnus said quickly and sheepishly.

"How...how did you get here?" Albert asked, woozy as he tried to process the comeback of his crush and the notion of resurrection.

"I had to defeat a time lobster in a battle that technically waged for centuries. And I won! But then the other time lobsters were actually okay with it. More than okay with it, actually. Stoked! They made me an honorary one, see?" she said, pointing to her tin star.

"Wow," Albert mumbled like an idiot.

Carl snorted and pointed his snout up at his cowboy hat.

"Okay, well, we'll talk about that later," Rosalind said. "My time lobster associates have told me what needs to happen here today. Shall we?"

They disembarked from their lobsters, tied them to some hitching posts, and prepared to enter the Patent Office, whose front door was adorned with a piece of cardboard that read, "Edison Labs," along with a crude little drawing of a dog.

"Oh, cute," Rosalind said. "It's *labs*, but there's a drawing of a Labrador."

"Very clever!" Magnus added. Albert ignored them both.

They entered the building. It was eerily quiet, and apparently devoid of life.

"Somebody's gonna get fired for that," Albert said, pointing to the door that had been left open, which led to a stairwell. Albert, Magnus, Rosalind, and Carl, silently and cautiously walked down the darkened stairs until they reached a glass door labeled "The Thomas Edison Hall of Ideas Too Good For An Ungrateful World."

"Oh, I've read about this!" Magnus said. "Edison always wanted to open a museum of all of his inventions that failed to take off."

"Like his flops?" Rosalind asked.

"This is gonna be great!" Magnus whispered to himself.

"You knew about this?" Albert asked incredulously.

"I've read two books in my life," Magnus boasted, "and both of them were about Thomas Edison."

They pushed open the door and entered the cavernous room, unlit but for the odd bit of ambient light, which made them aware of tall high metal shelves lining both sides of what appeared to be a long, wide room.

Something made of glass crashed to the floor. A child giggled.

The search party halted. Albert cautiously stepped forward, and his shoes crunched on the glass. He looked up just as he saw the outline of a child sitting on the top shelf pull on a metal chain to turn on an Edison-style light bulb. Fully illuminated in the small circle of light, Albert could see that the kid was dressed exactly like Thomas Edison — black jacket, loosely tied bow tie, white wig. When Albert spotted her, she reached into a big wooden box and pulled out a succession of light bulbs, throwing them at Albert in time to the song she sang.

"Mary had a little lamb, little lamb, little lamb!"

"Nice touch!" Magnus explained to his cohorts. "That was the song Edison recorded on the first phonog —"

Magnus was cut off by a light bulb smashing into his shoulder.

"That's very rude. You shouldn't throw —"

Magnus was cut off again, this time by the sound of a cat hissing. And then there were multiple cats hissing.

A dozen white cats ran at the group, although slowly and awkwardly because they were doing it on their hind legs. Still, it was really unsettling.

"What's on their hands?" Rosalind asked. "Or paws, I guess."

"Boxing gloves!" Magnus shouted, absolutely delighted.

A melee of cat screeches and horrible cat-fighting noises commenced, but cats can't really do much damage to three full-grown humans when their most potent weapon, their claws, are covered by tiny vinyl bags.

"You see," Magnus shouted above the din, "Edison trained

house cats to fight for his amusement, but he didn't want them to kill each other, so he fitted them with tiny boxing gloves!"

"I guess that's better than them scratching each other's eyes out," Rosalind said.

"Yeah, he wasn't *that* bad of a guy!" Magnus said with complete seriousness before catching himself. "I mean, back then. I guess."

Although the humans simply walked through the pack of boxing cats because they could, Carl was closer to their size and had to defend himself, and, in his mind, his human friends. He ran headfirst into the cat fracas and snorted angry snorts at the cats. They screeched and swatted at him with their gloved paws, which did no damage. They screeched some more and hissed as they ran away. Carl managed to hold onto one of the cats and deftly plucked off one of its boxing gloves and placed it on the cat's tail. He considered that a win.

"Cats really hate having their tails messed with," Albert deadpanned.

The party continued walking through the darkened museum of failure, slowly, carefully. Creepy children in Edison costumes, alternately giggling and singing "Mary Had a Little Lamb," threw light bulbs at them from high spots, except for the ones who threw milk bottles. Luckily, children, particularly ones who never exercised or played sports due to 20-hour workdays, had terrible aim. The closest hit landed right between Magnus's feet.

"Thomas Edison had diabetes, and for no discernible scientific reason, he thought the best way to treat it was to consume a pint of milk every three hours."

"How did that work out for him?" Albert asked.

"Oh, he died from complications of diabetes in 1931. Milk is full of sugar, which is very bad for diabetics. Speaking of which..."

Magnus took a packet of Brightly Colored Fizzy Candy Rocks

out of his pocket and grabbed the two-liter soda bottle off of his back. He poured the candy in the bottle, capped it, and shook it. "I think the smashing has gone on long enough."

"Wait!" Albert couldn't see much, but he thought he heard Magnus shaking his soda bottle. He grabbed what he hoped was Magnus's arm. "Save it for Edison."

"Please?" Magnus begged. "I really want to shoot these little jerks with my soda gun."

"No, save it for Edison," Rosalind said.

"Oh, sure, side with your *boyfriend*," Magnus petulantly responded. It was nearly pitch black in the museum, so Rosalind couldn't see Albert blush.

"Listen," Rosalind whispered.

"Pretty boy, pretty boy! Come and get me, you handsome son of a bitch."

"It's Edison!" Magnus whispered.

"He's taunting you," Albert said to Magnus.

"Yeah, come get me, I'm right around the corner," Edison continued.

Albert and Magnus peeked around the corner of a shelf unit. Another light bulb came at them but missed entirely. Then another milk bottle.

"Pretty boy, pretty boy. Come and get me, you handsome son of a bitch."

"That's weird," Magnus said. "He's just repeating himself."

"Yeah, come get me, I'm right around the corner."

Then Magnus figured it out, right as Albert jumped at the bay of shelves from where the voice came.

"Albert, stop!"

Albert didn't find Edison, only a doll: a creepy, shiny-faced porcelain doll with its eyes falling out and a speaker on its back.

"Pretty boy, pretty boy. Come and get me, you handsome son of a bitch."

That's when the 50 or so other dolls on the shelf started singing "Mary Had a Little Lamb," which would be an unnerving thing even in a well-lit room. It was so unsettling to Carl, as the dolls were bigger than he was, that he took off, back through from where they came, up the stairs, and out of Edison Labs entirely.

Albert turned around, hoping to face Rosalind and Magnus, but instead, a child dressed in an Edison costume jumped on him, attempting to stick its child-sized thumbs into Albert's adult-sized eyes.

"The road to hell is paved with good inventions!" it shouted.

This wasn't a child — it was the real Edison, or the real Edison clone, hiding in the shadows and lying in wait to attack Albert, Magnus, Rosalind, whoever fell for the trap he had set.

Forever and still a fan, Magnus laughed at Edison's aggressive pun.

Meanwhile, Albert tried to shake off Edison and twisted his head around wildly, trying to avoid Edison's thumbs. Rosalind found him in the dark and tried to pry Edison off, which was tough to do with only one arm.

"Get off him, Rosalind!" Magnus shouted. "Now!"

She did, and Magnus shook his soda bottle, ripped open a packet of fizzy rocks, poured it in the bottle, and shot the makeshift weapon directly at where he estimated Edison to be. He wasn't sure if and how hard he'd hit Edison — it was dark — but he heard a voice blubbering through liquid. It didn't matter much, because Edison had let go of Albert and took off and ran through another door in the distance, which he slammed behind himself.

Albert, Magnus, and Rosalind gave chase, trying to avoid all the milk, soda, and broken glass on the ground, as well as a lot of overturned cement furniture, last-ditch attempts by Edison to delay the pursuit.

"Edison didn't just make cement furniture," Magnus droned on, "but entire houses made of cement, with the appliances and even cement phonographs built right into the molds. The molds had to be the size of the house, of course, and there wasn't much of a market for —"

After feeling around in the dark for a minute, Rosalind found the door and kicked it open, revealing Edison's well-lit private workshop. Several workbenches sat covered in electronics, wood shavings, spare parts, and handfuls of wire. Albert noticed that the walls were lined with plaques, upon which had been mounted sheets of gold parchment and a placard denoting it had been awarded to "Thomas Edison, for sales of 500,000 units" of whatever each thing was.

"Wow, look at all these gold patents!" Magnus enthused. "There are even some platinum ones, too."

There were dozens of them, on the walls and on the ceiling, too. Albert noticed that some were for things the original Edison made, some for things the original Edison had muscled his way into getting credit for, and the rest for technology he'd stolen from the future.

"Is he even in here?" Rosalind asked.

"He could be anywhere," Albert said absent-mindedly, continuing to scan the patents, looking for one in particular while a theory took shape in his mind.

"I'm sitting at my desk, you incomparable buffoons!" yelled the tiny Edison, sitting in a desk chair five times his size behind a desk ten times his size. In front of him sat a large tin box resembling a fax machine.

"Hey, neat, what's that?" Magnus asked.

"This, you goon, is the patent-patenter. Cuts down the time it takes to file a patent by nearly 100 percent. It's almost completely instantaneous."

He picked up a piece of paper off the desk with some writing on it, scribbled on it a bit, signed it, and sent it through the patent-patenter, which shook and beeped and belched out smoke.

"What did you just do?" Albert asked in a panic.

"I patented that sugar-water cannon you shot me with. And I specifically designed it not to work, so it can't ever be produced."

"You filed a 'proof of concept' on us? *You monster!*" Magnus shouted. "That's seriously genius, though. Evil, but genius."

"Any moment now," Edison said, twiddling his thumbs. "Ah, and that should do it."

The patent-patenter stopped making noise, and a bell rang. The soda cannon disappeared from Magnus's person, and, in fact, all of existence. While it disarmed the group, it supported Albert's developing idea.

"It's okay, Magnus. There are other ways."

"There are?" Rosalind asked.

"Oh, yeah..." Magnus realized. "I just figured it out. If we kill him, it doesn't do anything. He's still got all the patents, and he's still got his legacy."

"Exactly," Albert grinned. "That's why we're gonna paradox him."

"Yeah," Rosalind said. "If you're gonna time travel, you're gonna have some paradoxes."

"It's unavoidable!" Magnus added.

"In what fashion?" Edison scoffed, and then he spat at them, but as he was very little, the spit just dribbled down to his chest. "There's no way you can stop me."

"Yes, I can," said Albert, looking around. "Yes, *we* can."

"Aww," mocked Magnus. Rosalind snickered.

"I'm looking around at all of these patents, and there's one I just don't see."

"Impossible," Edison sniffed. "I've got all of them. I've got everything!"

"Not the 3-D printer."

"A what? Oh, the printer. That was a redundancy. I saw a printer in action, it gave me the list of all of the inventions that are now in my name. I patented the printer. It's all done."

"But not a 3-D printer."

"That's the same thing as a two-dimensional printer. Paper has three dimensions."

"See, now this is why you go to school all the way through," Rosalind joked at Edison's expense. "To learn basic things like this."

"Look here!" Edison screamed, jumping up onto the desk to threateningly wave his finger in Rosalind's face. "Thomas Edison doesn't use shortcuts!"

Albert turned his back to Edison and whispered to Magnus and Rosalind.

"Do you guys see where I'm going here? We force him to patent the KopyRight!"

"No, but then I don't really know the entirety of the situation here," Rosalind said. "The time lobsters just told me to hit 1931 and stop Thomas Edison."

"That's all they said?"

"She was a very terse lobster."

"I got it!" Magnus shouted, who up to that point had been lost in thought. Then he let loose a diarrhea of words. All of them, Albert was pleased to note, were correct.

"If we make Edison patent the KopyRight!, a 3-D printer, under his own name, it creates a paradox, because I used the KopyRight! to create him, the new Edison," Magnus explained. "And paradoxes take care of themselves."

"And he would cease to exist, and everything he did would revert to its original year of patent, and its patent owner," Albert proudly added.

"Including the KopyRight!"

"Yep, that's what I was gonna say," injected Rosalind.

"I can hear everything you said," Edison shouted.

"Well, fine then," Albert said, taking the lead. "Don't bother patenting the 3-D printer. Even though it's a different invention entirely."

"Seeing as how you just stated in no uncertain terms that to do so would bring about my undoing, I don't think I will."

He walked over to Albert, and the height of the desk he stood on made them the same height.

"You can't make Thomas Edison do a goddamn thing he doesn't want to do," Edison said, annoyingly referring to himself in the third person.

"I can," Rosalind quipped, gently pushing Edison down to the desk with only a slight movement of her wrist. "I made you fall down."

"How clever," Edison said, righting himself. "Now then, there are about 30 more Thomas Edisons waiting for you in the room you came in here through, so do enjoy yourself on the way out and let me be."

"Magnus," Albert said, a mixture of real and exaggerated exasperation, "make Thomas Edison patent the KopyRight! so he'll disappear from existence."

"There's nothing you can do!" Edison screamed.

"Yes, there is!" Albert said. "Do to him what you did to me."

"Take him to the bowels of Gray Labs? Treat him to a meal prepared by El Robót?"

"No," Albert said half-whispering. "From earlier. In college."

"I don't see how humiliating you in front of the scientific community could or would help us in this situation, Albert."

"Oh, so you do remember?"

"I've done a lot of trepanning, and I can't always remember things so good, or right away, or at all. Just tell me what to do, okay?"

"Yeah, tell him what to do!" Rosalind shouted.

"Bah!" scoffed Edison before he sat down at the desk to take care of some paperwork.

"I didn't want to say it front of, you know," Albert replied, nodding his head in Edison's direction. Albert sidled up to Magnus and leaned in to whisper. His lips just millimeters from Magnus's spectacular ear was the most physical contact with another person Albert had experienced in, well, ever.

"*Steal...the...credit*," Albert whispered.

Magnus understood. Albert had spoken to him in a language he knew — that of professional science, in which all that really matters is whose name is on the thing.

"Time to publish...or perish," Magnus said to himself, sounding like a big-screen action hero but actually just quoting that episode of *The Scientist* where his character thwarted the efforts of an adjunct professor who'd built a doomsday device.

"Use the charisma!" Albert whispered so that everyone but Edison, he hoped, could hear. Magnus walked over to the desk, and as Edison busied himself, he sat down on the piece of furniture and stared down at his little hero.

"Hey, Edison," Magnus said. "All this talk about 3-D printers reminded me of something. What's interesting about that invention is that it's mine."

"It is?" Edison asked, incredulously. "It most certainly isn't!"

"No, it's a new printer. It's a better printer. Better than the old ones. It's probably the best printer that there ever was."

"Oh, you invented that?" Albert asked, playing along.

"Wow, nice job, Magnus," Rosalind said. "That's probably going to be your legacy."

"Oh, thank you so much," Magnus replied. "I think I'll go down in history as the world's finest inventor," he said, which didn't sound arrogant or like a lie at all, because his charisma was extremely powerful.

"And on the strength of just that one patent, too," Albert added.

Magnus, Albert, and Rosalind continued to discuss how 3-D printers are magnificent, and how neat it was that Magnus invented them. They pretended not to notice when Edison silently turned on the patent-patenter. He whistled "Mary Had a Little Lamb" to himself as he wrote down some things and signed his name. He placed it in the patent-patenter, and the machine shook and beeped and smoked.

"Wait, what's going on?" Magnus asked in a charming tone.

A bell rang.

"I've just patented the 3-D printer," Edison proclaimed.

"That's impossible!" Magnus gasped in mock surprise.

"That's *his* 3-D printer!" Rosalind shouted.

"Thief!" Albert added unnecessarily.

"Bully for me! Bully for Edison!"

He laughed maniacally, and he kept on doing that, up until the time a few seconds later, when he vanished with a faint "pop."

Albert and Rosalind cheered. Magnus deeply sighed.

"Aw, what's wrong, buddy?" Rosalind asked Magnus. "You realize you just fixed your big problem, right?"

"Yeah, I just miss him is all. He was like the father I never had."

"Magnus," Albert said with a sigh of his own. "Your father is alive. He's a good guy."

"Ugh. I *know*."

The lobsters returned their riders to the time-switching station, where Susan, the head time lobster, awaited them. Albert tried to not get too excited when he saw that she was holding two more cowboy hats and tin stars with clocks on them.

"I, Time Sheriff Susan Darden Cangrejo," she said as the humans approached on their lobsters, "hereby deputize thee, Albert Malfort, an Official Junior Time Lobster Deputy."

"Hey, just like me!" Rosalind said, tipping her hat to Albert.

"Ma'am," Albert said, returning the tip.

"Albert, Magnus, I sure would like to thank y'all for doing what you did today."

"Oh, well," Magnus said. "It was...kind of my fault."

"Kind of?" Albert teased.

"Well, sure, but y'all also restored the Great Depression, and in effect, time itself."

Albert's stomach sank once again.

"How is that a good thing?"

"Well, it's complicated, but see if y'all can keep up," the sheriff drawled. "Without the Great Depression, there woulda been no dang ol' lemon grove with a treehouse in it for Linus Pauling to live in, and then he woulda had a hard time getting to that place to give y'all those time-traveling secrets."

Carl came running up to the group from the direction of the storefront marked 1898, wearing his time lobster uniform of cowboy hat and tin star, but also a lei around his neck. He grunted quickly in acknowledgment to Albert and then Rosalind, and then politely nodded to Magnus because he didn't know him that well, and then grunted out a long litany to the sheriff.

"I reckon I better see to that. Thank you, Carl," the sheriff said. "Well, I best be hittin' this here trail to see a man about a horse. Thank y'all again. Carl?"

As the sheriff scuttled away, Carl snorted once, implying he would be a minute.

He trotted up to Albert and squealed as loud as Albert had ever heard him squeal. And then he ran off, catching up to the sheriff, and back into 1898.

Albert grinned.

"What did he say?" Rosalind asked.

"He said he wants to be a real time lobster, not, and I quote, 'this junior honorary deputy bullshit.'"

"Oh," Rosalind said, leaving Albert a moment of silence to collect his thoughts. Magnus, meanwhile, whistled "Mary Had a Little Lamb," and then the time station was silent.

"So...how do we get back?" Rosalind asked.

"Well, that depends. How did you get here?" Magnus inquired.

"Oh, Albert brought me here."

"When? I've been with him the whole time."

"No, she meant that my experiment opened up a time hole, and she got sucked down into it."

"Oh, cool, cool," Magnus said, then grinned. "So was that, like, your first date?"

"Well, there *was* drinking," Rosalind said.

"And lobsters," Albert added.

"Hey!" Magnus said. "I have an idea."

Magnus crouched down and then jumped up really high... then quickly landed on his feet.

"What was that?" Albert asked.

"Eh," Magnus said. "I thought that if the laws of time didn't apply here, then the laws of physics might not either."

Rosalind grabbed the tungsten rope hanging down from beyond the ceiling and gave it two firm tugs. She received two tugs back in return, and then she slowly started rappelling upward. Albert and Magnus, still attached to the rope, went along for the ride, and all three ascended out of the time station, and then through the dark tunnel of time, when the upward movement quickly picked up to face-ripping-off levels of speed.

44

Albert, Magnus, and Rosalind fell up through a hole on a hill and onto the wet morning grass. All three immediately freed themselves of their ropes, because holding on to tungsten rope as tightly as possible as it shoots up at light speed chafes like all get out.

"Okay," Albert said, feeling in control for a change, or at least for as long as he could ride out the day's glories. "We need to check all the equipment. See if it's still got the Edison logo, or if it's gone back to what it used to be."

Rosalind picked up a centrifuge and turned it over. "Gray."

Albert went over to the atomic clock and turned it over. "Gray!"

"Hooray, the slightly lesser of two evils wins!" Rosalind joked.

From inside his volcano car, Magnus shouted, flatly, "Gray here."

"Alright!" Rosalind and Albert shouted in unison, and high-fived.

"Are you guys kissing right now?" Magnus called out.

"I think we maybe were going to?" Albert joked, but not really, because he hoped the overwhelming emotions of the day would lead to an exchange of saliva and bacteria with Rosalind.

"It's not a good time," Magnus shouted.

"But we're exhausted, and I've got phantom limb pain, and there's some other dude hanging around," Rosalind said. "It's the romantic moment of which every girl dreams."

"You should probably just come over here," Magnus called out, his voice quivering.

Rosalind and Albert hurried over to the car. Magnus sat in the driver's seat. In the passenger seat was Eli Gray. Or what had become of him — no longer the muscular, virile, gleefully evil figure in a grey jumpsuit and helmet, this Eli Gray was what he looked like without his regular chronolyte treatments: a withered, bony thing in the vague shape of a man whose tight-fitting jumpsuit was now about five sizes too big. His face probably looked just as awful, but he still had the helmet on.

"Don't...steal...my lemons," Eli Gray croaked.

Albert and Rosalind each felt in their backs the barrels of whatever weapons Eli Gray's goonbots had.

"Oh, and one more thing," Eli Gray tried to say with as little breath and as much sarcasm as possible. "It floats."

Those were the last words Eli Gray, Elisha Gray, said before finally, at long last, without any more lemon-based chronolytes to preserve his incredibly old body, he died.

"Hey, *be bold*, man!"

Rosalind and Albert looked over their shoulders, which is hard to do when pinned against a car by angry robots, and caught a glimpse of a 10-foot-tall red cyborg jump into the still-open time hole.

"At least *he's* free," Albert said.

"Are they gonna put us in those floating jail cells?" Rosalind asked.

"Definitely," Albert replied.

"Even though he's dead? Magnus asked, nodding in the direction of Eli Gray, who had deteriorated even more, and now consisted of a loose jumpsuit topped with an overturned helmet filled with what looked like sand.

"I would say especially because he's dead," Rosalind offered.

The robots dragged them away, down through the hills and back into San Verguenza, and onto the campus of Gray Labs, where the entire staff had lined up along its pathways to shame, spit at, and curse Albert. They ignored Rosalind, who the robots had forcefully dressed in a lab coat with a giant letter "I" on it (for intern), and cheered for Magnus, who, if the rumors running through Gray Labs were true, had caught Eli Gray's killer.

Their march ended on the roof of Gray Labs. It turned out that Rosalind had been correct, as they each stared down a lesser-dimensional incarceration unit, or a blank space where they very much understood that a lesser-dimensional incarceration unit waited for each of them. Albert was thrown into his first, and it immediately floated up into the sky and lost one of its three dimensions.

A FEW WEEKS LATER

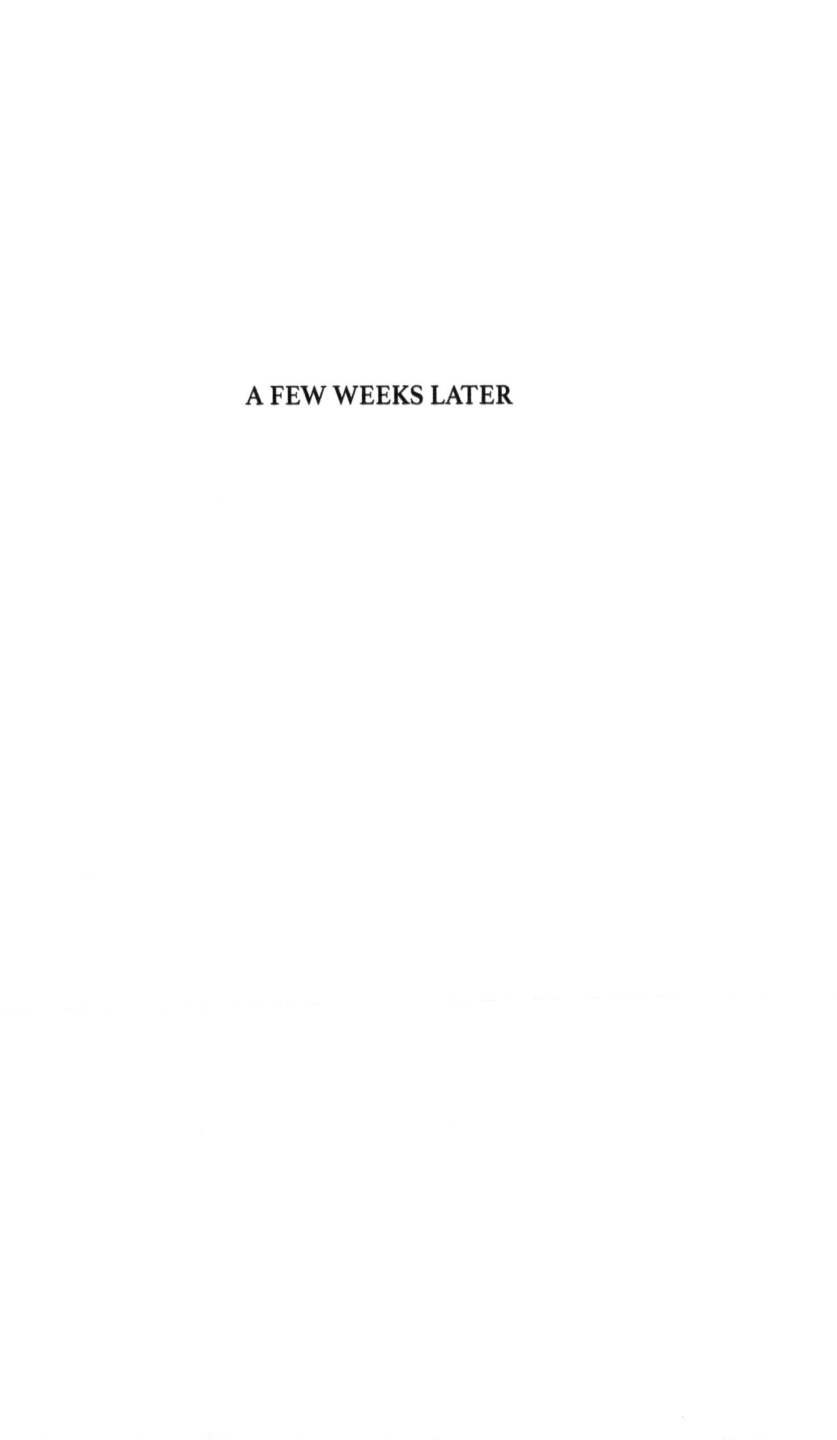

45

Immediately after the cell lost pressure and its imprisoning walls fell as if it had instantly dematerialized, there was nothing to hold Albert up in the sky, and he plummeted. Adding to the potent effects of gravity was the third-dimension, and all the weight that goes along with it, which had kicked back in the second that Albert's cell had malfunctioned and then disappeared. While prison breaks are always welcome for a prisoner, this one left something to be desired for Albert and that something was safety, as he found himself plummeting out of the sky at a tremendous velocity. Sure, he was free, but he was about to smash into the ground and shatter into a bunch of pieces, like a tomato frozen in liquid nitrogen, a Science Day street demonstration he could see going on as he fell to his certain death.

It takes only a few seconds to fall from even a great height, but it was enough time for Albert's life to flash before his eyes. The first 95 percent of it was so dull that he actually nodded off before waking up again, just in time to enjoy the greatest hits of the previous week. There was the traveling through time, first and foremost, but also time lobsters, seeing his mother again, and meeting people like Stephen Hawking, Linus Pauling, and Thomas Edison. Even if the latter were an evil, miniature clone version of Thomas Edison that he had to hunt down and kill, it was still an interesting experience.

And then there was Rosalind. And even Magnus. Not too long ago, he would have been enraged if Magnus Bigfaker Riptide made an appearance in his life's final moments, but right now, he was glad that somehow he had forged some kind of congenial arrangement with his sworn enemy.

Still, he was dying, about 70 years too early for his liking. He saw the hard pavement of San Verguenza, home of Gray Labs and Ron Malfort, getting closer and closer. As he prepared to face lasting unconsciousness, Albert extended the middle fingers of both hands, closed his eyes, and screamed.

Albert hit the ground. And then he bounced back up into the air about 10 feet, and then he hit the surface again. He bounced up once more, but not as far as he had the first time. All told, he hit the ground, surprisingly soft and rubbery and comfortable, and then flew back up into the air, about a dozen times before he settled into the safe but difficult to navigate terrain of what he finally realized was a Moonbounce.

"You wanna put those middle fingers away? I got kids here," Albert heard the peeved voice of an old man say.

"Come on, Dad. Give him a minute," said a familiar female voice.

Albert opened his eyes because he needed them to see, and to confirm that he wasn't dead, but also for some reason to confirm what his ears had already told him. There stood Rosalind, and Shuttle Commander Jimmy Howard, barking for new customers to try out "The Mobile Moonbounce."

"Hey, Albert, guess what?" Rosalind asked. "That space prison you invented has a design flaw." She held a large cannon behind her back but poked it up over her shoulder so Albert could see it. She put her finger to her mouth and made a *ssh* noise, long enough for Albert to see that the laser cannon had been surgically attached in place of her biological, bones-and-meat arm.

"Rosalind! You knew about the flaw?"

"I did?" she said, feigning ignorance.

"If you hit it at a 35-degree angle, the whole thing falls apart!"

"Oh, well, I was just broadly shooting. Just got this thing like three days ago, and it's still really fun," Rosalind explained, taking a couple of shots into the air and roasting a cloud. "I got lucky is all."

"That was *amazing!*" Albert heard Magnus shout from a distance before running up and jumping onto the Moonbounce. He was dressed in a black jacket and loosely tied black bow tie.

"Are you seriously dressed as Thomas Edison?"

"He's still my idol, Albert."

Rosalind and Magnus helped pull Albert up onto his feet on the trampoline surface. Rosalind did most of the work as Magnus kept getting distracted by how much fun it was to bounce on the Moonbounce. Albert suddenly realized that something didn't make sense.

"Wait, why aren't you guys in jail?"

Magnus hopped off the Moonbounce.

"We paid the fine, Albert," Magnus said.

"You can pay a fine?"

"You can always pay the fine, Albert."

"How much was it?

"A gentleman never tells," Magnus said.

"And if you have to ask..." Rosalind coyly added.

"You did, too? I figure you found some way to break out."

"I'm Commander Jimmy Howard's daughter. He's been to space. And so have I. It's like the ultimate diplomatic immunity."

"You've been to space?"

"Of course. I'll tell you later."

"No," Albert insisted. "You should tell me now. That's *amazing!*"

"Later," she said with a smile.

Albert, after struggling to get up upright, having been sitting on the Moonbounce surface, stabled himself on Rosalind but ended up pulling her down. Sensing that this was the right moment to do it, Albert decided, once and for all, to be bold. And so he kissed Rosalind.

She instantly pulled away in equal parts shock and disappointment.

"Look, Albert, you're really great, but —"

As she'd employed the universal language of gentle rejection, Rosalind expected Albert to cut her off with some excuse. But Albert had never been in a relationship, so he didn't know how being dumped went.

"Go on," he said.

"Oh!" she said, surprised. "It's just, you know, I've been through a lot lately, and I need some time to figure some things out. Does that make sense?"

"Sure, sure," Albert said, finally understanding. "Yeah, hey, of course."

"Also, you almost got me violently killed, and I lost my arm because of you."

"I get it," Albert said, really wishing that Rosalind would just stop talking.

"And I spent a lot of time with Magnus as well, and he's just so much more attractive than you."

"It's okay," Albert said, trying not to show any emotion of any kind, but failing, as he was showing off most of them, or at least the ones that make your face red.

"Albert, I'm kidding!"

Albert immediately felt his face cool down.

"Well, I mean, not all of it. I don't want to date you, that's true. But you cannot deny that Magnus is super-hot, and objectively, scientifically speaking, he is much more attractive than you."

"You can't argue the science!" Magnus yelled, jumping up and down.

"But I *like* you more than Magnus," Rosalind said. "As a friend."

And for Albert, whose life to that point that been an ordeal of meaningless cruelty alternating with crippling loneliness, that was enough.

He was distracted from feeling his feelings when out of the corner of his eye, he saw a flicker of activity in the sky.

And then he saw it again. The sunlight caught the edge of it just right, casting a shadow and small outline over the two-dimensional prison cell floating in the air, occupied by Ron Malfort. The mechanics of the cell are such that the person inside cannot hear anything on the outside, and people on the outside can't hear the person on the inside. But Albert was pretty sure he saw Ron look him in the eye and mouth the words, "Go suck a lemon!" in the kindest way possible.

"Hey, you guys, look!" Magnus shouted, pointing at the teacup pig running toward them at full speed. Carl was still dressed in his time lobster uniform of a cowboy hat and tin star. He looked so cute Albert had to bite his lip to keep from screaming.

Carl snorted, but he was so out of breath from running all the way from the stable time hole up in the hills to the Science Day festivities, so Albert had a hard time making out what he was trying to say.

"Carl, slow down."

Snort! Carl said, then paused to take a quick breath. *Snort!*

"Your squad has located Linus Pauling?" Albert translated.

"Oh, right! I forgot about that," Magnus said.

"Where is he?" Albert asked Carl.

Snort! Snort, snort…snort. After panting for a while, he added, *Snort.*

"The 1700s," Albert followed. "Chasing pirates?"

Snort. Snort snort, Carl snorted. *Snort. Snort. Snooooooort!*

"He's giving them lemons to fight off scurvy?"

Snort.

"They're…getting healthy enough to defeat the British Navy?"

"Oh, that could undo some history," Rosalind understated.

"A pirate adventure!" Magnus said, clapping his hands. "Are you telling me we get to go on a pirate adventure?"

Albert, Magnus, Rosalind, and Carl all hopped into Magnus's volcanic car, which he had conveniently but rudely parked in the middle of the blocked-off, "no cars allowed" area in the Science Day celebration zone. As they raced as best they could to get out of town and into the hills, Albert, for once, didn't think at all about the future. Instead, he contemplated the present, and he was shocked to discover that he was pretty happy with it.

The past was still shitty, but then it always had been.

ACKNOWLEDGMENTS

Immeasurable gratitude to my editor, Monica Sweeney, who tightened and cleaned up the book, and provided so many wonderful suggestions and offered so many astute changes, none of which involved sacrificing any humor or heart.

Tom Deja of Bossman Graphics, thank you for conceptualizing and delivering the most perfect and delightful cover, even though I didn't know how I wanted it to look apart from a particular feeling.

Thank you to the learned friends and illustrious colleagues who read various early drafts of this book and offered valuable and encouraging assistance: Jeremy Barker, Jeff Giles, Matthew David Brozik, and Eric Dodson.

To Brendan, who helped me ensure that this book was as funny as it absolutely could be.

And my eternal gratitude and undying love to Megan. Not just for being a true partner in everything, but for encouraging me to undertake the entire project, and to make exactly the book that I wanted to make, no matter what. You inspire me to keep climbing to such great heights.

ABOUT THE AUTHOR

Brian Boone has written for outlets such as Funny or Die, Someecards, McSweeney's Internet Tendency, Bunny Ears, CollegeHumor, *The Onion,* ClickHole, StarWipe, Weekly Humorist, Points in Case, Robot Butt, RiffTrax, and Splitsider. He's also created bits for the podcasts *Anna Faris is Unqualified, Minor Adventures with Topher Grace,* and the radio program *Paul Shaffer's Day in Rock.* On the informational end, he's contributed to How Stuff Works, Barnes and Noble Reads, PopDose, Looper, Grunge, NickiSwift, Vulture, and the *Uncle John's Bathroom Reader* series. His name also graces entries in the "101" series by Adams Media, a number of joke books for Sky Pony Press, and the snarky music trivia book *I Love Rock n' Roll (Except When I Hate It)* for Perigee. His theatrical works *The Egg Play* and *The Sea is a Restless Whore* have been performed around the country. Find him on social media: @brianbooone on Twitter, and @brianboone on Instagram.

www.ingramcontent.com/pod-product-compliance
Lightning Source LLC
Chambersburg PA
CBHW021112110726
47900CB00007B/2148